MYTHOLOGY
UNVEILED

A COMPLETE GUIDE TO
THE WORLD OF MYTH

ROBERT D. JONES

Contents

Figure 1: Pallas Athena & the Centaur by Botticelli (1481) shows us that wisdom can overcome instinct. The wise Athena leads the brutish centaur who cowers at her refined being.

The Mythic World Is Alive

The Breathe of Life

Mythology is the very breath of life, it is the essence of the world around us, the grand stories created and passed down, changed and distilled, told and interpreted over countless generations. They are the accounts of what were, the explanations for why things are, and they are the truth on what will be.

The mythic world is as real as ours, but it exists in a different place outside of time and space. It is a world of certain possibilities where one can divine the future by looking into the past. It is a realm of pure truths where archetypal forms can be observed. Mythology is the living fantasy where we can observe and play out all the different paths our life can lead.

But these broadly sweeping statements are far from an explanation of what mythology really is. We can observe that the mythological phenomena is found the world over. We can see its timelessness by reading the tales that date back to the advent of writing and even beyond through interpreting the inscriptions of our nomadic ancestors. And, it is clear to see that we are surrounded by mythology even in our modern lives. It appears that humanity is, and always has been, completely enveloped in the mythological world. But what is it? And why is it?

These questions are not so easy, for mythological stories are written and told for so many different reasons, that to categorize them under a single label would be a crime. We are lucky in our own age to be living with the accumulated knowledge of the generations before us. To borrow from Bernard of Chartres, we see more and farther than our predecessors, not because we have keener vision or greater height, but because we stand on the shoulders of giants. It is important to remember this, for as you read the fantastic stories of ancient people, do not fool yourself into believing it is nonsense and remember that they were just as clever as us, and hidden within the tales is a truth locked away.

Wrestling with Mythology

Our word mythology derives from the Greek mūthos which roughly means a speech or the plot of a story. Later in history, the Greeks began using the word logos with more frequency, which means logic. This shift in vocabulary gave rise to the idea that a mūthos or mythology was distinctly different from a logical explanation. Over time the ideals of a mūthos deteriorated until it became nothing more than a story of fantasy with no logic within it. But this idea is far from true, and the classical Greek philosopher, Plato, knew this. He had full faith in the uses of a mūthos, and so he began his great work Protagoras like this,

> *"Well, Socrates, "he said, "I won't refuse your request. Should I prove my point by telling a story (mūthos), as the elders do to the young, or by giving a rational argument (logos)?"*

Many in the audience responded that he should give his account in whatever way he wished.

"Then it seems to me," he said, "that it would be more pleasant if I told you a story. There once was a time..."

Immediately you can see how the Greek mind respected either way as an explanation for the world around them. Logos would give you an almost modern scientific reasoning, whereas mūthos an allegorical story to explain the world.

So in a round-a-bout way, we are seeing that the world around us can be explained in ways other than hard and fast facts. In fact, it can be argued that for a fuller explanation of the world to be available to an individual, you have to look at reality through a number of lenses, with mūthos and logos being just two. We see logos, or logic, as great at explaining how things are, a purely factual based methodology can tell us information like when a battle was fought, how the skeletomuscular system in a human functions, or how birds fly. But a mūthos gives you something different, it explains why things are. Why humans exist, why do we have to work, or what is love. These latter questions are far from quantifiable, so by their very nature cannot be answered through a scientific eye. There is no definitive answer for, what is love. Scientific knowledge could tell us the chemical changes associated with the emotion of love, logic thought may extrapolate the fact that the survival of kin is greatly increased through the protective presence of two parents, but everyone knows that love is more than that. The question of love has to be studied through numerous perspectives, and mūthos is one of these.

We are starting to understand the importance of mythology now, it is another lens in which the world can be studied. But despite our appreciation of its existence, we still do not really know what mythology is. Help might be found through the Oxford English Dictionary, which gives us this definition,

Mythology is a traditional story, typically involving supernatural beings or forces, which embodies and provides an explanation, aetiology, or justification for something such as the early history of a society, a religious belief or ritual, or a natural phenomenon. Myth is strictly distinguished from allegory and legend by some scholars, but in general use, it is often used interchangeably with these terms.

This definition is useful to us, but should not be completely relied upon. In the outer most layer, mythology is indeed a traditional story, and in many cases, it will be used to explain the world surrounding the author. But if this were all there was to it, then we would not be able to associate our lives today with the ancient tales of Homer. Yet it is as plain as day to see the rage of Achilles echo in the souls of modern humanity. We can feel the heartbreak of Orpheus as he loses his love forever. The helpless distraught of Hercules as he struggles with his long-held guilt. There are truths in these stories that do not merely belong to the world of the author, but are eternally alive, and will explain the ways of the world for all generations.

The Reality of Mythic Truth

As we saw above, Plato alludes to the idea that there is truth in mythology. The topic is explored in great detail by many scholars through time and boils down to this key idea. There are universal truths within the human condition that apply to all people and shape our reality. This means that every single one of us undergoes the same conditions and are subject to these overarching universal truths. We all experience the same emotions, we all go through physical hardships, and we all undertake the spiritual journey.

Figure 2: Perseus with the head of Medusa is a sculpture by Benvenuto Cellini (1554) depicting the victory of Perseus over the monstrous Medusa.

So what mythology does is portray the human journey in the form of a story. The stories let us read and understand what we are going through in our own lives by observing the mythic characters undergoing their own trials. The stories become a teaching tool, not just for moral guidance, but to open up a realization of what is happening to us personally in regards to the bigger picture.

Take for example the tale of poor Medusa. To paraphrase her story, we see her from the beginning in her human form, Medea, a woman famed for her beauty. She was so beautiful that it offended the super masculine goddess, Athena. So, Athena turned Medea's beauty against her, making her the monstrous Medusa with a head full of serpents for hair. Anybody who met the eyes of Medusa was petrified - instantly turned to stone, so no longer could people gaze on Medea's beauty. Further on, Athena sent Perseus to kill Medusa, and after cutting off her head, he returned it to the Goddess, where the head was placed on her shield, retaining its petrific power.

A very fanciful story, but when you cut through it you can see truths that we all endure. Medusa is often seen as Athena's "shadow" or darker side, the personality she tries to hide. She turns her own beauty into a monster, wearing it as a shield to defend herself. The myth is portraying the generic subduing of feminine beauty to survive in a male-dominated world. The journey of Medea is a lot longer and more complex than this, but you now have a taste of mythic reality. We can now appreciate that mythology is more than fantastic tale but speaks to a universal truth.

The Historicity of Mythology

Stepping back for a moment to the real world, let's look at how the phenomena of mythology came into being. Writing was first invented in ancient Sumeria, and soon after was found in Egypt from around 3000 B.C. It would make sense then that our first taste of mythology would date from around this period. This is partially true, our earliest records of mythic tales do date from this period, however, they did not originate from this time.

To date, the origins of mythology may as well be an impossible task. Our best assumption would be its coincidal birth with speech. I say this because mythology is linked with the oral tradition, a fact that we still observe today where a society passes down it mythology from generation to generation by speaking them. When

Europeans first came to the America's they noted the stories told by the native cultures, the same is still seen in many parts of Africa, Asia, and Europe. The Celtic tribes of Britain had a prevalent bardic culture, and the Greek Homer compiled his epics through the same means. So we see over and over this pre-literate telling of stories and can justify the statement that mythology predates the written word.

Why then were these myths being created? The answer is not easy, because there are so many reasons. As an overall answer, it's because the storyteller has an idea or message that they want to tell, like a tribal chief who wants to teach his people where they come from, or a football coach who wants his team to play fairly. The myths arise because the society needs something to be explained to them, and because of this, we see that mythology has been created ever since mankind has existed, and it is still being created today which we see in the form of books, songs, and movies to name but a few.

Why Mythology is so Fantastical

We have seen that myth has come from all peoples from all time and that it is an expression of the human condition and an explanation for the world around us, so then why do they contain such fanciful characters as gods and monsters? Why don't they just keep to using images and symbols from the real world around us? Well, to answer these I would like to ask you a question, how would I symbolize a man's uncontrollable rage in a story if that man was struggling with the emotion? You would need to find something fitting for him to fight that would resemble rage. For ancient cultures, you might look for similar things around you, like the wild beasts in the fields - for example, the bull. Now if this bull is really a human emotion it would seem fitting to humanize it so the audience can relate. All of a sudden a bull-man is created, the Minotaur.

Throughout mythology, this kind of process occurs, and not just in monsters, but a great variety of symbols are created to hold secondary meanings and soon enough the stories begin to resemble dreams instead of reality. It is up to you to form the interpretations to find out what the stories are really trying to say.

It should now be apparent to us that mythology is a real world. It predates the written history of man yet is always in a state of creation and renewal. The stories are used on different levels, to convey teachings and to guide the individual on the path of life. But it is not the only lens in which to observe the world, only another aspect of the universal reality.

Figure 3: Commonly found in mythology, the centaur can be interpreted as representing the boundary between civilization and the wild. (Laurent Marqueste, 1892) is aptly named, Centaure enlevant une nymphe.)

Theseus and the Minotaur

The young man muttered under his breath as he toiled in the fields. His bronze skinned glowing with sweat as he worked under the beating heat of the Mediterranean sun. Knowing no father, the burden of the home was his own and though his youthful body could bear the brunt of rural work with ease, his heart sung out for something more. For deep inside, Theseus yearned to see the world, yet his place was here in southern Greece, in a nameless village forgotten with time, tending to his aging mother.

He worked hard through the day plowing the fields as Helios guided his faithful chariot through the sky, and as the sun began its descent down the western mountains he left the field and began the trek home. This land was his and he knew every tree, every boulder, every craggy hillside. His home was no different to anyone else's in the village, smoke lazily wafting from the chimney and light spilling out from the small window by the door. His mother worked tirelessly inside and as he entered she greeted him kindly. Her warm smile soon slipped away and Theseus watched her lips tighten and eyes dance away from his.

"What is it mother, what do you have to say?"

He sat down at the kitchen table and watched as she turned her back as she busied herself with something in the kitchen. She had once been a beautiful woman, the daughter of King Pelos, but time had taken its toll as it does with all, and the burden of raising a son alone had not made her path an easy one. She turned slowly and looked on her son purposely, gazing into his eyes with motherly love.

"Theseus," she began. "I've watched you grown from a boy to a man. I've seen you sweating in the fields every day, working yourself to the bone. But there is something more about you that you don't know."

Theseus sat in silence, hanging on the words she said.

"You have a father." She paused giving her son space to take it in. "It is King Aegeas of Athens. He came here long ago looking for my father's council. He bedded me and you were conceived, but matters in Athens forbade him to stay."

She watched her son as he wrestled with what she said. His eyes seemed full of hope, his thoughts raced but he couldn't grasp the words to ask her what he needed to know.

"Your father never came back," she continued. "But he did not forget you either. Before he left he set up a test for you and had me swear to only tell you when you were of age. Before he left for Athens he buried his sword and sandals beneath the great boulder by the field. He claimed that if you could move it then you truly are his son and he would welcome you by his side in his city." She paused again looking into her son's eyes. "Theseus, it is time."

The dying sun slipped behind the craggy mountain peaks, illuminating them in a golden blaze more beautiful than any crown. Theseus knew the boulder, it was the greatest in the field, twice as tall as he and wider still. He looked upon it and marveled, beneath was his destiny, but how on earth could it be moved? He lay his back against it and heaved with all his might, he strained and flexed his powerful thighs but to no avail. Again he hurled himself at the beastly rock, sweat beads rolling down his body but the boulder would not shift. Theseus would not be beaten, but today he could not succeed either.

He returned home his mind racing with ideas. He lay down to rest but sleep would not come. As the morning light broke the horizon, Theseus began his task anew. He brought down his team of oxen and strapped them together. With great leather ropes, he secured the rock and hastened his animals forward. Grunting and snorting they took the strain, but again nothing. Theseus urged them on and again the ropes went tight, but this time the young hero threw himself at the rock with them and the great stone broke free from its earthly shackles. They kept the force up and before long it toppled over.

Theseus looked into the cavity long held captive by the boulder, a golden blade glistened in the morning sun and leather sandals sat neatly by its side. His heart leaped for joy as he took the tokens that secured his heritage. But as he took them back to his home, his heart sank. He found his mother inside and burst out to her,

"I can't just leave you, Mother! Who will tend the fields? Who will protect you? My place is here, not in far-off Athens."

His mother smiled and she looked down. Her heart was full for the love of her son.

"You cannot stay here, Theseus," she explained. "Your place is not with me anymore. You must set out and find your place in the world."

Theseus was taken aback, how could this be happening. He stalked around the small room wrestling with the weight on his shoulders.

"Why not take the sea, Theseus?" his mother begged. "It's a far safer way, the roads are dangerous and a ship could have you in the city by nightfall. You'd be out of harm's way and your father may have advice for you."

Theseus shunned the idea, how could he prove his worth if all he ever did was avoid danger? If he had to leave he would go by land and make a name for himself that would reach his father's ears before he did.

The two stood in silence, Theseus future seemed to be set. Tears welled up in the eyes of each, and with a final embrace, the boy left his mother and all he ever knew.

***

Theseus left his village heading north, the hills rolled on either side of him and before long he treaded land he had never known. It seemed the further he went the more alien his surroundings were as the tree's thickened into tight woods and the scrubland before him gave way to craggy hills and cliffs. He stopped along a trickling creek and made camp beside some wild olive trees. Before long sleep filled his eyes and he dreamed dreams of opulent magic. A man came to him, covered from head to toe in dark robes, his head deeply hooded so all that was seen was abyssal darkness. He called out to Theseus, speaking slowly with a voice of command.

"Trust your instincts, Theseus," he said. "The way is long and dangerous, but all you need is within you. Trust in yourself and no one else."

The words emanated through Theseus' soul, the man seemed to speak into him rather than to him yet Theseus felt no fear. The stranger was benign, he seemed to want nothing more than to help.

"Should you stray, I will set you straight," the robed man continued. "Should you need me, I will be there. But trust in your senses above all else, Theseus, for they will guide you through."

The dream dissipated and the mysterious figure was only left in Theseus' memory. The dream was so real he thought, and he pondered on the man's meaning, feeling reassured by his advice. Theseus got up and continued to follow the path, before long his mother's fears were made reality as Theseus neared the small town Epidaurus, sacred to the divine healers Apollo and Asclepius.

He walked the outskirts of the town, staying clear of entering the strange settlement when suddenly a roar bellowed out from the tree line to his left. No sooner than the cry echoed away an enormous man emerged from the thickets. Twice the size of young Theseus, the giant limped toward him revealing a single eye glaring from his forehead, a cyclops! The beast bellowed forth a speech so slurred and tangled the words were hard to make sense of,

"Y'ng man, y'ng man! Come 'ere a mom'nt!" he called.

Theseus' hand moved to the hilt of his blade, but as he eyed the giants gleaming club he knew he wouldn't stand a chance in a fight.

"You are so big, my friend," called Theseus, feigning friendship. "What is your name?"

The Cyclops laughed like rolling thunder.

"My name? Surely ev'n you 'ave 'eard of the great Periphetes! That's me! The club bea'er!"

Theseus swallowed hard, indeed the name of the bandit was famous. He would roam the roads between here and Athens stealing from travelers before bearing his club down on them grinding his prey into the earth. Theseus kept his cool,

"Periphetes, of course! Is it true that you are the son of the mighty Hephaestus? That your club is solid bronze? May I see it, can I touch and hold it?"

Periphetes laughed again, he saw no harm in letting the small boy hold his pride before returning him to the earth. He handed over the club and its weight strained Theseus' arms. Again The Cyclops bellowed his laughter like rolling thunder, the boy could barely take the strain!

But Theseus smiled, his arms hardened from years of labor regained their strength as he lifted the bronze club and felt its power. He looked at the alarm in Periphetes face and without a word swung the full weight of the weapon catching the Cyclops off guard. Periphetes head exploded in a mass of crimson pulp and he's bulk collapsed to the ground where he stood.

***

Theseus kept the club of Periphetes and continued his journey. He made his way north and soon the forests were dominated by tall, looming pines. The air freshened as his path came closer to the sea and he could smell the salt of two different waters as he closed on Corinth's Isthmus. As he walked the trail, a figure ahead became visible, sitting by the wayside. He approached the stranger who stood to greet Theseus.

"Hello young man," he called out. "Would you have time to help a poor man out?"

Theseus replied in kind and agreed to help the man. The stranger explained he was picking pinecones from the trees above and needed someone to help him bend one down. They moved through the forest together and chatted for some time. The man revealed himself as Silas, though he did not know his reputation had preceded him. Wary of his new companion, Theseus remembered the tales he had been told of the 'Pine-bender', of how he would fling his victims from the cliffs, using the pines as catapults, or even split a man in two by tying an arm to two separate trees and releasing them together. Theseus didn't give away his knowledge and they continued to wander the forest.

Silas smiled as he picked out a young pine, still flexible in its youth, he worked its trunk and bent the tip to the floor asking Theseus to tie it to the ground. He did as he was asked. Theseus bent the second tree down and Silas worked to tie it down. As the stranger pressed his weight on the tree, Theseus let go. The man screamed, but held on, pushing his weight down to keep the pine from flinging away.

Theseus cried out, knowing the bandit's game was up and called him out for all that he had done. Silas begged for his life as Theseus strapped each hand to the opposing pines. As he released them together, the trees arched up and flew apart from each other ripping Silas down the middle, leaving two bloody halves hanging harmlessly in the fresh sea breeze.

**

The journey to Athens continued, as did the challenges to Theseus' life. North of the Isthmus, he dispatched Phaea's Crommyonian Sow that was ravaging the region. Traveling along the cliffs of Megara, he outwitted the bandit Sciron, presenting him the same fate he had given his victims as he tumbled toward the craggy rocks in the sea below.

Theseus kept traveling and eventually came to Eleusis, ruled by the sadistic King Cercyon. The king met Theseus on the road, as he did with all travelers passing through his township, and offered him the same deal he gave to all the others.

"You must wrestle me," he explained. "If you win, I will be sacrificed and you will take my kingdom, but if I win, you will be sacrificed to ensure a prosperous year!"

There was little choice for Theseus, he had to wrestle, but Cercyon was famously strong, the son of Poseidon. The two began their dance of death, and before long Theseus' fears were proven true, there would be no way for him to overpower the King. They grappled and locked for hours but Theseus could not keep his man down. He tried something new, Cerycon bore down on Theseus taking the advantage, but the boy used his wit, he shifted his weight and used the Kings own strength to throw him weightlessly over his shoulder. Cerycon winded himself on the fall down and Theseus won the match using his brains, rather than his brawn and received the Kingdom of Eleusis as his reward.

Before reaching Athens, Theseus encountered one last challenger, Procrustes the stretcher. Like each of his challengers before him, Procrustes was outwitted by Theseus and easily dispatched. And so, after six victories and a long journey, Theseus was free to enter Athens and his father's home.

***

The trials had opened Theseus' eyes to the hostility of the world around him. He entered Athens, and indeed his name had found its way here long before he did. The city was huge and bustling with people coming and going, a site very unfamiliar to the young man. He kept his true identity uiet but found his fame had brought him to the kings court anyway. Here he dined with Aegeas, who begged for him to tell his stories over and over, and his wife Medea who leered in disgust at the young hero. For Medea knew who Theseus truly was, and feared he would take the inheritance of the throne from her own son. The night went on and Medea leant over to Aegeas, whispering in his ear.

"My King, if the boy is who he says he is, then send him to Marathon to slay that Cretan Bull that lays waste to the land."

The challenge was put forth and at once and Theseus left to dispatch the menace. Once he had left, Medea spoke at length of how Theseus had come to steal the throne and that Aegeas should be wary. Days passed and the king and queen agreed to poison the young hero should he return alive. One morning the townspeople cried out in joy. Theseus marched through the Athenian gates with the hulking Marathonian Bull slumped across his shoulder. Again the king invited him to feast with him and tell the tale of his great feat.

At dinner, the preparations were made, as Theseus told his tale, Medea poured him poisoned wine. He took the glass, but in his animated telling of how he overcame the bull, Aegeas noticed something strapped to the boys belt. The glimmering gold sword shone out to him, and the craftsman's work became clear. He peered down and indeed the leather sandals were his! This was his son! Theseus lifted the cup to drink, and in those seconds Aegeas slapped the wine away, cried out in joy and distress and turned on his wife. Medea had fled. Aegeas smiled on Theseus and greeted him anew as his son and the two made up for lost time.

***

Weeks passed and Theseus tended to the roles of a heroic prince, doing his father proud. He had seemed to finally have found a place in the world and his new position led a myriad of potential wives to pass his way. Theseus lost himself in the loves and lusts and desires of his heart but could find no woman that truly satisfied his craving. Each lover was more beautiful than the last but Theseus found them lacking in one way or another. On one of the nights, after his lovers had left and he lay alone, sleep troubled young Theseus. He dreamed of a terrible world of burning flames and putrid smells where his senses were tortured by the onslaught of filth. As he stood weeping, the robed stranger appeared to him.

"Why do you weep, Theseus? Have your senses been overwhelmed? Can you not trust them to see what is real anymore?"

Theseus answered the man, in turn, explaining his desires and loss of reason. He could no longer find satisfaction.

"Can you not see the truth, Theseus?" asked the man. "All things in this world are a delight, but you poison them with your incessant need for more! You are the fly in the ointment, Theseus, you must humble yourself."

Theseus wept, waking himself from his nightmare. The morning sun's rays pierced the skies and he set out to find his fathers council. He found Aegeas atop his cliff top, watching the sea. His father's eyes were deeply troubled and something most peculiar appeared on the horizon. The two watched for some time as the silhouettes of black sails became clearer to their eyes.

"Minos..." whispered the king, "...seven years already?"

"What is it father?" pressed Theseus. "What worries you so? surely you are not fearful of these pirates?"

Aegeas sighed deeply and looked at his son, "They are not pirates my boy. Across the sea, there is a land far away, with people far greater than we. For years they come and pick the best of our youth, sailing them away in their black hulls. There is nothing we can do, nothing you can do. They will make port and we will deliver them youths who will be taken away for their rituals. They take them back to their island land and deliver them to their monster. Put it out of your mind, Theseus. This is the way it is."

Theseus raged, he raged at his fathers hopelessness, he knew he could fight the beast and free Athens and Greece from the tyrannies of these people. He begged to be volunteered, but each request was denied. Theseus kept it up, how could he be great if he were held back he'd say, how could a king do nothing as his people were picked away? Slowly the king gave in.

"You will go Theseus, on a ship with black sails and I will mourn your death. But, should you return in health, put up white sails, for I will wait every day, my heart breaking until I know of your demise. Will you promise me this?"

Theseus agreed and made the preparations.

The sea voyage was long, but the waters strangely calm as he and several of his countrymen and women were ferried away. The crew around them were dark-skinned, they spoke a strange language and slurred awful Greek when an order was needed. For three days they were at sea, and on the third night, the ocean was alight with flames that danced across the waters like stars in the sky. The little lights climbed atop each other and it was clear they were looking at a town built into and on top of a craggy islands cliff face. They were approaching Crete.

The ships made port and the human cargo was forced onshore. The sailors led them in parade up the street into the main town. The alleys and roads were lined with people, and a great calamity filled the ear as if they were the prized guests of a great festival. The winding streets led up to a center filled with even more alien faces, and the captives were pulled in front of a stage from where a man of some status stood and spoke out his alien tongue to the thronging crowd. Theseus took it all in his stead, his father had told him what would happen, the strange customs and what it all meant. His voice echoed in his memory,

"The Minoans are an old people, Theseus. They are full of customs and traditions older than any of our ancestors, older than Greece itself! But this rite, this ritual you are head longed for is different. For you see King Minos did something no one should do, he challenged the gods, he dismissed Poseidon himself and kept the sacred bull for himself. Do you know what Poseidon did, Theseus? He had Minos' wife, Pasiphae, fall in love with the animal, she lusted for it with such burning desire they bedded, all while Poseidon laughed his last laugh! Nine months later she gave birth to baby Asterion, with the body of a man but the head of a raging bull! Minos' son and heir to the throne was a monster. He took his greatest engineer, Daedalus, and built a complex maze, the labyrinth, to hold his son, and every seven years he takes seven of Athens greatest boys and seven of its most beautiful maidens and puts them to their doom inside those twisting walls. That is where you are going, Theseus. You cannot get lost down there. Even if you kill Asterion, you might never find your way back out."

His father's warnings circled through his head. Theseus stood in front of the crowd, watching them, taking in their

Figure 4: Theseus and the Minotaur, from The Story of Greeks, H.A. Guerber, 1896.

faces. But it was the eyes that met his that took him back. Beautiful green emeralds watching his every move, belonging to a girl no older than he yet dressed in clothes of royalty.

The night wore on and the prisoner were taken to their cells. Tomorrow they would meet their fate. Theseus paced his cell, he could not sleep. Time wore on until a small knock at his door broke his thoughts. The emerald-eyed woman slipped into his room pressing her finger to her lips for silence.

"I don't have much time, Theseus," she said. "I am Minos' daughter Ariadne, and you must listen to me carefully. I know the maze and I know the beast that awaits you. You will not defeat it with your bare hands and you will never find your way out. When you enter the labyrinth take the first three right turns, I have hidden a sword and a ball of wool there beneath a rock. Take them and return to the entrance. Tie the wool fast, it will guide you home. Use the blade and free the creature from this world."

Theseus was dumbfounded at his luck. He started slowly and quietly,

"How can I ever repay you?" he questioned.

"When you come out victorious, Minos will know I helped, you must take me away with you, it's all I ask!"

"Fair Ariadne! I will take you with me to Athens and make you my queen!"

A smile broke across the princess' face and she slipped back through the door, bolting it behind her.

The next morning broke with Helios rising his sun and the sound of a hundred trumpets and drums pounding through the air. Theseus was the last to enter the labyrinth and followed Ariadne's instructions. He wound his way through endless corners and dead ends of the labyrinth, it's walls decayed and decrepit through age and lack of maintenance. Oil lamps burned endlessly through the tunnels, throwing shadows and fear as Theseus crept his way around. He held his breath straining for sound, but in the dark cavern, there was nothing but silence. He made his way through, sword in one hand, wool in the other. Without warning the minotaur stormed around a bend and faced off with Theseus.

The beast was huge, his body was indeed that of a man, but terrifying huge. Its skin was dark and its muscles flexed in the flickering light. His neck gave way to the head of a bull, its eyes red with rage, its great horns protruding outward offering death to any who stood in its way. The Minotaur charged, bearing down the tight corridor like a cannonball. Theseus managed a side step narrowly missing the great horns as they flew by his body. Again the bull came around, and again he missed. Over and over the two danced, neither gaining the upper hand. For hours they wrestled and fought, charged and dodged until both were completely worn away. Asterion fell to one knee, thick breath snorting from his nostrils, his strength waned and his head slumped forth revealing the back of his neck.

Theseus took the opportunity and plunged his blade deep into the man-beast. Hot blood spurted up, and Asterion's life fled from his mortal body.

Theseus collapsed in ecstatic relief. He was completely worn by the battle but had come through on top. As he rested, back against the caverns wall, he felt for the first time a kind of contempt he was unfamiliar with. All the fear he had held in flooded away, rushing from his mind and body, and in the silence, he felt inner peace. He had faced death countless times, yet it had never snatched him away, and in the flickering lights of the passageway he questioned if death was really t be feared? He had survived again, he was alive still. He would keep living.

Theseus returned in triumph, the head of the bull held high from his victorious arms. The people outside were in silent shock. The creature had finally fallen, and the man before them was something new. An aura of strength and knowledge surrounded Theseus and wasting no time, he led the surviving Athenians and Ariadne back to the ships.

The trip back was long and the sea's were troubled with turbulence. Mighty Poseidon had watched Theseus take his son's life within the catacombs of Minos' labyrinth and demanded retribution. The god swirled the seas and set wave upon wave crashing down on the small boat. The adventurers made port at the island of Naxos, escaping the storm in its cove and stayed for the night sleeping on the beach. Theseus' dreams were troubling, the goddess Athena came to him, begging him to leave at once and leave his bride, Ariadne. A crack of lightning broke the sky, the earth shook and forced Theseus upright, waking him from his slumber. Storm clouds were regathering and the crew were making ready to leave as the waves found their way into the coves safety. Theseus hurried to his ship to find what the plan was when the winds came gushing across the island. He cried out to the beach but the heavy sleepers slept away. The winds howled and the ships sails were filled until they broke the ties anchoring them still. Helplessly he sat aboard as the winds carried them off, his young bride, Ariadne, stranded alone on the shore became a distant figure as they were carried away. Poseidon laughed heartily for Theseus had lost his beloved just as he had lost his son, and so calmed the storm and the ship sailed for Athens. Theseus full of sorrow and heartache sat on the decks weeping as the crew hurried toward home.

That same morning, King Aegeas, sat atop the cliffs watching the ocean as he had every day since his son's departure. He squinted his eyes and prayed to the gods for Theseus' safe arrival. No sooner had his prayer been sent into the morning winds did he spot a ship on the horizon. He held his breath. It came closer and closer until he could see it for sure. Black Sails. His son was dead. Aegeas howled out in pain, he cursed the gods and wept some more. His son was dead, and so was he. In his sorrow, Aegeas stood at the cliff edge and spied the rocks below. Nothing in this world could keep him anymore, he jumped. His body dashed on the crags below, his blood feeding the sea.

However, Theseus was very alive. He inherited his father's kingdom but never returned for Ariadne. He continued his heroic journeys and exploits uniting the land of Attica under Athens. The land prospered under his rule, and his fame became widespread. But constant travel saw Theseus fall out of favor in Athens. Eventually, the people drove him away and he died alone. But the stories of Theseus after his return are best left for another time.

The Varying Perspectives of Mythological Interpretation

Theories of Myth

Mythology is full of fantastic tales of heroes fighting monsters, long quests far from home, and the ever-looming presence of danger, and on the surface, there is this entertaining narrative that everyone loves. The stories strike a chord in our heart, from our earliest childhood readings all the way to old age, there is something about mythology that mystifies us, leaving a yearning to know more about this dream world.

Yet the true beauty of the stories lies underneath what appears on the surface. It is the personalities that enthrall us, the good and bad decisions of the hero that make us cringe or cry for joy, the impossible challenges faced, and that final triumph of victory. It is reading into what the myth is really trying to say that keeps us coming back. These underlying principles of the tale sing verses to our soul that we are consciously unaware of, yet it is crucial to hear what is being said to truly grasp the importance of mythology.

The ageless tales of mythology have been studied for as long as they have been told, and we now enjoy the interpretations of countless scholars that came before us. It is with their knowledge that we can dive deeper into the tales than anyone before us ever could. We can peer into the tales with numerous lenses, each giving a different perspective of what is being told. And by putting the various viewpoints together, we might be able discern the flickering flame of truth which is buried in the heart of every great tale.

But alas, we must walk before we run, and using the tale of Theseus we will look into a brief overview of some of the methods which will aid us in our journey. To begin, we will split mythological interpretation into two broad categories; external theories and internal theories.

External Theories

Euhemerism

By far the oldest methods of interpreting mythology fall into the category of the external theories. They deal with myth in the 'real world' or perhaps better described as the physical, perceivable world. Broadly speaking, the external theories deal with any historical value that may exist in the stories, they might interpret the characters as natural phenomena, or give explanations for cultural values and rituals, and are also used to explain the cause of things around us.

Very early on, myths were interpreted as historical fact. Herodotus was a Greek living in the

Figure 5: Herodotus. Illustration for The Universal Historical Dictionary by George Crabb (Baldwin, 1825).

fifth century BC who wrote a series of writings call the Histories. These writings give us great incite to the historical events of his day, yet the accounts are thoroughly laced in mythology. For example, when he discusses the cause of the Persian Wars, he states that it originated in the rape of Io by Zeus. The events of mythology seem to hold a place in the mind of early man as a literal incident. This idea of a living mythology is further exemplified by the Greek custom of tracing family lines back to heroes of the Trojan War. Sharing the bloodline of a famous Greek hero was a status symbol for these people, so it was popular for mythology to be seen as historical truth. This custom was long-lived, and we see at the time of the writing of Virgil's Aeneid, that the Roman emperor Augustus was very keen to tie his, and the Roman nation's, lineage to the Trojan hero Aeneas. What this resulted in of course was the peoples want, and the political need, for mythology to be unquestionably historic.

People reassured their historical belief in a number of ways, the retelling of stories, writing them down as 'history' and also keeping relic like evidence of the true life of their heroes. Plutarch wrote an account called The Life of Theseus where he informs the reader that the ship that returned Theseus to Athens was kept in the harbor for several centuries. This kind of 'relic keeping' kept the literal account of Theseus' life alive for the Athenians. So we see these ancient mythologies being linked to everyday life in an attempt to validate the literal truth behind them.

This belief or rationale for bringing mythology and history together is called euhemerism. Though he was far from the first person to do so, the interpretive style is linked to the Greek scholar, Euhemerus and is an approach to the understanding of mythology where mythological accounts are presumed to have originated from real historical events.

The difficulties of pulling the euhemeristic threads out of a tale are in deciding what is historical and what is not. It is usually found in the realm of speculations and assumption, and this guesswork is a dangerous place to stake any solid theories – though that is not to say that there isn't historical reality in the stories. After all, the archaeologist Heinrich Schliemann supposedly found the ancient city of Troy through his euhemeristic interpretations of Homer's Iliad.

Looking into Theseus and the Minotaur, we see a number of euhemerism's jump straight out of the page. The story itself is connected with historical sites, we know that the Minoan civilization existed on Crete and the possible structures for the labyrinth at Knossos. We know that at the height of their power, the Minoans were the greatest sea power in the Mediterranean and it was quite likely they were demanding tribute from smaller cities like Athens. We also see a myriad of art concerning the possible worshipping of bulls within Minoan civilization which explains the symbolic use of the Minotaur. In fact, with a bit of imagination, you could picture a priest wearing the head of a bull in ceremony. Historically speaking, the earliest authors of the Theseus mythology could have been using these facts as influence for his narrative. These examples are few, but instantly we see how historical facts can almost be pulled straight out of the story with careful reading. However, it is also a precaution because we cannot definitively say, 'yes this is what happened', from these stories either, not without further corroborating evidence anyway.

Nature Theory

Like euhemerism, nature theory is a very old way of looking at mythology, yet often gives resounding results in interpretation. In essence, nature theory is the process of attributing natural phenomena to mythic characters and seeing how they relate to each other. In its simplest form, it is something like attributing lightning to Zeus, or earthquakes to Poseidon. In a more complicated version, it is seeing Persephone as the fertility cycle of crops, which we will discuss in depth later.

Figure 6: Jupiter de Smyrna was a statue of unknown origin, brought to King Louis XIV as a restored Zeus around 1686. You can see the chief gods association with lightning.

Reading out of Theseus and the Minotaur again, we see an interesting relationship between Poseidon's bull and Pasiphae. Let's assume the bull is a symbol of Poseidon, and we know Poseidon is symbolic of the sea, so, we can say that the bull is symbolic of the ocean (from which it came to Minos in the first place). Pasiphae being the mother goddess figure in the story can be used to represent the moon. So what we see is an unnatural relationship between the ocean and the moon – perhaps an explanation for the tides? This is an interesting theory, especially when we consider the euphemistic theories above, for we know the Minoan's power came from the sea, and so did their destruction. So using nature theory, we might conclude that the tale is a mythological reasoning for the downfall of the Minoan civilization which originated with King Minos' disrespect of the ocean.

Using the Gods as metaphor helps us understand many of the mythologies, but we can't fit everything under this banner. For example, nature theory simply cannot be used to explain the deeper meanings within Sophocles tale of Oedipus Rex. So it appears that you cannot successfully interpret any myth with any one theory.

Aetiology

The third theory in the interpretation of myth is called aetiology. Etymologically the word comes from the Greek aiton (cause) and logos (logic/study) and is an attempt to explain the cause of things. It can almost be expressed as a 'proto-science' where the world around us is given reason through mythology. For example, in Egyptian mythology, the firmament above us is the goddess Nuit, who is believed to be arching her body over the earth in protection of it. The stars are imprinted onto her, and so there is an explanation for the sky and the celestial bodies. Aetiological reasoning can also be used to see myth as an explanation for the human condition, like how Prometheus' theft of fire in Hesiod's Work and Days led to the fall of humanity and suffering as the human condition. Aetiology is usually easy to find in mythology for it is the explicit reasoning for why something is as it is. In Theseus and the Minotaur, we see that the reason the Aegean Sea has its name is from King Aegeas plunging himself into it.

Ritual Theory

Ritual theory was developed by a man named Sir James Frazer through his extensive study on mythology called The Golden Bough. The idea is that mythology was developed to explain the strange rituals and rites that people were already performing. Frazer posed that man has always believed in magic and the spiritual world, but over time lost faith and needed explanations for the old customs they were still holding onto.

Ritualistic explanations do appear in the story Theseus and the Minotaur. The greatest being the bull worship on Crete. We know through archaeology that there was great importance given to bulls, and also to the labrys, the double-headed ax. The human sacrifice within the story is ritualistic, as is the labyrinth itself, which mirrors the mazes found on the floors of Knossos, Crete, and in temples found throughout the world. Frazer specifically looks at the episode with Theseus and Cerycon as it is a theme that is played in other mythologies. He proposes that the Cerycon is a "year-king" where he must annually do battle and be victorious for the prosperity of his

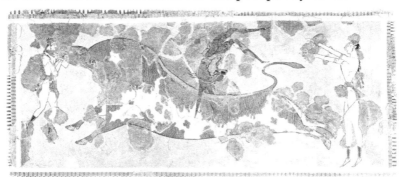

Figure 7: The Bull Leaping Fresco (c. 1450 B.C.) was found in the ruins of Knossos on Crete and suggests a very early form of bull worship.

kingdom and himself. The ritual is known to have existed, and the myth seems to explain it.

It is also interesting to note that many of these early cultures had no Bible as we know it today. There were no canonical books to definitively say how to worship your god. Their rituals were found in their mythology in an attempt to justify their ceremonies, and one must be careful when reading to realize that many mythologies are in fact sacred texts.

Charter Theory

The last of the external explanations is called charter theory. It proposes that mythology is an explanation to its audience for why things are the way they are within a society. This can be observed in Theseus and the Minotaur, it's an obscure reference but we know Pasiphae was worshipped in Laconia and Athens. Her worship included the yearly marriage of a woman to the bull-god, Dionysus, in a building called "the cattle-stall". The myth gives us a possible origin of this rite. A less obscure example can be given through the paraphrased myth below.

Once upon a time, the people of Athens were in need of a patron deity. The people cried out and Poseidon and Athena came to compete for the role. The Athenians looked at the two gods and asked, "What can you do for us?" Poseidon announced an endless supply of clean water, and a beautiful spring broke forth from the ground. The Athenians sang with joy and gulped down generous mouthfuls before vomiting it back up and spitting in disgust, "Salty sea water, yuck!" Athena laughed and offered the people her olive tree. The Athenians accepted her gracious gift and took her on as their patron goddess.

The story shows us how Athens explains its choice of patron deity while also explaining the salt water springs that surround the city. In another related theme, charter theory can be used to explain why some groups of people make a claim for certain lands. For example, in the Biblical Exodus, YHWH promises the Hebrews the land of Canaan, and so the Hebrew people still claim the land of Israel as their own.

Internal Theories

Freudian Interpretation

The internal theories are those that explain the psychological aspect of mythology and really took off when Sigmund Freud published his Interpretation of Dreams in 1913. Freud argued that dreams resemble mythological tales in their imagery and the way they are structured. He likened the way myths could jump between time and places to the way our dreams do and how a dream could be enthralled on the most minute details before blowing out into an overview of things, just as myth does. Freud interpreted myth (like dreams) as the subconscious fulfilling the conscious wish. A basic example of this is Medusa hair which could be symbolizing the phallus, so an interpretation of Medusa is a woman in control of her sexuality. Being portrayed as a monstrous figure, perhaps Medusa is to be seen as symbolic for a woman in control of her sexuality and strong enough to hold her own in a male dominant world, thus striking fear into the hearts of men.

Archetypal Theory

The psychologist Carl Gustav Jung further built on the work of Freud. After studying mythology he found an uncanny similarity between the characters of myth and the figures within dreams. He developed his archetype theory where the same types of heroes, monsters, situations, and places reoccurred within dreams and mythologies. Archetypes will be discussed in detail in chapter 5, but the chart below will give an idea on how his theory worked in mythology.

Hero

The central figure, such as Theseus.

Mentor

The positive figure who teaches and guides the hero, such as the mysterious dream figures, Aegeas and Ariadne.

Threshold Guardians

The stepping stone villains building up to the main villain. They must be overcome, the way this is done relates to the hero type. The six chthonic monsters Theseus encounters on his way to Athens hold this role.

Shadow

What the hero is trying to overcome. This is usually the darker side of himself – the repressed/unacknowledged side, in our case, the Minotaur.

Herald

Delivers the call to action. How the hero is called, and the hero's reply tell a lot of the hero's character. For Theseus, it is his mother.

Trickster

A comic relief character whose motivations are sometimes doubtful - he could have any agenda and is not found in this story, but for example, the Norse god Loki is often a trickster.

Shapeshifter

Usually the same as the trickster but the shapeshifter adds suspense to the story. In our case, it is is Athena within the dream.

Anima

The female element inside the male. Ariadne (within Theseus).

Animus

The male element inside the female. Theseus (within Ariadne).

The important detail about archetypes is that they are the generic character types found in all mythologies and dreams, and because of this, they can be recognized by people regardless of time and culture. In this, we can see that the archetype speaks not to our conscious senses that are reading the story, but a deeper subconscious, and it is through this deeper aspect of the psyche that Jung suggests that all archetypes exist in the collective unconscious of humanity.

Monomyth

Joseph Campbell worked on Jung's idea and further observed that the archetype phenomena spanned across cultures, and were not only found in the classical mythological tradition. Campbell discovered that the structural makeup of a mythology was essentially the same in every tale, despite varying cultures and times. This breakthrough led to his theory of the monomyth. Through this, he drew up a kind of heroic cycle from beginning to end, and though not every stage is found in every myth, or in his stated order, the majority of mythologies could still fit within his model. This was explained by the ideas brought forward by Freud and Jung that mythology was born out of the deep psychology of all men, from a kind of collective unconscious which is why myth resonates with all people across space and time.

Stage I - Departure

1. The Call to Adventure

The hero is living in his normal world when information is received that he must head off. This is Theseus learning of his royal heritage and the trial of moving the boulder.

2. Refusal of the Call

The hero might not take the call to adventure, this is due to fear or duty or insecurity. Theseus questions whether it is right for him to leave.

3. Supernatural Aid

Early in his quest, the hero will encounter a mysterious helper who will give aid or advice that can be counted on through the journey. The mysterious dream figure and also Ariadne offering help and advice to overcome the labyrinth and minotaur.

4. Crossing the Threshold

The hero's first step into the unknown, leaving the safety of his known life into the unknown of his quest. Theseus leaving his home village and setting upon the trail to Athens. Also, Theseus' journey to Crete.

5. Belly of the Whale

Crossing the threshold, the hero undergoes a metamorphosis. He is not stepping outward into the world, but rather into himself, into his psyche. Accepting the challenge, the hero is re-entering a 'womb' from where he will be reborn. Theseus entering the labyrinth is synonymous with entering the dark places of his mind. Here he faces his inner demons in the form of the minotaur. His re-emergence is akin to rebirth.

Stage II - Initiation

6. *The Road of Trials*

This is the main body of mythology where the hero is challenged over and over. These small challenges are preliminary steps showing glimpses of ultimate glory before the final challenge is met. The road to Athens presents a set of trials to Theseus, each one building his confidence and teaching him lessons needed later in life.

7. *The Meeting with the Goddess*

Once the trials have been overcome, the hero is united with a being of unconditional love. This test leads to the acceptance of happy fulfillment for eternity. Ariadne takes the form of the goddess with her love for Theseus and gives him guidance on overcoming the minotaur.

8. *Woman as Temptress*

Woman here is metaphorical, she is representing all the earthly desires the hero yearns for, that unknowingly corrupt him from the divine. For the hero to overcome this temptation he must realize that the corruption is not from the outside world, but from within himself as it is he who falls to temptation. Theseus' many suitors in Athens corrupt his purity. As he is given more and more of the physical world, he wants more and more. The cycle had to be broken.

9. *Atonement with the Father*

This step is central to the hero's journey, it is the ultimate confrontation with the all-powerful masculine figure that dominates the hero's life. This is usually god, but can be represented as a father. The hero must bare all before the father and relies only on the loving protection of the 'goddess' encountered earlier. Upon confrontation, the hero gazes upon the source of life and is contempt with the answers and reasons he finds. Theseus' struggle with the minotaur is a metaphor for his struggle within. When he overcomes his inner beast through the guidance of Ariadne, he is freed from what terrifies him on the physical plane and can take in the beauty of the spiritual.

10. *Apotheosis*

Having found the answers to life, the hero sheds his former mortal skin and in a way dies and is reborn in knowing that he and all things live forever. At this stage, the hero can relax before returning to the world. The labyrinth itself is Theseus' chthonic experience from which he is reborn a new man.

11. *The Ultimate Boon*

The ultimate prize is only gifted to those who are pure and have passed the cleansing of every challenge preceding this one. The prize itself is not immortality but a uniting with the energy source of life. This is personified through god's grace, the elixir of life, the holy grail, et cetera. Theseus learns the fear of death is but a veil hiding life through his experiences in the labyrinth.

Stage III - Return

12. Refusal of the Return

Once the hero has received his prize of understanding, he is obliged to return to his community and share for the prosperity of all. However, this is commonly refused, the hero unwilling to leave the realm of bliss or doubting his ability to explain what he knows. Theseus does return home, but if he hadn't he may well have stayed within the labyrinth where he first felt his ecstasy.

13. The Magic Flight

The prize is not always given to the hero, sometimes he has to take it through confrontation, and if the guardian resents him or the world he wishes to return to, the hero's return will be blocked and further challenges overcome. Poseidon did not agree with Theseus killing his son and so threw up storms and winds to stop his return to Athens.

14. Rescue from Without

The hero may not want to return home, or he may be unable to due to weakness. In these cases, the community often sends help to bring its man back to them. This can be seen as Theseus lays aboard his return ship weeping for Ariadne, the Athenians man the ship and carry him home.

15. The Crossing of the Return Threshold

Once returned to normality the hero has perhaps the greatest challenge yet, he must present his findings to an ignorant audience. He must find finite ways to explain infinite truths that are essential for the furthering of civilization. This is not seen in Theseus, but other common examples are the tales of Buddha, Jesus, and other religious leaders.

16. *Master of Two Worlds*

The hero is able to accept and manage all realities at once, the physical and the spiritual. He can dance between them with ease and becomes a kind of ascended master. As above, this is not seen in Theseus, but other common examples are again the tales of Buddha, Jesus, and other religious leaders.

17. *Freedom to Live*

Having mastered both worlds, the hero is free to live as he no longer fears death. He can live in the moment not regretting the past nor fearing the future. Theseus does not think back of Aegeas or Ariadne but keeps his mind on the present. Continuing his heroic lifestyle could be seen as thoughtlessness and leads to his ultimate demise.

Structuralism

The last of the internal theories is structuralism. Developed by Claude Levi-Strauss who explained that as a result of our physical structure we automatically project a binary significance onto experience, dividing everything into polar opposites. For example, we see light and dark, sweet and sour, raw and cooked, good and evil et cetera. What we also see are certain elements that come to resolve these oppositions. A quick example of this is the human intelligence of Theseus against the animal strength of the minotaur. The feminine Ariadne verses the masculine Theseus. The mortal Minos verses the immortal Poseidon. The good Athenians against the evil Minoans.

So there we have it, the basic tools for interpreting mythology. I will briefly sum them up here for quick reference, but you will find they become second nature the more you read these stories and ponder their deeper meanings yourself.

External Theories

Euhemerism – Myth as a historical account.

Nature Theory – The gods are symbolic for forces of nature.

Aetiology – Myth as an explanation or form of 'proto-science'.

Ritual Theory – Myth formed as an explanation for religious rituals.

Charter Theory – Myth as an explanation for state customs.

Internal Theories

Freudian Interpretation – Myth as symbolic of the subconscious mind.

Archetypal Theory – Reoccurring figures within myths and dreams.

Monomyth – Reoccurring themes within myths and dreams.

Structuralism – the projection of duality and singularity within myth.

A Word of Warning

Along the roadside, in a little cottage lived a man name Procrustes. A hospitable man, he would offer his home to anyone who passed by, and would go on to brag how comfortable his guest bed was, and that it would perfectly fit any who lay upon it. What he would leave out, however, was the magic behind the bed. If the guest was a little too long,

Procrustes would go to work on his legs, cutting the guest to size, and if they were too short, stretch them on the rack...

Don't be Procrustes. You cannot stretch or cut away a myth to fit your interpretation. The myth is what it is, and it is your job to interpret it with what is at hand.

Symbolic Secrets & Attaining Higher Wisdom

Hidden Symbols

Why is the understanding of symbolism so important in revealing the truth within mythology? It seems that in every story, no matter how simple, there is a mysterious hidden meaning meant only for those who look for it. These mysteries are as plain as day, but how can this hidden knowledge be attained for those uninitiated in symbolic interpretation?

It come as no surprise to learn that mythology is symbolic. In fact, mythology is heavily symbolic, and if you are going to read it and understand it you have to understand what symbolism is. There is no mystery here for the definition though, symbolism is simply a way to convey ideas between people. It occurs in many ways, but usually through the use of something mundane to represent something more complicated. For example, a picture of a heart representing the emotion love.

As simple as the definition is, the practice of symbolic representation is incredibly diverse. By this, I mean there are a plethora of ways to present an idea, from writing it down, to pictures, to music, to rituals, plays and movies, and of course through oral traditions such as fables, parables and mythology. All these methods can convey ideas directly or indirectly, which leads to layers of meaning. A mythology may have a simple message in its direct reading, but by decoding the symbolism held within, deeper layers of meaning will start to emerge.

Symbols hold different levels of meaning and understanding based on who the author is and who is reading. For example, a picture of the sun might be representing the star in the sky, but it could equally be portraying the life-giving energy that the sun gives earth. This life-giving energy, in turn, may be symbolic of the soul, or the divine creator. In one image of the sun, you can see multiple layers of meaning emerge.

So what we begin to see

Figure 8: The Square and Compass is a common symbol found within freemasonry. Using their heritage as master builders, devices from that profession have been used to represent means of attaining higher knowledge. One interpretation is that the fixed square is symbolic of the physical, or, material world, while the compass represents that of the spirit as it is variable in its movements. The two combined can be used for the individuals self mastery. The central G may stand for God, or the Hebrew letter gimmel tying in with kabalistic beliefs.

is that symbolism is simply a way to convey ideas that otherwise might not be able to be conveyed. An example of this would be trying to explain an experience to someone who has not shared the same experience. You could help give them an understanding of that experience by explaining it to them through an allegorical story, using images they know to symbolize the meaning you are trying to convey.

This thought carries on to practical symbolism as found through initiation rites and religious ceremonies. For example, initiates of the Eleusinian Mysteries undergo a nine-day ritual that is symbolic of the nine months during pregnancy. The completion of the nine-day ritual, therefore, symbolizes rebirth in the individual who becomes a member of the cult with a new understanding on life.

Symbolic representation undoubtedly predates writing. This is shown by caves that are scrawled with pre-historic paintings and pictograms, by the rituals of illiterate tribes, and the stories passed down through countless oral cultures. The mere fact that something can be used to mean something else is most likely what gave rise to writing in the first place. After all, the letters of the alphabet are symbols and when you put them into the correct order they form words and ideas that the reader can understand. Egyptian hieroglyphs are symbolic in the same way, the images have meanings, and if you have been taught the meanings, you can read the sentences and understand what is being conveyed. This is symbolism at its heart.

But symbolic representation really comes into its own when what is written takes more than one meaning. For example, think about this sentence,

"His heart belongs to the girl."

Now it should be quite obvious by the context that his heart does not literally belong to the girl, but rather that he is in love with her. Using the word heart, therefore, is synonymous for his love. The sentence is symbolic. Now context is important in deciphering the symbolism, perhaps his heart, the literally organ, does belong to her, you have to decide that based on what is going on in the story. But along with this, a level of cultural understanding is needed to understand the symbolism. What I mean is that Greek mythology will use symbols quite differently to that of Chinese mythology, or any other different culture for that matter.

How To Decipher Mythic Symbolism

Now, symbolism does take various forms in the way it is presented and can be very hard to spot, especially if you are uneducated in the culture you are reading from. The only real way to resolve this is to read that cultures works, look for repeating patterns and read about other people's interpretations of the stories. However, there is a kind of formula you can use to get you started.

1. Read the story and look for things that stand out. Look for something that is odd or that is repeated and associate the context in which it is found.
2. What does this thing resemble? Does it share qualities with something else in the story or in the real world? You may have just found a link through symbolism.
3. How does the author feel about this thing? How is it being portrayed? The author wants you to feel the same way and to carry this feeling on to the real world and onto what this thing really represents.

Symbolic representation, especially in mythology, is layered and connected. By finding one symbol, you will usually find it connected later on with another symbol, and slowly a second, or third, or fourth layer to the narrative is revealed. The crux of symbolic representation is that it is only open to those that think. To connect the symbolism is not a work of facts and learning, but of meditation and thought. This means the deeper teachings, the secrets, and true knowledge is only available to those of us who stop to think.

Plastic Mythology

As I said earlier, it is very helpful to read the interpretations of others even though the original meanings of the myth may very well be completely different from what the interpreter has come up with. When symbolism is interpreted, the interpreter will naturally see things that will strike a chord with them, but this does not make their interpretation wrong, but rather adds further layers of meaning, all of which are true and valuable.

Even though the interpretation may not be what was initially intended, it is still valuable. This is because mythology has a certain plasticity, there are no definite facts within it. Unlike history which is something that has happened in a certain place and time, mythology is something that we live again and again. It is universal to the human condition in that it is an archetypal representation of certain patterns that we experience.

In other words, mythology is a way to explain our living experiences, which means all interpretations are correct because they explain the experience of the interpreter. And the reasons another person's interpretations are important to you is because we all share the same reality and the same archetypal representations.

Therefore, it is irrelevant whether the events of mythology ever really took place in a historical sense. It does not matter if Judas really betrayed Jesus, or if Osiris was betrayed by Set. What matters is that betrayal is a universal theme experienced by all people, it is universal to the human condition. And understanding every interpretation of these stories brings you closer to understanding the true meaning of the original story and therefore the reality of the experience.

To bring it full circle, mythology is the symbolic representation of the human experience that is life.

Symbols In Mythology

Now that we have an understanding on what symbolism is in mythology, it wouldn't be any fun if we didn't actually look at some. I will explain some of the symbols that the meanings are largely agreed on. But keep this in mind, the key to mythology is in its plethora of interpretations, and that not one is solely right, and that none is truly wrong. Don't get too dogmatic in what you believe. Symbolism is a way to represent and express different ideas and concepts, so their meanings by nature will continually evolve.

Wild Animals and Primal Urges

Wild or primal animals are representative of humanities primal urges. The ferocity of the beast is indicative of fear, hatred, rage, lust and all other urges that need to be controlled for civilized life. The primal animal becomes the exaggerated mythic monsters in grand stories, but they still represent the blown up primal urge of the hero trying to destroy it. Just look at the stories of Mithras and the Tauroctony, Hercules, and the Cretan Bull, or Gilgamesh and the Bull of Heaven. The reason these animals are wild is because they cannot exist in society, in the same way, that the emotions they symbolize cannot exist in a harmonious civilization.

Figure 9: Here we see the Persian Mithra killing the sacred bull. Interpretations of the tauroctony are widespread and become complex. In some versions we see the bull representing primal urges and so Mithra is overcoming or subduing his base instincts. In astro-mythology the bull may represent the age of Tauros to which Mithra is taking humanity out of. This relief comes from a double sided alter piece from the second century A.D. found near Fiano Romano, Italy.

Snakes, Wisdom, and Immortality

Snakes are hugely symbolic throughout the world and hold various meanings to different cultures. Though it seems universal that they stand for wisdom and immortality. It was largely believed that the shedding of the snake's skin was its way of giving itself rebirth and living forever. This is first recorded in the Sumerian, Epic of Gilgamesh, where the snake steals the fruit of life. The snake's immortality later led it to symbolize medicine, and it can be seen coiling around the caduceus of Asclepius, God of Medicine, and on modern medical insignia. Its wisdom is also universal, the Biblical Genesis shows the snake offering the fruit of knowledge to man.

Picking Flowers and the Loss of Innocence

This symbolism is particularly true for Greek mythology (and every culture they influenced...) and is quite strong. You will often see young girls picking flowers in the fields with their friends. This is symbolic of youth, immaturity, and innocence. However, the scene is almost always tragic in that the youth will be kidnapped, stolen, or raped. Picking flowers is a foreshadowing of innocence lost, but also of the evolution of character. We will look at the Homeric Hymn to Demeter later, but you will see Persephone picking flowers before her abduction by Hades. However, the story shows her transform from immaturity to womanhood.

Fighting and the Internal Struggle

Internal struggles of the mind can be represented as external struggles between people. For example, two brothers fighting could be representative of an individual struggling with them self. This becomes obvious when you consider the expected strength of a family unit, where all members of the family should work together for success. When there is discordance within the family, it no longer functions healthily. The mind works in the same way, despite popular belief, the mind is actually a parliament of various voices. For example, if an individual is trying to quit smoking then some voices in the individuals head will scream the need to smoke, others will rationalize the need to quit, some debate the need for pleasure, others the need for restraint. Different voices in the one head create the struggle of the mind, often represented by the struggle of the family unit. Just look at the Labors of Hercules, Cain killing Abel, Horace fighting Set, or Jacob wrestling the Angel. These can all be symbolic for the internal struggle.

Towers, Beliefs, and Starting Anew

Towers, walls, and fortifications are usually representative of the ideas or beliefs built up in your mind that defend your beliefs and understanding in the world. The destruction of the tower in mythology can represent the tearing down of these beliefs to start a new. This is clearest in the Tarot, where the Tower card represents just this, a huge unpredictable fall or failure. As bad as this sounds though, it is actually good, through death and destruction, rebirth and change can occur. The structured beliefs we have held on to sometimes become outdated, and it is then that they need changing, and the destruction of the tower becomes a beneficial event. You can see through this how destruction and creation are critically linked together. Look at the Tower of Babel in Genesis, this could easily symbolize the ego growing to such size that it thinks it is like a god. Only its destruction can bring it back to reality where the individual can function healthily again.

Naturally, this is only a taste of symbolic representation in mythology. The topic is literally endless, and we will discuss it further as we continue to look at different mythologies. Always keep in mind that no interpretation is 100% right or wrong, but that they are all parts of the whole in understanding the meaning of the story.

Creation Mythology

Enuma Elish

This is the beginning of the Babylonian creation myth, Enuma Elish. It is not the entire document but gives a good account of their beliefs on the beginnings of the universe and the birth of humanity.

***

In the beginning, neither heaven nor earth had names. Apsu, the god of fresh waters, and Tiamat, the goddess of the salt oceans, and Mummu, the god of the mist that rises from both of them, were still mingled as one. There were no mountains, there was no pasture land, and not even a reed-marsh could be found to break the surface of the waters.

It was then that Apsu and Tiamat parented two gods, and then two more who outgrew the first pair. These further parented gods, until Ea, who was the god of rivers and was Tiamat and Apsu's great-grandson, was born. Ea was the cleverest of the gods, and with his magic, Ea became the most powerful of the gods, ruling even his forebears.

Apsu and Tiamat's descendants became an unruly crowd. Eventually Apsu, in his frustration and inability to sleep with the clamor, went to Tiamat, and he proposed to her that he slay their noisy offspring. Tiamat was furious at his suggestion to kill their clan, but after leaving her Apsu resolved to proceed with his murderous plan. When the young gods heard of his plot against them, they were silent and fearful, but soon Ea was hatching a scheme. He cast a spell on Apsu, pulled Apsu's crown from his head, and slew him. Ea then built his palace on Apsu's waters, and it was there that, with the goddess Damkina, he fathered Marduk, the four-eared, four-eyed giant who was god of the rains and storms.

The other gods, however, went to Tiamat and complained of how Ea had slain her husband. Aroused, she collected an army of dragons and monsters, and at its head, she placed the god Kingu, whom she gave magical powers as well. Even Ea was at a loss how to combat such a host until he finally called on his son Marduk. Marduk gladly agreed to take on his father's battle, on the condition that he, Marduk, would rule the gods after achieving this victory. The other gods agreed, and at a banquet, they gave him his royal robes and scepter.

Marduk armed himself with a bow and arrows, a club, and lightning, and he went in search of Tiamat's monstrous army. Rolling his thunder and storms in front him, he attacked, and Kingu's battle plan soon disintegrated. Tiamat was left alone to fight Marduk, and she howled as they closed for battle. They struggled as Marduk caught her in his nets. When she opened her mouth to devour him, he filled it with the evil wind that served him. She could not close her mouth with his gale blasting in it, and he shot an arrow down her throat. It split her heart, and she was slain.

After subduing the rest of her host, he took his club and split Tiamat's water-laden body in half like a clamshell.

Half he put in the sky and made the heavens, and he posted guards there to make sure that Tiamat's salt waters could not escape. Across the heavens, he made stations in the stars for the gods, and he made the moon and set it forth on its schedule across the heavens. From the other half of Tiamat's body, he made the land, which he placed over Apsu's fresh waters, which now arise in wells and springs. From her eyes, he made flow the Tigris and Euphrates. Across this land he made the grains and herbs, the pastures and fields, the rains and the seeds, the cows and ewes, and the forests and the orchards.

Marduk set the vanquished gods who had supported Tiamat to a variety of tasks, including work in the fields and canals. Soon they complained of their work, however, and they rebelled by burning their spades and baskets. Marduk saw a solution to their labors, though, and proposed it to Ea. He had Kingu, Tiamat's general brought forward from the ranks of the defeated gods, and Kingu was executed. Kingu's blood was mixed with clay from the earth, and with spittle from the other gods, Ea and the birth-goddess Nintu created humans. On them, Ea imposed the labor previously assigned to the gods. Thus the humans were set to maintain the canals and boundary ditches, to hoe and to carry, to irrigate the land and to raise crops, to raise animals and fill the granaries, and to worship the gods at their regular festivals.

***

Figure 10: Tiamat fights Marduk. Black and white crop of full plate scan, from Austen Henry Layard's 'Monuments of Nineveh, Second Series' plate 19/83, London, J. Murray, 1853

The Babylonian creation myth, Enuma Elish, shares many qualities that are seen in all stories that explain the birth of the Cosmos and the creation of humanity. Paralleling the much older Australian Aboriginal Creation Myth (discussed later), we see that in the beginning that events are initiated by a masculine 'active' deity (Apsu), who sets things in motion by interacting with a feminine 'passive' deity (Tiamat). A number of deities are born through several generations and then there is a cosmic battle that results in a new hierarchy of gods, with the youngest deity from the third generation taking the role of leader (Marduk). This series of events is later retold in Hesiod's Theogony. Finally, the birth of humanity is explained and the human condition of suffering is told to be a result of the gods needs for mortal slaves. In this story, the divine hierarchy is symbolic for what is found on earth, with the Babylonian social order being divided into slave, workers, aristocrats, and the monarch. By telling the Enuma Elish, the structure of Babylonian society is justified and people can accept their roles in life because it appears to be sanctioned by the divine world.

Through observing the many ways in which mythology can be interpreted, it makes sense that there is a huge variety of topics discussed in the various stories. In this way, mythology becomes a 'virtual reality' in that it is an imaginary realm where various ideas can be thrown around and experimented with. The interactions of various personalities can be experimented with, different situations can be played out, and explanations for the world can be trialed with in a way to understand the world around us. These experimental mythologies are distilled down and told to audiences in a way that can impart lessons on how to live a purposeful and happy life.

Categorizing mythology is not such an easy task, where the primary motive for one may be an explanation for the universe, the same myth may impart teachings on ethics and morality. The stories twist and turn, interweaving with one another to create a complex web of beliefs and a sometimes frustrating system of religious doctrine. But despite this, we will do our best to break these mythologies down into understandable segments.

In The Beginning

Have you ever stopped to ask yourself what life is? What is this reality we are all experiencing? Have you ever pondered the origins of the universe? Or do you think it has always been here, existing outside the limits of linear time? Do gods really exist, and if they do, what are they? These are humanities primal questions, they are the mysteries of reality that have no definitive answer. We have approached them in every way, through science, logical philosophy, through religion, and most importantly to us, by means of mythology. The questions predate civilization and they exist in our earliest writings where we see some of mankind's earliest stories attempting to define the origins of existence.

To learn about these early stories it is beneficial for us to learn about the cultures they came from and how these cultures came to be in the first place. If we travel back some five thousand years and observe an area known as the Fertile Crescent in modern day Iraq, we see a profound change in the way humans have lived. Humanity to date has always survived as either hunter-gatherers or nomadic herders, but here, between the mighty Tigris and Euphrates rivers, people learned that if they planted seeds in fertile ground, then they could grow their own food. By growing our own food, people were able to stay in the one place instead of constantly being on the move. The agricultural revolution was born. People began to aggregate together and small villages turned into small towns. The farms grew in size and allowed for more people to come and live. Soon the small towns turned into small cities and slowly civilization was born.

We now call this land Mesopotamia, and the people we are speaking about are known as the Sumerians. As agriculture developed it soon came to pass that the farmers could produce more food than they could eat themselves. This meant that within these cities, people were freed from trying to feed themselves and could specialize in other skills. We see leaps in metal work and art, and perhaps most importantly the advent of writing. It seems that the Sumerians were the first to experiment with writing, literally putting marks into wet clay that symbolized sounds they would make from their mouths. The Sumerians could write sounds! And by writing them down, this meant that the words could last forever.

The wet clay tablets were held in great royal libraries. Some of these libraries burnt down and the huge fires acted as kilns baking the wet tablets hard. These hardened tablets remained in the burnt out libraries and were buried by the desert sands until of course they were rediscovered in the 19th century by western archaeologists. These archeologists took the records and sent them back to European libraries and museums, and eventually, the Sumerian writing was deciphered. Millions and millions of these tablets were recovered and slowly they were translated from the ancient cuneiform script into modern languages that the world could read once more.

As these texts were translated a huge amount of information was discovered. The bulk of texts were accountant like records of where wealth was being distributed and who owned what. The content is dry, but it still gives us a snapshot of what it was like to live in humanities first civilization. Among the vast majority of business tablets, there were also the highly sacred, and significantly rarer religious texts. They contained the sciences of the day, documents on worship and belief, and the arts of life. Among the ancient relics, we were blessed to have found the Epic of Gilgamesh, the oldest work of epic writing and our first account of a heroic story. Written around 2100 BC, it is often regarded as the oldest piece of great literature, but it was not found in a single piece. Rather, it was recovered from various sources and pieced back together. Most interestingly, the epics Sumerian name actually translates to He Who Sees The Unknown.

Pantheistic Worldview

Prior to the development of a monotheistic worldview, most of humanity held a pantheistic belief where there were many gods that ruled over various stations in the universe. From Mesopotamia, we see the story of the creation told in the Babylonian mythology, Enuma Elish, a complex document full of highly specialized language and symbolism specific to their culture. Despite its cultural specificity, the Enuma Elish does not stand alone in its theories or overarching message. The tale it tells is found in all pantheistic societies and can be found in Greek society through Hesiod's Theogony, in the Maori myth of Rangi and Papa, or the Norse stories of Niflheim, Ginnungagap, and Muspelheim, to name but a few of the worlds cultures.

Because the creation myth is generally the same throughout the world, many cultures shared a similar belief in the way that the universe was made up. The universe was composed of layers, the lowest layer was the underworld, Hades, or hell. Above this, the earth populated by mortals. The sky sits on top of us, then there is the firmament which was a kind of barrier between the inhabited world below and the original primordial soup that is the origins of everything. The stars are printed on the firmament, and the rest of the astral bodies were seen as living beings. These beings were the wanderers - the

Sun, the Moon and the five planets, Mercury, Venus, Mars, Saturn, and Jupiter. These wanderers moved through the firmament into and out of the primordial soup as they are divinely ordered to do.

Topographically, the Mediterranean people believed the earth was divided into three sections - Europe, Asia and Africa, the Mediterranean Sea in the middle, and the world river/ocean surrounds the continents, giving us a flat, plate-like earth, with a snow-globe roof being the firmament.

The creation of the world always starts with the primordial soup. It could today be likened with space but was often described as being composed of a watery like substance. It is what all creation originated from. This water housed two great forces, like yin and yang, there was a creative feminine force and an active masculine force. The two forces were symbolized as primordial gods, the masculine father initiates action by procreating with the mother, and she creates a second set of primordial gods, and usually another race of beings that we might associate with demons or monsters. The original father is threatened by the second generation of gods and attempts to destroy them. One of the second generation gods, usually the youngest male, makes a stand, rallies his siblings and overcomes the parents. This youngest son takes leadership and begins to create order out of the primordial forces. He separates the waters of the primordial soup, making a space to create the earth and gives the gods divine tasks such as moving the planets in a set way or keeping the balance of life on earth. The earth is then populated by humanity and mortal life and the young leader god becomes the patriarchal deity of the universe.

What has occurred that is significant for the people who accept this belief is that no god is mightier than the other. The gods are more seen as immortal super-humans, they have good and bad personalities and are free to overpower each other. The primordial soup is also seen as the original pure substance, and the gods too are under its power. Magic can exist as an attempt to circumnavigate the gods and tap into the powers of the primordial substance. In this way, the gods are not all powerful, but still, hold power over human affairs, so need to be kept satisfied. It is a complex affair.

Australian Aboriginal Creation Myth

The Australian continent is incredibly large and the native cultures that inhabit it are widespread and diverse. They all share a mythological custom called the Dreamtime and this tale of creation is common to many of the Aboriginal cultures.

***

At the beginning of time, everything was still. All the spirits of the earth were asleep - well nearly all. The only one awake was the great Father of all Spirits. He gently awoke the Sun Mother. She opened her eyes slowly and a ray of warm light shot off toward the sleeping earth. Then, the Father of All spirits said to the Sun Mother,

"Sun Mother, I have some work for you to do. Go down to the Earth and wake up the sleeping spirits. Give them forms."

The Sun Mother descended down to Earth, which at the time was bare and began to walk in all directions and everywhere she went the plants started to grow. After returning to the field where she had begun her work the Sun Mother rested, pleased with what she had done. The Father of All Spirits came and saw her work, but instructed her to go into the caves and wake the spirits there as well.

She ventured into the dark caves and the bright light that shone from her awoke the spirits. After she left, every different kind of insect flew out of the caves. The Sun Mother sat down and watched the wonderful sight of her insects mingling with her flowers. Once again the Father came to her and urged her to keep going.

The Sun Mother ventured into a very deep cave, spreading her light around her. Her heat melted the ice which created the rivers and streams of the world. Then she created fish and small snakes, lizards and frogs. Next, she awoke the spirits of the birds and animals and they burst into the sunshine in a glorious array of colors. Seeing this the Father of All Spirits was now pleased with all the work that the Sun Mother had done.

She called all of her creations to her and instructed them to enjoy the earth and to live peacefully with one another. Then she ascended back into the sky and became the sun.

The living creatures watched the Sun in awe as she crept across the sky towards the west. But when she sunk beneath the horizon, all of the creatures became horrified believing that she had deserted them. All night they stood frozen in their places, thinking that the end of time had come. After what seemed to them like a lifetime the Sun Mother arose her head above the horizon in the East. After this first night, the children of the earth learned to expect her coming and going and were no longer filled with fear.

At first, the children lived together peacefully, but after a time, jealousy crept into their hearts. They began to argue with each other. The Sun Mother was forced to come down from her home in the sky to intervene with their constant fighting. She gave each creature the ability to change their form to whatever they chose. The results were a nightmare, and the Sun Mother was saddened by what she saw. The rats she had made had formed into bats; giant lizards and fish gave themselves blue tongues and feet. And all sorts of odd amalgamations of animal occurred.

The Sun Mother looked down upon the Earth and thought to herself that she must create new creatures lest the Father of All Spirits be angered by what had occurred. She gave birth to two children who were divine. The god was the Morning Star and the goddess was the moon. From these god, two more children were born and these children the Sun Mother sent down to Earth. They became our ancestors. She made them superior to the animals because they had part of her mind and would never want to change their shape.

Figure 11: Rock art is common in Australian Aboriginal culture. Here we see the mythology of the Mowanjum tribe represented in art. Depicted here are the rain and cloud gods called Wondjina who created the landscape during the dreamtime.

Hesiod's Theogony

What follows is selected sections of Hesiod's Theogony
which is the Greek creation myth. You will see many
parallels in its themes with the Babylonian Enuma Elish.
The translation comes from Hugh G. Evelyn-White (Loeb
Classical Library, 1914).

***

(ll. 104-115) Hail, children of Zeus! Grant lovely song and
celebrate the holy race of the deathless gods who are
forever, those that were born of Earth and starry Heaven
and gloomy Night and them that briny Sea did rear. Tell
how at the first gods and earth came to be, and rivers, and
the boundless sea with its raging swell, and the gleaming
stars, and the wide heaven above, and the gods who were
born of them, givers of good things, and how they divided
their wealth, and how they shared their honours amongst
them, and also how at the first they took many-folded
Olympus. These things declare to me from the beginning,
ye Muses who dwell in the house of Olympus, and tell me
which of them first came to be.

(ll. 116-138) Verily at the first Chaos came to be, but next
wide-bosomed Earth, the ever-sure foundations of all the
deathless ones who hold the peaks of snowy Olympus, and
dim Tartarus in the depth of the wide-pathed Earth, and
Eros (Love), fairest among the deathless gods, who
unnerves the limbs and overcomes the mind and wise
counsels of all gods and all men within them. From Chaos
came forth Erebus and black Night; but of Night were born
Aether and Day, whom she conceived and bare from
union in love with Erebus. And Earth first bare starry

Heaven, equal to herself, to cover her on every side, and to be an ever-sure abiding-place for the blessed gods. And she brought forth long Hills, graceful haunts of the goddess-Nymphs who dwell amongst the glens of the hills. She bare also the fruitless deep with his raging swell, Pontus, without sweet union of love. But afterwards she lay with Heaven and bare deep-swirling Oceanus, Coeus and Crius and Hyperion and Iapetus, Theia and Rhea, Themis and Mnemosyne and gold-crowned Phoebe and lovely Tethys. After them was born Cronos the wily, youngest and most terrible of her children, and he hated his lusty sire.

(ll. 139-146) And again, she bare the Cyclopes, overbearing in spirit, Brontes, and Steropes and stubborn-hearted Arges, who gave Zeus the thunder and made the thunderbolt: in all else, they were like the gods, but one eye only was set in the midst of their foreheads. And they were surnamed Cyclopes (Orb-eyed) because one orbed eye was set in their foreheads. Strength and might and craft were in their works.

(ll. 147-163) And again, three other sons were born of Earth and Heaven, great and doughty beyond telling, Cottus and Briareos and Gyes, presumptuous children. From their shoulders sprang an hundred arms, not to be approached, and each had fifty heads upon his shoulders on their strong limbs, and irresistible was the stubborn strength that was in their great forms. For of all the children that were born of Earth and Heaven, these were the most terrible, and they were hated by their own father from the first.

And he used to hide them all away in a secret place of Earth so soon as each was born, and would not suffer them to come up into the light: and Heaven rejoiced in his evil doing. But vast Earth groaned within, being straitened, and she made the element of grey flint and shaped a great sickle, and told her plan to her dear sons. And she spoke, cheering them, while she was vexed in her dear heart:

(ll. 164-166) `My children, gotten of a sinful father, if you will obey me, we should punish the vile outrage of your father; for he first thought of doing shameful things.'

(ll. 167-169) So she said; but fear seized them all, and none of them uttered a word. But great Cronos the wily took courage and answered his dear mother:

(ll. 170-172) `Mother, I will undertake to do this deed, for I reverence not our father of evil name, for BNhe first thought of doing shameful things.'

(ll. 173-175) So he said: and vast Earth rejoiced greatly in spirit, and set and hid him in an ambush, and put in his hands a jagged sickle, and revealed to him the whole plot.

(ll. 176-206) And Heaven came, bringing on night and longing for love, and he lay about Earth spreading himself full upon her.

Then the son from his ambush stretched forth his left hand and in his right took the great long sickle with jagged teeth, and swiftly lopped off his own father's members and cast them away to fall behind him. And not vainly did they fall from his hand; for all the bloody drops that gushed forth Earth received, and as the seasons moved round she bare the strong Erinyes and the great Giants with gleaming armor, holding long spears in their hands and the Nymphs whom they call Meliae all over the boundless earth. And so soon as he had cut off the members with flint and cast them from the land into the surging sea, they were swept away over the main a long time: and a white foam spread around them from the immortal flesh, and in it there grew a maiden. First, she drew near holy Cythera, and from there, afterward, she came to sea-girt Cyprus and came forth an awful and lovely goddess, and grass grew up about her beneath her shapely feet. Her gods and men call Aphrodite, and the foam-born goddess and rich-crowned Cytherea, because she grew amid the foam, and Cytherea because she reached Cythera, and Cyprogenes because she was born in billowy Cyprus, and Philommedes because sprang from the members. And with her went Eros, and comely Desire followed her at her birth at the first and as she went into the assembly of the gods. This honor she has from the beginning, and this is the portion allotted to her amongst men and undying gods, — the whisperings of maidens and smiles and deceits with sweet delight and love and graciousness.

(ll. 207-210) But these sons whom be begot himself great Heaven used to call Titans (Strainers) in reproach, for he said that they strained and did presumptuously a fearful deed and that vengeance for it would come afterward.

***

This section which I have omitted goes into lengthy details on the births of other divine beings. Many of which are pseudonyms for worldly phenomena like Sleep and Dreams and others include moral or ethical features like Doom, Famine, and Toil. Also explained is the birth of some monsters like Echidna and Typhon who become important features in later Greek mythology.

***

(ll. 453-491) But Rhea was subject in love to Cronos and bare splendid children, Hestia, Demeter, and gold-shod

Figure 12: Painting by Sir Peter Paul Rubens (1577 - 1640) of Kronos eating one of his children.

Hera and strong Hades, pitiless in heart, who dwells under the earth, and the loud-crashing Earth-Shaker, and wise Zeus, father of gods and men, by whose thunder the wide earth is shaken. These great Cronos swallowed as each came forth from the womb to his mother's knees with this intent, that no other of the proud sons of Heaven should hold the kingly office amongst the deathless gods. For he learned from Earth and starry Heaven that he was destined to be overcome by his own son, strong though he was, through the contriving of great Zeus. Therefore he kept no blind outlook, but watched and swallowed down his children: and unceasing grief seized Rhea. But when she was about to bear Zeus, the father of gods and men, then she besought her own dear parents, Earth and starry Heaven, to devise some plan with her that the birth of her dear child might be concealed, and that retribution might overtake great, crafty Cronos for his own father and also for the children whom he had swallowed down. And they readily heard and obeyed their dear daughter, and told her all that was destined to happen touching Cronos the king and his stout-hearted son. So they sent her to Lyetus, to the rich land of Crete, when she was ready to bear great Zeus, the youngest of her children. Him did vast Earth receive from Rhea in wide Crete to nourish and to bring up. Thither came Earth carrying him swiftly through the black night to Lyctus first, and took him in her arms and hid him in a remote cave beneath the secret places of the holy earth on thick-wooded Mount Aegeum; but to the mightily ruling son of Heaven, the earlier king of the gods, she gave a great stone wrapped in swaddling clothes. Then he took it in his hands and thrust it down into his belly: Wretch! he knew not in his heart that in place of the stone his son was left behind, unconquered and untroubled, and that he was soon to overcome him by force and might and drive him from his honours, himself to reign over the deathless gods.

(ll. 492-506) After that, the strength and glorious limbs of the prince increased quickly, and as the years rolled on, great Cronos the wily was beguiled by the deep suggestions of Earth, and brought up again his offspring, vanquished by the arts and might of his own son, and he vomited up first the stone which he had swallowed last. And Zeus set it fast in the wide-pathed earth at goodly Pytho under the glens of Parnassus, to be a sign thenceforth and a marvel to mortal men. And he set free from their deadly bonds the brothers of his father, sons of Heaven whom his father in his foolishness had bound. And they remembered to be grateful to him for his kindness, and gave him thunder and the glowing thunderbolt and lightening: for before that, huge Earth had hidden these. In them he trusts and rules over mortals and immortals.

(ll. 507-543) Now Iapetus took to wife the neat-ankled mad Clymene, daughter of Ocean, and went up with her into one bed. And she bare him a stout-hearted son, Atlas:

71

also she bare very glorious Menoetius and clever Prometheus, full of various wiles, and scatter-brained Epimetheus who from the first was a mischief to men who eat bread; for it was he who first took of Zeus the woman, the maiden whom he had formed. But Menoetius was outrageous, and far-seeing Zeus struck him with a lurid thunderbolt and sent him down to Erebus because of his mad presumption and exceeding pride. And Atlas through hard constraint upholds the wide heaven with unwearying head and arms, standing at the borders of the earth before the clear-voiced Hesperides; for this lot wise Zeus assigned to him. And ready-witted Prometheus he bound with inextricable bonds, cruel chains, and drove a shaft through his middle, and set on him a long-winged eagle, which used to eat his immortal liver; but by night the liver grew as much again every way as the long-winged bird devoured in the whole day. That bird Heracles, the valiant son of shapely-ankled Alcmene, slew; and delivered the son of Iapetus from the cruel plague, and released him from his affliction — not without the will of Olympian Zeus who reigns on high, that the glory of Heracles the Theban-born might be yet greater than it was before over the plenteous earth. This, then, he regarded, and honored his famous son; though he was angry, he ceased from the wrath which he had before because Prometheus matched himself in wit with the almighty son of Cronos. For when the gods and mortal men had a dispute at Mecone, even then Prometheus was forward to cut up a great ox and set portions before them, trying to befool the mind of Zeus. Before the rest he set flesh and inner parts thick with fat upon the hide, covering them with an ox paunch; but for Zeus, he put the white bones dressed up with cunning art and covered with shining fat. Then the father of men and of gods said to him:

(ll. 543-544) `Son of Iapetus, most glorious of all lords, good sir, how unfairly you have divided the portions!'

(ll. 545-547) So said Zeus whose wisdom is everlasting, rebuking him. But wily Prometheus answered him, smiling softly and not forgetting his cunning trick:

(ll. 548-558) `Zeus, most glorious and greatest of the eternal gods, take whichever of these portions your heart within you bids.' So he said, thinking trickery. But Zeus, whose wisdom is everlasting, saw and failed not to perceive the trick, and in his heart he thought mischief against mortal men which also was to be fulfilled. With both hands he took up the white fat and was angry at heart, and wrath came to his spirit when he saw the white ox-bones craftily tricked out: and because of this the tribes of men upon earth burn white bones to the deathless gods upon fragrant altars. But Zeus who drives the clouds was greatly vexed and said to him:

(ll. 559-560) `Son of Iapetus, clever above all! So, sir, you have not yet forgotten your cunning arts!'

(ll. 561-584) So spake Zeus in anger, whose wisdom is everlasting; and from that time he was always mindful of the trick, and would not give the power of unwearying fire to the Melian race of mortal men who live on the earth. But the noble son of Iapetus outwitted him and stole the far-seen gleam of unwearying fire in a hollow fennel stalk. And Zeus who thunders on high was stung in spirit, and his dear heart was angered when he saw amongst men the far-seen ray of fire. Forthwith he made an evil thing for men as the price of fire; for the very famous Limping God formed of earth the likeness of a shy maiden as the son of Cronos willed. And the goddess bright-eyed Athene girded and clothed her with silvery raiment, and down from her head she spread with her hands a broidered veil, a wonder to see; and she, Pallas Athene, put about her head lovely garlands, flowers of new-grown herbs. Also she put upon her head a crown of gold which the very famous Limping God made himself and worked with his own hands as a favour to Zeus his father. On it was much curious work, wonderful to see; for of the many creatures which the land and sea rear up, he put most upon it, wonderful things, like living beings with voices: and great beauty shone out from it.

(ll. 585-589) But when he had made the beautiful evil to be the price for the blessing, he brought her out, delighting in the finery which the bright-eyed daughter of a mighty father had given her, to the place where the other gods and men were. And wonder took hold of the deathless gods and mortal men when they saw that which was sheer guile, not to be withstood by men.

(ll. 590-612) For from her is the race of women and female kind: of her is the deadly race and tribe of women who live amongst mortal men to their great trouble, no helpmeets in hateful poverty, but only in wealth. And as in thatched hives bees feed the drones whose nature is to do mischief — by day and throughout the day until the sun goes down the bees are busy and lay the white combs, while the drones stay at home in the covered skeps and reap the toil of others into their own bellies — even so Zeus who thunders on high made women to be an evil to mortal men, with a nature to do evil. And he gave them a second evil to be the price for the good they had: whoever avoids marriage and the sorrows that women cause, and will not wed, reaches deadly old age without anyone to tend his years, and though he at least has no lack of livelihood while he lives, yet, when he is dead, his kinsfolk divide his possessions amongst them. And as for the man who chooses the lot of marriage and takes a good wife suited to his mind, evil continually contends with good; for whoever happens to have mischievous children, lives always with unceasing grief in his spirit and heart within him; and this evil cannot be healed.

(ll. 613-616) So it is not possible to deceive or go beyond the will of Zeus; for not even the son of Iapetus, kindly Prometheus, escaped his heavy anger, but of necessity strong bands confined him, although he knew many a wile.

(ll. 617-643) But when first their father was vexed in his heart with Obriareus and Cottus and Gyes, he bound them in cruel bonds, because he was jealous of their exceeding manhood and comeliness and great size: and he made them live beneath the wide-pathed earth, where they were afflicted, being set to dwell under the ground, at the end of the earth, at its great borders, in bitter anguish for a long time and with great grief at heart. But the son of Cronos and the other deathless gods whom rich-haired Rhea bare from union with Cronos, brought them up again to the light at Earth's advising. For she herself recounted all things to the gods fully, how that with these they would gain victory and a glorious cause to vaunt themselves. For the Titan gods and as many as sprang from Cronos had long been fighting together in stubborn war with heart-grieving toil, the lordly Titans from high Othyrs, but the gods, givers of good, whom rich-haired Rhea bare in union with Cronos, from Olympus. So they, with bitter wrath, were fighting continually with one another at that time for ten full years, and the hard strife had no close or end for either side, and the issue of the war hung evenly balanced. But when he had provided those three with all things fitting, nectar and ambrosia which the gods themselves eat, and when their proud spirit revived within them all after they had fed on nectar and delicious ambrosia, then it was that the father of men and gods spoke amongst them:

(ll. 644-653) `Hear me, bright children of Earth and Heaven, that I may say what my heart within me bids. A long while now have we, who are sprung from Cronos and the Titan gods, fought with each other every day to get victory and to prevail. But do you show your great might and unconquerable strength, and face the Titans in bitter strife; for remember our friendly kindness, and from what sufferings you are come back to the light from your cruel bondage under misty gloom through our counsels.'

(ll. 654-663) So he said. And blameless Cottus answered him again: `Divine one, you speak that which we know well: nay, even of ourselves we know that your wisdom and understanding is exceeding, and that you became a defender of the deathless ones from chill doom. And through your devising we are come back again from the murky gloom and from our merciless bonds, enjoying what we looked not for, O lord, son of Cronos. And so now with fixed purpose and deliberate counsel we will aid your power in dreadful strife and will fight against the Titans in hard battle.'

(ll. 664-686) So he said: and the gods, givers of good things, applauded when they heard his word, and their spirit longed for war even more than before, and they all, both male and female, stirred up hated battle that day, the Titan gods, and all that were born of Cronos together with those dread, mighty ones of overwhelming strength whom Zeus brought up to the light from Erebus beneath the earth. An hundred arms sprang from the shoulders of all alike, and each had fifty heads growing upon his shoulders upon stout limbs. These, then, stood against the Titans in grim strife, holding huge rocks in their strong hands. And on the other part the Titans eagerly strengthened their ranks, and both sides at one time showed the work of their hands and their might. The boundless sea rang terribly around, and the earth crashed loudly: wide Heaven was shaken and groaned, and high Olympus reeled from its foundation under the charge of the undying gods, and a heavy quaking reached dim Tartarus and the deep sound of their feet in the fearful onset and of their hard missiles. So, then, they launched their grievous shafts upon one another, and the cry of both armies as they shouted reached to starry heaven; and they met together with a great battle-cry.

(ll. 687-712) Then Zeus no longer held back his might; but straight his heart was filled with fury and he showed forth all his strength. From Heaven and from Olympus he came forthwith, hurling his lightning: the bold flew thick and fast from his strong hand together with thunder and lightning, whirling an awesome flame. The life-giving earth crashed around in burning, and the vast wood crackled loud with fire all about. All the land seethed, and Ocean's streams and the unfruitful sea. The hot vapour lapped round the earthborn Titans: flame unspeakable rose to the bright upper air: the flashing glare of the thunder- stone and lightning blinded their eyes for all that there were strong. Astounding heat seized Chaos: and to see with eyes and to hear the sound with ears it seemed even as if Earth and wide Heaven above came together; for such a mighty crash would have arisen if Earth were being hurled to ruin, and Heaven from on high were hurling her down; so great a crash was there while the gods were meeting together in strife. Also the winds brought rumbling earthquake and duststorm, thunder and lightning and the lurid thunderbolt, which are the shafts of great Zeus, and carried the clangour and the warcry into the midst of the two hosts. An horrible uproar of terrible strife arose: mighty deeds were shown and the battle inclined. But until then, they kept at one another and fought continually in cruel war.

(ll. 713-735) And amongst the foremost Cottus and Briareos and Gyes insatiate for war raised fierce fighting: three hundred rocks, one upon another, they launched from their strong hands and overshadowed the Titans with their missiles, and buried them beneath the wide-pathed earth, and bound them in bitter chains when they had conquered them by their strength for all their great spirit, as far beneath the earth to Tartarus. For a brazen anvil falling down from heaven nine nights and days would reach the earth upon the tenth: and again, a brazen anvil falling from earth nine nights and days would reach Tartarus upon the tenth. Round it runs a fence of bronze, and night spreads in triple line all about it like a neck-circlet, while above grow the roots of the earth and unfruitful sea. There by the counsel of Zeus who drives the clouds the Titan gods are hidden under misty gloom, in a dank place where are the ends of the huge earth. And they may not go out; for Poseidon fixed gates of bronze upon it, and a wall runs all round it on every side. There Gyes and Cottus and great-souled Obriareus live, trusty warders of Zeus who holds the aegis.

(ll. 736-744) And there, all in their order, are the sources and ends of gloomy earth and misty Tartarus and the unfruitful sea and starry heaven, loathsome and dank, which even the gods abhor.

It is a great gulf, and if once a man were within the gates, he would not reach the floor until a whole year had reached its end, but cruel blast upon blast would carry him this way and that. And this marvel is awful even to the deathless gods.

***

Hesiod was a Greek man writing in the early 7th century BC, he can almost be seen as the counter author to the more famous Homer. Where Homer was writing slightly earlier and covering great narratives that included snippets of mythology, Hesiod dedicated an entire work to the creation of the universe (cosmogony) and the birth of the gods (theogony).

The Theogony opens with an ode to the Muses. They form what is essentially the ultimate force of the universe - fate. Nobody, not even the gods can control this force, no one can escape their destiny. The work then explains the primordial soup, in this case, it is called chaos, which is where the English word chasm comes from. So the primordial chaos can be seen as a kind of chasm or opening in space that allows for existence to take place. Out of the chaos, a complex string of births come into existence. First, the earth was formed known as the deity, Gaia. Gaia gave birth to her first son Ouranos which is seen as the heavens and firmament. Now a space within chaos was stable enough for significant creation, and from the intercourse of Gaia and Ouranos came a plethora of monsters and gods. Ouranos feared his offspring and forced them into the middle of the earth. Gaia was offended by this act and implored her children to fight back. Her youngest son, Kronos, accepted the challenge and with Gaia's help, castrated his father Ouranos. Tossing his severed loins to the ocean, and so Kronos became the savior for his siblings.

All the personalities we have seen fall into the category of primordial god or Titan to the Greek minds, and as of yet none of their divine Olympians had come into creation. However, this changes with coming of Kronos for he becomes head of the pantheon at this time. He takes his sister Rhea as a partner, and together they produce a third generation of gods whose names are more likely to be known. First was Hestia and Demeter, Hera, Hades, then Poseidon and finally Zeus. Kronos feared his children and ate them one by one as they were born. Rhea was distraught by this and begged her parents to distract Kronos as Zeus was born, this was done and a plan was put in place to save the youngest son. Rhea dressed a stone in baby's clothes and fed it to Kronos who under the pretense that it was the baby Zeus, ate it unknowingly. Zeus came to age and forced his father Kronos to vomit forth all his siblings.

A great battle ensued called the Titanomachy, where the Greek Olympians (under the leadership of Zeus) overcame the Titans who fought against them. Victorious, Zeus took sole leadership and brought order to the universe. He divided creation into three sections, he would rule the heavens, Poseidon the sea and Hades the underworld, and in this way, each of the brothers held a powerful station, but none had complete dominion over the earth and the people that inhabited it.

The creation of living mortals was given to the Titan Prometheus (for not all titans fought against Zeus), and so humanity was brought into the world. Hesiod goes into great detail about the creation of man and their subjugation to the gods, the creation of woman and the decline of the human condition - all are very interesting and profound topics.

Many themes are presented in the above story that can be explained through the external and internal theories of mythology discussed earlier. There is an underlying theme within the Theogony of an establishment of order. The world starts out with chaos, the first powers are aggressive and immature. The base attributes of these powers are refined with the next generation of gods, who are again refined by the third generation. This third generation is that of the Olympians who bring a sense of order and justice to the universe, creating a world suitable for human existence. It is a story of how the universe can go from a chaotic nothing to an ordered paradise.

A knowledge of the original language of the myth also gives great insight as the names of characters often give clarity to their roles. For the pantheist, the gods are more than just personalities, everything is god, or represented by a god. Let us look at this closer, Kronos is the Greek word for time. So when the god Kronos consumes his offspring, we are really looking at the negative attributes of time. So, what are the offspring's of time? Well, what are the attributes of the other gods? Collectively they symbolize the attributes of civilization, so in a way, the story is saying that time creates and consumes civilizations, however, there is a twist, for what overcomes Kronos is Zeus. Zeus symbolizes law/order and justice, so the saving grace of civilization from the ravages of time is a society steeped in justice and order.

Still looking at language, Prometheus translates to forethought and his brother Epimetheus to afterthought. It is Prometheus' ability to think of the future that led him to attempt a deceiving trick against Zeus at Mecone. This, of course, fell flat leading to the fall of humanity. Later in the story, it is Epimetheus' inability to think ahead that has him accept the present of Pandora and doom the world by her actions. In the ancient world, names have great meanings and are terribly important to understanding the roles of individuals.

We won't go too deep into analyzing Hesiod's Theogony for the subject can become quite in depth. But some things to think about are Zeus' hurling down of the stone to Delphi, is this an aetiological link for the famous prophet there and the divine world? The deception at Mecone, is that a ritual explanation for the presenting of meats to the gods? And finally, I think you would agree that Freud would have something to say about the continual theme of the son overcoming the father. Read through the entire account of Hesiod's Theogony yourself and see if you can pull out some of the threads and find their meanings.

One God

The profound shift of faith from believing in a chaotic creation to an ordered process of one divinity is deeply argued among scholars. We are in particular talking about how the mythologies and beliefs of the Hebrew people came about. The argument is one along the lines of a religious evolution versus a prophetic revolution. Literal belief of the Hebrew scripture leads one to believe that the Hebrew God made himself apparent to the people, and revealed certain mysteries of the world to them which led to a revolution in the way people saw the creation of the world. The evolution theory differs widely by suggesting the shift from a pantheon of gods to a singular all-powerful god was inevitable. Both theories have strengths and weaknesses.

The evolution/revolution debate brings up an interesting myth that I will leave here for your enjoyment, but keep in mind, this is far from proven but is a nice anecdote. Egypt was a traditionally pantheistic society, worshipping around 80 gods until

Figure 13: Pharoah Akhenaten worships the Aten under his new proto-monotheistic religion of Atenism. He is surrounded by his family who join him with their prayers.

Ankhenaten became Pharaoh (c.1330 B.C.). Ankhenaten shared the prophesy that only one god was the true god - the sun and that Egypt was to stop worship of all other deities except the sun. Egypt is held to be the birthplace of Moses, the traditional writer of the Torah, the sacred book of the Jewish people, whom also pushed the idea of one god. The idea some scholars allude to is that Moses and Ankhenaten were one and the same. For only a few years after his historical rule, Ankhenaten was overthrown by the disembodied priest caste of Egypt, and we lose references of him. This mirrors the Biblical story of Moses' exodus out of Egypt.

The creation story of Genesis in itself is a quantum leap from the creation myths of Hesiod and the older Mesopotamians. In Genesis, we witness the creation of the world as a will of a supreme being. There is no primordial soup or higher power, what this being created from is unstated, but the process of his creating is discussed vividly.

This idea of one all-powerful divinity did not originate in a vacuum though, the Greek philosopher Aristotle (384 - 322 B.C.) theorized an 'unmoved mover' or a primary god which enacted all action, and he may have taken the idea from Aeschylus (525 - 456 B.C.) who wrote,

Zeus is sky, Zeus is earth, Zeus is heaven;
Zeus is everything and all that is beyond these things.
- Aeschylus, Daughters Of Helios (fr. 70 Nauck)

This thought itself probably came from the even older philosopher, Xenophanes (570 - 475 B.C.) who eluded to monotheistic tendencies that have been pieced together through various fragments of his poetry,

There is one god, greatest among gods and human beings,
not at all like mortals in form nor yet in mind [...]
All of him sees, all of him thinks, all of him hears [...]
But, far from toil, with the thought of his mind, he puts all
things in motion [...]
Always he remains in the same place, moving not at all,
nor does it befit him to go at different times in different
directions.
- Xenophanes, fragments 23 - 26 D-K

So we see as early as the 6th century B.C. that the idea of a single omnipresent and omniscient god has begun to filter into the Greek philosophical mind. The original Egyptian creation myths also discuss a divine creator, Atum (sometimes Ptah), who willed himself into existence from nothing. But the argued difference between all of these and the Hebrew belief in the presence of a 'primordial soup'. For the Jewish faith, there is no question that God was the beginning and this 'soup' did not exist before him. This essential detail is what differentiates the faiths and allows Judaism to lay claim for the first truly monotheistic religion.

The Big Bang Myth

People today still believe these creation myths. And sitting alongside of them is modern sciences attempts to explain the origins of the universe. The scientific mythology is also one of beautiful faith. Like the priestly writings of Enuma Elish, the complexity of the Theogony or the theology of the Torah, it is hard for the ordinary person to understand the language of science. Despite that, most of us would know and understand the ideas that make up The Big Bang. In the beginning, everything was in existence, but so closely compacted that it was infinitely small. When the energy of everything became too much, it exploded, expanding at unprecedented speeds, creating time and space as it did so. The idea is steeped in mysterious physics that the layman takes on faith, but is in its own rights a great attempt at the explanation of the universe.

Obviously, the story I give of The Big Bang would be bawked at by a physicist or mathematician who knows the theories much better than I, but the point remains - we are not 100% sure that this is the truth. In fact, we simply do not know, there are too many questions, and the theory itself is only working off the observations we are able to make today. Tomorrow we might have new technologies and new theories and a completely new understanding of reality, the universe and creation. In another five thousand years, humanity might look at The Big Bang Theory in the same way that we read Enuma Elish today.

Fertility Mythology

The Great Change

When man shifted from a nomadic lifestyle of moving across the world hunting and gathering to a domestic life of agriculture, the myths of people also changed. All of sudden, the seasons became incredibly significant, the fertility of the soil for crops to grow, the regularity of the rains or flood waters and the general motions of the earth had the ability to give life or take it away. This is the theorized period of the matriarchal society, where womanhood and fertility were revered and worshipped. The land was seen as the womb, and the impregnation of it by the rain gave life, and people lived off of this.

The association between the fertility of the land and the reproduction of mankind quickly became apparent to people. Symbolically the rain was seen as sacred sperm, falling into the mother earth impregnating her, giving birth to crops. In our attempt to keep this cycle consistent, we developed a form of sympathetic magic in the form of rituals. The rituals were a way of people playing out different forms of fertility as an example for nature to follow.

The forms of these rituals differ from culture to culture. Some saw it necessary to give a gift of blood to the gods, others to re-enact the cycles of nature through drama or dance, and others through the divine sexual act. For

Figure 14: The Return of Persephone, by Frederic Leighton (1891)

example, the Canaanites saw it fit to boil a kid goat in the milk of its mother, and the Aztecs inflicted pain on children to provoke tears (mimicking the falling rain) before sacrificing them. In Greek culture, the Eleusinian Mysteries were very popular using dramatic rituals and symbolism to mimic fertility. Seasonal dances and the mimicking of animals is very popular worldwide and still seen in Australian Aboriginal, American Indian and Tengri cultures. The sexual act was also widely used, one example is that of ancient Babylon where every woman would have to sit at the shrine of Ishtar once in her lifetime and follow the passage of sacred prostitution. These are a small sample of fertility rituals, but it shows its universal importance in human culture.

The Homeric Hymn To Demeter

What follows is The Homeric Hymn To Demeter, translated by Hugh G. Evelyn-White (Loeb Classical Library, 1914).

***

I begin to sing of rich-haired Demeter, awful goddess — of her and her trim-ankled daughter whom Aidoneus [Hades]

88

rapt away, given to him by all-seeing Zeus the loud-thunderer. Apart from Demeter, lady of the golden sword and glorious fruits, she was playing with the deep-bosomed daughters of Oceanus and gathering flowers over a soft meadow, roses and crocuses and beautiful violets, irises also and hyacinths and the narcissus which Earth made to grow at the will of Zeus and to please the Host of Many, to be a snare for the bloom-like girl — a marvellous, radiant flower. It was a thing of awe whether for deathless gods or mortal men to see: from its root grew a hundred blooms and it smelled most sweetly that all wide heaven above and the whole earth and the sea's salt swell laughed for joy. And the girl was amazed and reached out with both hands to take the lovely toy; but the wide-pathed earth yawned there in the plain of Nysa, and the lord, Host of Many, with his immortal horses sprang out upon her — the Son of Cronos, He who has many names.

He caught her up reluctant on his golden car and bare her away lamenting. Then she cried out shrilly with her voice, calling upon her father, the Son of Cronos, who is most high and excellent. But no one, either of the deathless gods or of mortal men, heard her voice, nor yet the olive-trees bearing rich fruit: only tenderhearted Hecate, bright-coiffed, the daughter of Persaeus, heard the girl from her cave, and the lord Helios, Hyperion's bright son, as she cried to her father, the Son of Cronos. But he was sitting aloof, apart from the gods, in his temple where many pray, and receiving sweet offerings from mortal men. So he, that Son of Cronos, of many names, who is Ruler of Many and Host of Many, was bearing her away by leave of Zeus on his immortal chariot — his own brother's child and all unwilling.

[Line 33] And so long as she, the goddess, yet beheld earth and starry heaven and the strong-flowing sea where fishes shoal, and the rays of the sun, and still hoped to see her dear mother and the tribes of the eternal gods, so long hope calmed her great heart for all her trouble. . . . and the heights of the mountains and the depths of the sea rang with her immortal voice: and her queenly mother heard her.

Bitter pain seized her heart, and she rent the covering upon her divine hair with her dear hands: her dark cloak she cast down from both her shoulders and sped, like a wild-bird, over the firm land and yielding sea, seeking her child. But no one would tell her the truth, neither god nor mortal man; and of the birds of omen, none came with true news for her. Then for nine days, queenly Deo wandered over the earth with flaming torches in her hands, so grieved that she never tasted ambrosia and the sweet draught of nectar, nor sprinkled her body with water. But when the tenth enlightening dawn had come, Hecate, with a torch in her hands, met her, and spoke to her and told her news:

"Queenly Demeter, bringer of seasons and giver of good gifts, what god of heaven or what mortal man has rapt away Persephone and pierced with sorrow your dear heart? For I heard her voice, yet saw not with my eyes who it was. But I tell you truly and shortly all I know."

[Line 59] So, then, said Hecate. And the daughter of rich-haired Rhea answered her not, but sped swiftly with her, holding flaming torches in her hands. So they came to Helios, who is watchman of both gods and men, and stood in front of his horses: and the bright goddess enquired of him: "Helios, do you at least regard me, goddess as I am, if ever by word or deed of mine I have cheered your heart and spirit. Through the fruitless air, I heard the thrilling cry of my daughter whom I bare, sweet scion of my body and lovely in form, as of one seized violently; though with my eyes I saw nothing. But you — for with your beams you look down from the bright upper air over all the earth and sea — tell me truly of my dear child if you have seen her anywhere, what god or mortal man has violently seized her against her will and mine, and so made off."

So said she. And the Son of Hyperion answered her: "Queen Demeter, daughter of rich-haired Rhea, I will tell you the truth; for I greatly reverence and pity you in your grief for your trim-ankled daughter. None other of the deathless gods is to blame, but only cloud-gathering Zeus who gave her to Hades, her father's brother, to be called his buxom wife. And Hades seized her and took her loudly crying in his chariot down to his realm of mist and gloom. Yet, goddess, cease your loud lament and keep not vain anger unrelentingly: Aidoneus, the Ruler of Many, is no unfitting husband among the deathless gods for your child, being our own brother and born of the same stock: also, for honour, he has that third share which he received when division was made at the first and is appointed lord of those among whom he dwells."

So he spake, and called to his horses: and at his chiding they quickly whirled the swift chariot along, like long-winged birds.

[Line 90] But grief yet more terrible and savage came into the heart of Demeter, and thereafter she was so angered with the dark-clouded Son of Cronos that she avoided the gathering of the gods and high Olympus, and went to the towns and rich fields of men, disfiguring her form a long while. And no one of men or deep-bosomed women knew her when they saw her, until she came to the house of wise Celeus who then was lord of fragrant Eleusis. Vexed in her dear heart, she sat near the wayside by the Maiden Well, from which the women of the place were used to draw water, in a shady place over which grew an olive shrub. And she was like an ancient woman who is cut off from childbearing and the gifts of garland-loving Aphrodite, like the nurses of king's children who deal justice, or like the house-keepers in their echoing halls. There the daughters of Celeus, son of Eleusis, saw her, as they coming for easy-drawn water, to carry it in pitchers of bronze to their dear father's house: four were they and like goddesses in the flower of their girlhood, Callidice and Cleisidice and lovely Demo and Callithoe who was the eldest of them all. They knew her not, — for the gods are not easily discerned by mortals, but startling near by her spoke winged words:

"Old mother, whence are you of folk born long ago? Why are you gone away from the city and do not draw near the houses? For there in the shady halls are women of just such age as you, and others younger; and they would welcome you both by word and by deed."

[Line 118] Thus they said. And she, that queen among goddesses answered them saying: "Hail, dear children, whosoever you are of woman-kind. I will tell you my story; for it is not unseemly that I should tell you truly what you ask. Doso is my name, for my stately mother gave it me. And now I am come from Crete over the sea's wide back, — not willingly; but pirates brought me thence by force of strength against my liking. Afterwards they put in with their swift craft to Thoricus, and these the women landed on the shore in full throng and the men likewise, and they began to make ready a meal by the stern-cables of the ship. But my heart craved not pleasant food, and I

fled secretly across the dark country and escaped my
masters, that they should not take me unpurchased across
the sea, there to win a price for me. And so I wandered and
am come here: and I know not at all what land this is or
what people are in it. But may all those who dwell on
Olympus give you husbands and birth of children as
parents desire, so you take pity on me, maidens, and show
me this clearly that I may learn, dear children, to the house
of what man and woman I may go, to work for them
cheerfully at such tasks as belong to a woman of my age.
Well could I nurse a newborn child, holding him in my
arms, or keep house, or spread my masters' bed in a recess
of the well-built chamber, or teach the women their work."

So said the goddess. And straightway the unwed maiden
Callidice, goodliest in form of the daughters of Celeus,
answered her and said:

[Line 147] "Mother, what the gods send us, we mortals
bear perforce, although we suffer; for they are much
stronger than we. But now I will teach you clearly, telling
you the names of men who have great power and honour
here and are chief among the people, guarding our city's
coif of towers by their wisdom and true judgements: there
is wise Triptolemus and Dioclus and Polyxeinus and
blameless Eumolpus and Dolichus and our own brave
father. All these have wives who manage in the house, and
no one of them, so soon as she had seen you, would
dishonor you and turn you from the house, but they will
welcome you; for indeed you are godlike. But if you will,
stay here; and we will go to our father's house and tell
Metaneira, our deep-bosomed mother, all this matter
fully, that she may bid you rather come to our home than
search after the houses of others. She has an only son, late-
born, who is being nursed in our well-built house, a child

of many prayers and welcome: if you could bring him up until he reached the full measure of youth, any one of womankind who should see you would straightway envy you, such gifts would our mother give for his upbringing."

So she spake: and the goddess bowed her head in assent. And they filled their shining vessels with water and carried them off rejoicing. Quickly they came to their father's great house and straightway told their mother according as they had heard and seen. Then she bade them go with all speed and invite the stranger to come for a measureless hire. As hinds or heifers in springtime, when sated with pasture, bound about a meadow, so they, holding up the folds of their lovely garments, darted down the hollow path, and their hair like a crocus flower streamed about their shoulders. And they found the good goddess near the wayside where they had left her before and led her to the house of their dear father. And she walked behind, distressed in her dear heart, with her head veiled and wearing a dark cloak which waved about the slender feet of the goddess.

[Line 184] Soon they came to the house of heaven-nurtured Celeus and went through the portico to where their queenly mother sat by a pillar of the close-fitted roof, holding her son, a tender scion, in her bosom. And the girls ran to her. But the goddess walked to the threshold: and her head reached the roof and she filled the doorway with a heavenly radiance. Then awe and reverence and pale fear took hold of Metaneira, and she rose up from her couch before Demeter, and bade her be seated. But Demeter, bringer of seasons and giver of perfect gifts, would not sit upon the bright couch, but stayed silent with lovely eyes cast down until careful Iambe placed a jointed seat for her and threw over it a silvery fleece. Then she sat down and held her veil in her hands before her face. A long time she sat upon the stool without speaking because of her sorrow, and greeted no one by word or by sign, but rested, never smiling, and tasting neither food nor drinks because she pined with longing for her deep-bosomed daughter, until careful Iambe — who pleased her moods in aftertime also — moved the holy lady with many a quip and jest to smile and laugh and cheer her heart. Then Metaneira filled a cup with sweet wine and offered it to her; but she refused it, for she said it was not lawful for her to drink red wine, but bade them mix meal and water with soft mint and give her to drink. And Metaneira mixed the draught and gave it to the goddess as she bade. So the great queen Deo received it to observe the sacrament.

[Line 212] And of them all, well-girded Metaneira first began to speak: "Hail, lady! For I think you are not meanly but nobly born; truly dignity and grace are conspicuous upon your eyes as in the eyes of kings that deal justice. Yet we mortals bear perforce what the gods send us, though we be grieved; for a yoke is set upon our necks. But now, since you are come here, you shall have what I can bestow: and nurse me this child whom the gods gave me in my old age and beyond my hope, a son much prayed for. If you should bring him up until he reach the full measure of youth, any one of woman-kind that sees you will straightway envy you, so great reward would I give for his upbringing."

Then rich-haired Demeter answered her: "And to you, also, lady, all hail, and may the gods give you good! Gladly will I take the boy to my breast, as you bid me, and will nurse him. Never, I ween, through any heedlessness of his nurse shall witchcraft hurt him nor yet the Undercutter:

for I know a charm far stronger than the Woodcutter, and I know an excellent safeguard against woeful witchcraft."

When she had so spoken, she took the child in her fragrant bosom with her divine hands: and his mother was glad in her heart. So the goddess nursed in the palace Demophoon, wise Celeus' goodly son whom well-girded Metaneira bare. And the child grew like some immortal being, not fed with food nor nourished at the breast: for by day rich-crowned Demeter would anoint him with ambrosia as if he were the offspring of a god and breathe sweetly upon him as she held him in her bosom. But at night she would hide him like a brand in the heart of the fire, unknown to his dear parents. And it wrought great wonder in these that he grew beyond his age; for he was like the gods face to face. And she would have made him deathless and unaging, had not well-girded Metaneira in her heedlessness kept watch by night from her sweet-smelling chamber and spied. But she wailed and smote her two hips because she feared for her son and was greatly distraught in her heart; so she lamented and uttered winged words:

[Line 248] "Demophoon, my son, the strange woman buries you deep in fire and works grief and bitter sorrow for me."

Thus she spoke, mourning. And the bright goddess, lovely-crowned Demeter, heard her and was wroth with her. So with her divine hands, she snatched from the fire the dear son whom Metaneira had born unhoped-for in the palace and cast him from her to the ground; for she was terribly angry in her heart. Forthwith she said to well-girded Metaneira:

"Witless are you mortals and dull to foresee your lot, whether of good or evil, that comes upon you. For now in your heedlessness you have wrought folly past healing; for — be witness the oath of the gods, the relentless water of Styx — I would have made your dear son deathless and unaging all his days and would have bestowed on him ever-lasting honour, but now he can in no way escape death and the fates. Yet shall unfailing honor always rest upon him, because he lay upon my knees and slept in my arms? But, as the years move round and when he is in his prime, the sons of the Eleusinian shall ever wage war and dread strife with one another continually. Lo! I am that Demeter who has share of honor and is the greatest help and cause of joy to the undying gods and mortal men. But now, let all the people build me a great temple and an altar below it and beneath the city and its sheer wall upon a rising hillock above Callichorus. And I myself will teach my rites, that hereafter you may reverently perform them and so win the favor of my heart."

[Line 275] When she had so said, the goddess changed her stature and her looks, thrusting old age away from her: beauty spread round about her and a lovely fragrance was wafted from her sweet-smelling robes, and from the divine body of the goddess a light shone afar, while golden tresses spread down over her shoulders, so that the strong house was filled with brightness as with lightning. And so she went out from the palace.

And straightway Metaneira's knees were loosed and she remained speechless for a long while and did not remember to take up her late-born son from the ground. But his sisters heard his pitiful wailing and sprang down from their well-spread beds: one of them took up the child in her arms and laid him in her bosom, while another revived the fire, and a third rushed with soft feet to bring their mother from her fragrant chamber. And they gathered about the struggling child and washed him, embracing him lovingly; but he was not comforted, because nurses and handmaids much less skillful were holding him now.

All night long they sought to appease the glorious goddess, quaking with fear. But, as soon as dawn began to show, they told powerful Celeus all things without fail, as the lovely-crowned goddess Demeter charged them. So Celeus called the countless people to an assembly and bade them make a goodly temple for rich-haired Demeter and an altar upon the rising hillock. And they obeyed him right speedily and harkened to his voice, doing as he commanded. As for the child, he grew like an immortal being.

[Line 301] Now when they had finished building and had drawn back from their toil, they went every man to his house. But golden-haired Demeter sat there apart from all the blessed gods and stayed, wasting with yearning for her deep-bosomed daughter. Then she caused a most dreadful and cruel year for mankind over the all-nourishing earth: the ground would not make the seed sprout, for rich-crowned Demeter kept it hid. In the fields, the oxen drew many a curved plow in vain, and much white barley was cast upon the land without avail. So she would have destroyed the whole race of man with cruel famine and have robbed them who dwell on Olympus of their glorious right of gifts and sacrifices, had not Zeus perceived and marked this in his heart. First, he sent golden-winged Iris to call rich-haired Demeter, lovely in form. So he commanded. And she obeyed the dark-clouded Son of Cronos and sped with swift feet across the space between. She came to the stronghold of fragrant Eleusis, and there finding dark-cloaked Demeter in her temple, spake to her and uttered winged words:

"Demeter, father Zeus, whose wisdom is everlasting, calls you to come join the tribes of the eternal gods: come therefore, and let not the message I bring from Zeus pass unobeyed."

Thus said Iris imploring her. But Demeter's heart was not moved. Then again the father sent forth all the blessed and eternal gods besides: and they came, one after the other, and kept calling her and offering many very beautiful gifts and whatever rights she might be pleased to choose among the deathless gods. Yet no one was able to persuade her mind and will, so wroth was she in her heart; but she stubbornly rejected all their words: for she vowed that she would never set foot on fragrant Olympus nor let fruit spring out of the ground until she beheld with her eyes her own fair-faced daughter.

[Line 334] Now when all-seeing Zeus the loud-thunderer heard this, he sent the Slayer of Argus whose wand is of gold to Erebus, so that having won over Hades with soft words, he might lead forth chaste Persephone to the light from the misty gloom to join the gods, and that her mother might see her with her eyes and cease from her anger. And Hermes obeyed and leaving the house of Olympus, straightway sprang down with speed to the hidden places of the earth. And he found the lord Hades in his house seated upon a couch, and his shy mate with him, much reluctant, because she yearned for her mother. But she was afar off, brooding on her fell design because of the deeds of the blessed gods. And the strong Slayer of Argus drew near and said:

"Dark-haired Hades, ruler over the departed, father Zeus bids me bring noble Persephone forth from Erebus unto the gods, that her mother may see her with her eyes and cease from her dread anger with the immortals; for now she plans an awful deed, to destroy the weakly tribes of earthborn men by keeping seed hidden beneath the earth, and so she makes an end of the honours of the undying gods. For she keeps fearful anger and does not consort with the gods, but sits aloof in her fragrant temple, dwelling in the rocky hold of Eleusis."

So he said. And Aidoneus, ruler over the dead, smiled grimly and obeyed the behest of Zeus the king. For he straightway urged wise Persephone, saying:

[Line 360] "Go now, Persephone, to your dark-robed mother, go, and feel kindly in your heart towards me: be not so exceedingly cast down; for I shall be no unfitting husband for you among the deathless gods, that am own brother to father Zeus. And while you are here, you shall rule all that lives and moves and shall have the greatest rights among the deathless gods: those who defraud you and do not appease your power with offerings, reverently performing rites and paying fit gifts, shall be punished for evermore."

When he said this, wise Persephone was filled with joy and hastily sprang up for gladness. But he on his part secretly gave her sweet pomegranate seed to eat, taking care for himself that she might not remain continually with grave, dark-robed Demeter. Then Aidoneus the Ruler of Many openly got ready his deathless horses beneath the golden chariots And she mounted on the chariot and the strong Slayer of Argus took reins and whip in his dear hands and drove forth from the hall, the horses speeding readily. Swiftly they traversed their long course, and neither the sea nor river-waters nor grassy glens nor mountain-peaks checked the career of the immortal horses, but they crave the deep air above them as they went. And Hermes brought them to the place where rich-crowned Demeter was staying and checked them before her fragrant temple.

[Line 384] And when Demeter saw them, she rushed forth as does a Maenad down some thick-wooded mountain, while Persephone on the other side, when she saw her mother's sweet eyes, left the chariot and horses, and leaped down to run to her, and falling upon her neck, embraced her. But while Demeter was still holding her dear child in her arms, her heart suddenly misgave her for some snare, so that she feared greatly and ceased fondling her daughter and asked of her at once: "My child, tell me, surely you have not tasted any food while you were below? Speak out and hide nothing, but let us both know. For if you have not, you shall come back from loathly Hades and live with me and your father, the dark-clouded Son of Cronos and be honoured by all the deathless gods; but if you have tasted food, you must go back again beneath the secret places of the earth, there to dwell a third part of the seasons every year: yet for the two parts you shall be with me and the other deathless gods. But when the earth shall bloom with the fragrant flowers of spring in every kind, then from the realm of darkness and gloom thou shalt come up once more to be a wonder for gods and mortal men. And now tell me how he rapt you away to the realm of darkness and gloom, and by what trick did the strong Host of Many beguile you?"

[Line 405] Then beautiful Persephone answered her thus: "Mother, I will tell you all without error. When luck-bringing Hermes came, swift messenger from my father the Son of Cronos and the other Sons of Heaven, bidding me come back from Erebus that you might see me with your eyes and so cease from your anger and fearful wrath against the gods, I sprang up at once for joy; but he secretly put in my mouth sweet food, a pomegranate seed, and forced me to taste against my will. Also I will tell how he rapt me away by the deep plan of my father the Son of Cronos and carried me off beneath the depths of the earth, and will relate the whole matter as you ask. All we were playing in a lovely meadow, Leucippe and Phaeno and Electra and Ianthe, Melita also and Iache with Rhodea and Callirhoe and Melobosis and Tyche and Ocyrhoe, fair as a flower, Chryseis, Ianeira, Acaste and Admete and Rhodope and Pluto and charming Calypso; Styx too was there and Urania and lovely Galaxaura with Pallas who rouses battles and Artemis delighting in arrows. We were playing and gathering sweet flowers in our hands, soft crocuses mingled with irises and hyacinths, and rose-blooms and lilies, marvellous to see, and the narcissus which the wide earth caused to grow yellow as a crocus. That I plucked in my joy; but the earth parted beneath, and there the strong lord, the Host of Many, sprang forth and in his golden chariot he bore me away, all unwilling, beneath the earth: then I cried with a shrill cry. All this is true, sore though it grieves me to tell the tale."

[Line 434] So did they then, with hearts at one, greatly cheer each the other's soul and spirit with many an embrace: their hearts had relief from their griefs while each took and gave back joyousness.

Then bright-coiffed Hecate came near to them and often did she embrace the daughter of holy Demeter: and from that time the lady Hecate was minister and companion to Persephone.

And all-seeing Zeus sent a messenger to them, rich-haired Rhea, to bring dark-cloaked Demeter to join the families of the gods: and he promised to give her what rights she should choose among the deathless gods and agreed that her daughter should go down for the third part of the circling year to darkness and gloom, but for the two parts should live with her mother and the other deathless gods. Thus he commanded. And the goddess did not disobey the message of Zeus; swiftly she rushed down from the peaks of Olympus and came to the plain of Rharus, rich, fertile corn-land once, but then in nowise fruitful, for it lay idle and utterly leafless because the white grain was hidden by design of trim-ankled Demeter. But afterward, as spring-time waxed, it was soon to be waving with long ears of corn, and its rich furrows to be loaded with grain upon the ground, while others would already be bound in sheaves. There first she landed from the fruitless upper air: and glad were the goddesses to see each other and cheered in heart. Then bright-coiffed Rhea said to Demeter:

[Line 459] "Come, my daughter; for far-seeing Zeus the loud-thunderer calls you to join the families of the gods, and has promised to give you what rights you please among the deathless gods, and has agreed that for a third part of the circling year your daughter shall go down to darkness and gloom, but for the two parts shall be with you and the other deathless gods: so has he declared it shall be and has bowed his head in token. But come, my child, obey, and be not too angry unrelentingly with the dark-clouded Son of Cronos; but rather increase forthwith for men the fruit that gives them life."

So spake Rhea. And rich-crowned Demeter did not refuse but straightway made fruit to spring up from the rich lands so that the whole wide earth was laden with leaves and flowers. Then she went, and to the kings who deal justice, Triptolemus and Diocles, the horse-driver, and to doughty Eumolpus and Celeus, leader of the people, she showed the conduct of her rites and taught them all her mysteries, to Triptolemus and Polyxeinus and Diocles also, — awful mysteries which no one may in any way transgress or pry into or utter, for deep awe of the gods checks the voice. Happy is he among men upon earth who has seen these mysteries; but he who is uninitiated and who has no part in them never has lot of like good things once he is dead, down in the darkness and gloom.

[Line 483] But when the bright goddess had taught them all, they went to Olympus to the gathering of the other gods. And there they dwell beside Zeus who delights in thunder, awful and reverend goddesses. Right blessed is he among men on earth whom they freely love: soon they do send Plutus as guest to his great house, Plutus who gives wealth to mortal men.

And now, queen of the land of sweet Eleusis and sea-girt Paros and rocky Antron, lady, giver of good gifts, bringer of seasons, queen Deo, be gracious, you and your daughter all beauteous Persephone, and for my song grant me heart-cheering substance. And now I will remember you and another song also.

Demeter & Eleusis

Let's look more into the Eleusinian Mysteries, it is, after all, a myth of great importance and deserves a deeper look. The Homeric Hymn to Demeter was written at a point in time where the mystery rituals were already well established but portrays them and their meanings very well. This myth has multiple levels of understanding, and that the agricultural/fertility connotations are only of the surface reading, we will revisit this myth later to explore its deeper meanings.

Demeter is the Greek god of the crop. She has a daughter named Kore/Persephone. Persephone is kidnapped by Hades and forced to marry him and dwell in the underworld. Distraught, Demeter travels the land with a heavy heart, she makes her way to Eleusis and after an episode, there forces the people to make her a temple. She resides in the earthly temple away from the other divine gods. Her bitter attitudes stops her from fertilizing the earth so no crops will grow. The people starve from famine and can give no sacrifices to the rest of the gods. The Olympians, angry and weakened by this beg Demeter to relent. She does not do so until she barters the return of her daughter. Persephone during this time has however eaten the pomegranate fruit given to her by Hades, she cannot wholly return to earth. However, a deal is organized that she may return nine months of the year, before returning to the underworld for three. With this, Demeter continues her responsibilities and keeps the crops growing each year.

It is a great story and gives a great many lessons in its allegories and symbolism. Specific to fertility, the myth shows that after a nine-month period of growth, life must return to the underworld for a period of time as it is obligated to do so before returning again. This, of course, mimics the seasons, with 9 months of spring, summer, and autumn allowing for life and growth, with 3 months of winter symbolic of death. It is a continual cycle of reincarnation, of life and death. The people at Eleusis would portray this by telling the stories and play them out in dramatic ways. In this case, the myth and the rituals were portraying the sympathetic magic discussed earlier, but more importantly, it was a method to educate people in the mysteries of the world.

This is not the end of the Homeric Hymn to Demeter, we will look at its deeper layers in the next chapter.

Dionysus/Bacchus

At some point in history, Dionysus joined Demeter in worship at Eleusis and was integrated into her mysteries. Chronologically this makes sense as the cultivation of vines and the fermentation of wine post dates that of grain.

The tragic backstory is that while Zeus and Semele were having their affair, Zeus offered to grant Semele any wish she asked for and having swore on the waters of the Styx, Zeus was under an unbreakable oath to grant any wish. Now prior to this, Hera had given Semele the desire to know Zeus in all his power, that of the horrific lightning god, and this is what Semele asked for. Powerless to stop himself, Zeus gave her what she wanted of him and as no mortal could withstand such a force she was destroyed in a furious flash. Semele was with child at the time, and Zeus took the tiny infant and placed him within his thigh so it could come to term, and so, Dionysus was born through Zeus' leg.

Hera's hate did not cease with the death of Semele, she took action against baby Dionysus too and sent the Titans to tear him apart. Rhea put the young demi-god back together and Zeus gave the child to the mountain nymphs to be raised in safety.

Dionysus grew into manhood but could never forget the mother he never knew. His existence was one of misery, so he decided to go to the underworld and demand her back. With Zeus' blessing, he underwent the journey and having collected her, escorted Semele back to Olympus where she was allowed to live among the gods.

These two episodes of Dionysus were celebrated at the Eleusinian rituals. The connection to fertility lay in the simile of his death and rebirth to the death of the grape vines each winter. The vines must be torn apart back to the stump, but in spring they again come back to life. So the teaching of rebirth is revealed to the worshippers. Dionysus' return from the underworld also showed that life was stronger than death and would always overcome it.

Figure 15: Pentheus torn apart by Agave and Ino. Attic red-figure lekanis (cosmetics bowl) lid, c. 450-425 BCE (Louvre).

Transitional Mythology

A State Of Flux

An individual person is constantly in a state of flux. Our mind and our body are always changing, we are forever growing older and our mind is always developing. The change never ends, but there is a need for people to define themselves, to be able to state what they are, a child, a woman, a warrior, an old man, etc. These labels give purpose to life and allow the individual to have a certain sense of identity. But because we are in a constant state of change, it is hard to clearly state where we are at any point in time. When does the child become an adult? When does the apprentice turn into the master? In reality, there is no black and white definitive times of 'being' any of these things, but instead, we exist in a hazy grey area that is between states. If left like this, then the individual cannot find appreciation for themselves and loses a sense of identity. To counter this issue, it is commonplace for all cultures to develop a form of ritual known as the rite of passage.

There are specific times of change in every person life, the most profound being the transition from childhood to adulthood. In the hazy stage of adolescence, when does one 'grow up' and what does that even mean? When does one shed the innocence of youth to become an adult with responsibilities? Traditionally, cultures would stage a rite of passage, a specific time when the youths of a culture would be taken away, undergo a trial and return an adult.

Rites of Passage

Specific rites of passage exist for every station of life, whether a judge is being sworn into office, or a soldier celebrating the initiation into an army. People define their positions in life by successfully passing through these rites. Mentally what is occurring is a person is going from a state of being on the 'outside' of a group, passing through a test, and being accepted be part of the 'inside' group effectively giving a sense of belonging.

One of the universal, and perhaps the most important, of these transitions between stations in life, is the passing from childhood to adulthood. Generally, for boys, this included violence, a trial of strength where they must be successful in a fight against stronger opponents or even being forced to survive in the wild for a period of time. These acted as tests of competent, but it was also important to bear the marks of this change and so scarring, tattooing, circumcision and the like are commonplace to physically change the body from that of a boy in to that of a man.

In the television series Joseph Campbell and the Power of Myth (1988), Campbell recites a story about the initiation rites of boys in certain Polynesian tribes. Throughout their childhood, the children are told the traditional stories and learn to fear their local gods. When the boy comes of age, around the age of twelve, the tribe deems him to be ready to take on the responsibilities of manhood. During the dead of the night, the men of the tribe adorn their cultural dress and masks of the gods and burst into the boys hut. They terrorize the adolescent and drag him into the villages open area. The boy kicking and screaming begs his mother for help but she does not come to his aid. The gods surround the boy and begin to taunt him, they attack him with controlled violence and strike the uttermost fear into his heart. The boy is induced into an extreme state of terror and despair as the very gods themselves surround and assault him. After some time of this, the chief god enters the circle and faces off with the boy, he challenges him to single combat. With nowhere to go, the child must stand his ground and so a fight occurs. The chief god forces the boy to fight with all his might, but in the end, allows the adolescent to win. The god kneels down in a sign of surrender and takes off his mask. The boy's father reveals himself as the man behind the mask, and in a symbolic gesture places the mask of the god onto the boys own head. The boy has not only confronted and overcome his deepest fears, having defeated the very gods themselves but has successfully gained an equality with his father and thus has passed into adulthood.

The female body naturally changes with puberty and so the period of change does not have the ritual grandeur of that which boys endure. Blood is sacred to all cultures, and at the first signs of menstruation the girl is 'hidden away', not being allowed to touch the earth or see the sun for a period of time. During the hiding period, the girl would be taught by older woman of her future roles as a wife and mother. After the predetermined time of hiding has passed, the girl leaves the hiding place (usually a hut or dwelling) and is symbolically reborn into the society as a woman.

The rites of passage have slowly diminished in western culture. Shadows of the practice still exist in the form of the Jewish Bar/Bat Mitzvah, the Christian Confirmation and the popular celebration of the western world's sweet sixteenth, but they do little to truly empower a child growing into adulthood. It is however interesting to note a return of the initiation practice which can be seen in the cultures of urban gangs. It is common for individuals in this lifestyle to not come from traditional families, and with a lack of parental role models, youths look to each other to fill the void of family and tribe. One such initiation observed is when members are 'beaten in' and perform other acts of violence or strength to prove themselves and gain admission into the gang.

Figure 16: Boys of nine and 10 years of age undergoing the initiation rituals of the Yao tribe in Malawi which will involve circumcision. Photograph by Steve Evans from Citizen of the World.

Transitional Qualities of The Homeric Hymn to Demeter

Returning to The Homeric Hymn to Demeter, we can now look into a deeper layer of the myth, one that portrays the transitions of people to different stations of life.

Most important of all is the transition of Demeter's daughter from the child Kore to the adult Persephone. Kore is the Greek word for girl, and the Hymn starts out with her picking flowers and playing childlike games with her friends. She is kidnapped without warning by Hades who takes her to the underworld making her his Queen. Here Kore is given equal responsibility over the realm of the dead whilst her mother still searches for her on the earth. Hades offers the girl a seed of the pomegranate which she eats. When Demeter bargains her back, the act of eating the seed prevents her daughter from returning to earth permanently. Kore has transitioned into Persephone and in doing so has taken on new responsibilities and a new independence.

The kidnapping and marriage is a great transition from her former life of carefree childhood to the responsibilities of adulthood. Persephone takes on the role of wife at the snap of a finger, and though she can return to earth to be with her mother, she is no longer an innocent child. She has eaten the seed by her own will and takes on the responsibility of the act. She can exist on the earth, but never again as Kore for she is now a woman.

Demeter undergoes her own transitional period through the myth, she is no longer the mother whose sole duty is to raise and care for her child but must learn to let go and let her daughter find her own path in the world. The myth goes into details about this acceptance of change. Demeter goes through the classic symptoms of loss - unacceptance as she frantically searches for Kore, sorrow as she wanders the earth, anger as she starves the world, and acceptance when Persephone returns. It is a mirror of human psychology and a roadmap for humanity as we undergo the same journey. Persephone also shows the audience how we must accept the repercussions of our actions and must go with the flow of natural change, accepting the events that are outside of our control.

Demeter & Persephone: Life & Death Unveiled

The Greek myth of Demeter and Persephone is vitally important in understanding life and death. It is a story often overlooked and barely remembered but holds the keys to some of western societies greatest philosophies. Wrestling with ideas of life and death, hardship, and hope, masculinity and femininity, Demeter's mythology is a keystone in western mythology and philosophy.

Not actually written by Homer, the hymn is one of 33 separate poems written by anonymous poets in the same style Homer used for his Iliad and Odyssey. For those interested, the hymns were first labeled Homeric by Thucydides because they follow the same epic rhythm found through dactylic hexameter and use the same dialect as the great poet. Each of the 33 poems is its own, celebrating separate deities, and the one we're interested in is dedicated to Demeter, goddess of fertility and crops.

Homeric Hymn to Demeter in Summary

1. Persephone, Demeter's daughter, is innocently picking flowers in a field with her friends before Hades, lord of the underworld, opens up the

earth, charging forth in his chariot. Hades scoops up Persephone, kidnapping her, takes her back to the underworld and make her his queen. Zeus has given Hades the okay to do this.

2. Demeter is distraught with the loss, having no idea where her daughter has gone or who has taken her. She seeks for her daughter for nine days. The gods Hecate and Helios give her help in telling her what has happened. Helios, as he is the sun god, see's all things that occur on earth.

3. In her wanderings, Demeter is invited to the palace of Metaneira and Keleus, the king and queen of Eleusis. Demeter takes the form of an old lady as is offered to look after the baby prince Demophon.

4. Demeter tries to make the baby Demophon immortal by putting him in the fire. She is caught by one of the maids and the ritual is disrupted.

5. Upon the disruption, Demeter returns to her divine form and demands that the people of Eleusis build her a temple. Once built, she stays in the temple, refusing to return to Olympus, and denies the fertility of crops creating a famine.

6. Meanwhile, Persephone is still in the underworld, and Hades is treating her well, establishing her as a queen. He offers her food but she refuses to eat. He keeps offering and she accepts a single pomegranate seed.

7. The gods take note of what Demeter is doing. They beg Zeus to take action and put a stop to the famine.

8. Zeus orders Hermes to go to the underworld and to order Hades to return Persephone to her mother. However, because Persephone has eaten food from Hades table, she cannot return permanently.
9. A deal is struck where Persephone may live on the earth for nine months but must return for three months every year.
10. The myth ends here, and I the author give myself a pat on the back for squeezing 495 lines of Greek poetry into 10 bite-sized pieces.

This is the basic plot of the Homeric Hymn to Demeter, and the story is great as it is, but the devil really is in the detail. It is the small things that count in this myth (which is why it is useful to read the original) because there is so much symbolism within it. Let us look at some of the themes that are intertwined within this myth.

A Female Hero

Greek myths are abound with heroes, but because they originate from a Greek society which was male-dominated, the heroes themselves are almost always male. Here we find that the feminine Demeter is the heroic character. But what is more, myths like this usually see the child saving the parent, again it is reversed in the mother saving her daughter. This can be seen as a kind of commentary on the strengths of motherly love. The mythic mold of the helpless female is broken, and the Homeric Hymn to Demeter still fills all the necessary characters of Joseph Campbell's mythic cycle, but we are seeing it through feminine eyes. This should not be underestimated, in this myth, a mother forces change on a pre-arranged marriage set up by a father and uncle. This would have been shocking to Greek cultural norms.

Emotional Understanding

The Homeric Hymn to Demeter displays an extraordinary understanding of human emotion. The myth tracks the mentality of Demeter through her lose, displaying her sadness, grief, and anger in an accurate chronology. Her sadness is seen in her wanderings and pleading the gods for help. She refuses to enjoy the bliss of Olympus, and clothes herself in rags. She hides herself away as an infertile old woman and dwells in her depression. The tale clearly shows the void left in her heart from the loss of her daughter. Her grief lasts for nine days - a cultural custom in Greece at the time. But her anger is what defines the story. She lashes out at humanity and the gods and this is what eventually secures her victory.

An Episode at Eleusis

The fact that Demeter arrives at Eleusis appears very specific for a myth that is otherwise quite broad in scope. This is no accident, mythologists call this aetological reasoning, and the reason the author included the episode is to justify why the worship of Demeter takes place at Eleusis. The hymn as we know it was probably written well after the festivities had started at Eleusis, by having Demeter come to the town in the myth links the story directly to the worship. It explains why Eleusis is a holy site, and why the temple is situated there.

An Episode with Demophon

This section of the tale confuses most, why is it included and what does it mean? Why does Demeter want to burn a baby alive? The answer works logically in the ancient Greek belief system. Hades is king of the underworld, his power rest in the souls he collects and rules over. He stole a life from Demeter, so she sees it fit to steal a soul from him. The ritual she was performing with Demophon would secure his immortality, this means he would never die and Hades could never claim his soul. That explains why she is doing it, but how does burning a baby make it immortal? This is up for evaluation too, but some ideas suggest that the flames would scorch off the mortality of the baby, and the ritual has even been paralleled with blacksmithing. By placing the child in the flames, the impurities will burn out and the soul will harden to be equal to that of the gods.

Starving the Gods

When Demeter's plan to take revenge against Hades through Demophon fails, she has to rethink what she is going to do. She is the goddess of fertility and the crop, she has the power to feed or starve humanity. The gods, in turn, feed on the offerings and sacrifices that humanity supplies to them. So Demeter takes action by refusing to raise the crops. Now humans can no longer afford to sacrifice to the gods because food is so scarce. The gods begin to starve and Demeter now has their attention. Once she has taken away something that they need, they are more willing to take action to help her. It is through this that Zeus is placated into discussing the terms of Persephone's marriage, and Demeter has leverage to make a bargain with.

The Pomegranate Seed

Hades wants Persephone to eat in the underworld because it was commonly believed that once you had accepted something from that realm, you could never leave. However, Persephone continually refuses him and only accepts the tiny seeds from the pomegranate fruit, why is such an insignificant food so significant? The seed is symbolic of fertility (remember Demeter, and therefore Persephone, is the goddess of fertility), by accepting the seed from Hades, she is symbolically taking his fertility. This act elevates Persephone from a girl to a woman, she successfully separates herself from her mother by becoming a mother herself.

Life, Death, and Rebirth

Persephone exists in a halfway point between mortality and immortality. She lives forever like a goddess but dies every nine months. This makes her an intermediary between the divine and mortal realms and gives her the exemplary role to humanity showing them that life, death, and rebirth are all part of the cycle of existence.

The Eleusinian Rites

The Homeric Hymn To Demeter was first recorded over three thousand years ago, and Greek mystics revealed the truth of life and death through the ancient tale. Setting up a secret school at Eleusis, they divulged the truth of these mysteries only to the purest of heart. With the coming of Christianity, this pagan knowledge was lost for over a millennia. Since then, fragments have been uncovered and lost writings interpreted.

Mankind has always grappled with the stark reality that one day we will all die. Death is perhaps the greatest motivator of all, how can one attain all there is in this world while spending such little time on it. What is the fate of the soul, after the corporal body has rotted away? The Sumerians asked the question over 5000 years ago through their mythology The Epic Of Gilgamesh, and since then we are no closer to understanding what lays beyond the veil. Not that humanity hasn't tried, religious texts and human philosophy has long attempted to bridge the gap between life and death, promising everything from paradise to the cessation of existence altogether.

Early in the development of civilization, a dark, shadowy entity emerged, mostly hidden to the outside world and people. It was the advent of a special kind of school, bringing faith and rationalism together so that the two could work together in the search for tangible answers to the divine mysteries surrounding our existence. Secret societies, mystery schools, call them what you wish, they were organized groups with a clear mission to understand life, death, the world around, and beyond us.

What is the Cult of Demeter?

In its most basic description, the Cult of Demeter was a pagan festival occurring at Eleusis, Greece. It is estimated that worship began around 1500 B.C. and lasted until 395 A.D. when the Roman Emperor, Theodoros, banned the practice in preference for Christianity. A side note, it was around this time that the people of the region began to legally worship the Christian St. Demeter instead.

The pagan festival was originally only open to women, but after a period of time men were allowed to take part, so long as they took a feminine name. Members were to know the Greek language and hold no impurity by blood guilt. The leniency of the terms and the secrets the cult promised to divulge to members meant that the festival rapidly grew in size with people traveling from every corner of the known world to take part.

The Cult of Demeter promised its initiates a better life and for something to be hopeful about after death. Cicero wrote,

'We have been given a reason not only to live in joy but also to die with better hope.'

And Isokrates,

'Those who take part in them possess better hopes in regard to the end of life and in regard to the whole lifespan.'

It is clear to us that once initiated into the Cult of Demeter, one could attain higher knowledge and an understanding of life that added meaning to it.

The Eleusinian Rites

The mysteries were revealed to individuals through ceremonial rituals, unlocking the secrets within the mind of the person through a real experience. The society was secret with the initiated persons swearing an oath of silence with severe consequences of breaking that promise. It is because of this that we do not know in detail what occurred during the festivals. However, we know enough through interpreting the Homeric Hymn to Demeter and the testimonies of some members.

It is known that there were two festivals in the year, the lesser occurring in spring, the greater in autumn. The festivities held great purifications, processions, and sacrifices for nine straight days, leading up to the final night, where initiates would enter the temple of Demeter. All parts of the festival and rituals were highly symbolic, the nine days of initiation parallel Demeter's nine days of mourning and mimicked the nine months of pregnancy, where finally the initiate would be reborn a new individual. Writing from the experience of his own initiation, Plutarch gives perhaps the greatest firsthand account of these rites,

> "...Wandering astray in the beginning, tiresome walkings in circles, some frightening paths in the darkness that lead nowhere; then immediately before the end all the terrible things, panic and shivering and sweat, and amazement. And then some wonderful light comes to meet you, pure regions and meadows are there to greet you, with sounds and dances and solemn, sacred words and holy views; and there the initiate, perfect by now, set free and loose from all bondage, walks about crowned with a wreath, celebrating the festival together with the other sacred and pure people, and he looks down on the uninitiated, unpurified crowd in this world in mud and fog beneath his feet."
> - Plutarch (168 Sandbach = Stobaeus Anthologium 4.52.49)

This topic relies heavily on the interpretation of the myth as it is a blueprint for the rituals themselves. The teachings discussed below are modern interpretations and theories on the significance of the Eleusinian Mysteries found within the Homeric Hymn To Demeter.

Inevitable Change

All things in this world are transient in that they are in a state of constant change. This is clear through the stages of Persephone's development in the myth. She is introduced as Kore, an affectionate name for "girl", and is picking flowers carelessly with her friends. Kidnapped, she evolves into Persephone, shifting to the role of a married lady and queen of Hades. Her mother, Demeter, struggles with the reality, trying to save her daughter and restore her innocence. However, it is in vain, for change usually only travels one way in this world and it is not backward. What Demeter does succeed in though, is evolving Persephone further to allow her to return to the earth from the underworld for nine months of the year. The initiate is taught that change should not be feared, and it cannot be stopped. Even if a poor situation manifests itself, it too cannot last forever because it is subject to change as well.

More Than The Material

With the loss of her daughter, Demeter refuses to eat, drink, or sleep reminding us that there are greater things in this world than just the material. Demeter refuses to join the gods at Olympus with all their divine pleasures, teaching the audience that pleasure is also subject to a state of change. What the episode is trying to show us is that there is a hierarchy of importance in the world, and that pleasure and material wealth is below things like love, family, and loyalty. It is a reminder of morality over materiality.

Hope & Strength

Hope is a huge theme throughout the myth and is a massive theme through the teachings. Demeter loses a lot, but she holds on to the hope of saving her daughter. She doesn't rest on her laurels and wait for fate though, she sets out into the world and takes action. This legend come from a highly male-dominated society, and it is important to remember this when you consider what Demeter does. She actively rebels against the patriarchal gods of Olympus. She refuses to raise the crop essentially starving humans on earth. Without food, the humans cannot give gifts and sacrifices to the gods, so in turn, they starve too. Demeter held on to hope, took action, and outwitted Zeus, leading to the recovery of her daughter. It is a serious lesson to humanity, that no matter how daunting the task, to always hold hope in your heart, and to never stop trying.

Life After Death

Because change is a constant, death should not be feared, for even the cessation of existence cannot be permanent. The deal struck that allowed Persephone to live on earth for nine months before returning to the underworld for three shows the initiate that rebirth is simply a way of the world. These times, nine and three months, were not accidentally picked either. The priests studied the workings of nature and noted the cycle of crops. Starting from seed, the plant slowly grows, changing through the seasons, and reaching maturity it dies after nine months and returns to the earth. For three months the land lays barren with no life, until again in spring, the cycle starts anew. It was the final lesson at Eleusis, by simply lifting a stalk of wheat above his head, the priest shows the initiate the cycles of existence. This is the deeper understanding of Demeter being the patron deity of the crop.

The rituals and beliefs of the Eleusinian Mysteries are not to be taken lightly. Many of history's greatest minds, philosophers, playwrights, mathematicians, and politicians were initiates of the school. It taught them new ways of understanding the world in a method that reading and writing simply cannot. To experience the lesson leaves a purer understanding. We cannot recreate the Eleusinian Mysteries, their secrecy has been sealed away, but we can try and understand them through the material we have. Perhaps over time, new secrets will be revealed and greater truths unlocked.

Psychological Mythology

Transitory Periods

Transitory periods of life are not limited to the natural changes of the body. There are many times in a person's life where they will change through the actions they take or the choices they make and these too are explored in mythology. The stories act as roadmaps for the audience, seeing that they are not alone they can take example from the myths to make the right decisions or see the greater picture of what is occurring in their life.

Psychological theory in ancient times was a deeply debated subject. There were a great number of ideas in existence at the same time, and philosophers argued on what they believed was the true workings of the human psyche. These varied in details, but a common ground for most was the existence of the soul and what it was composed of. In the 2nd century A.D., a man named Galen of Pergamum distilled these ideas into a working theory that lasted for at least the next 1600 years and is finding a resurgence in popularity today. Galen was a famed Greek physician who was working out of Rome, following the medical theories of Hippocrates. He took his psychological theories from Plato, and it is through this school that we will find interest in discussing.

Plato believed in a triadic system of the mind. He theorized that there are three parts to the psyche which

Figure 17: The Chariot Tarot card is a perfect representation of Plato's psychology. The driver represents the rational mind which needs to control the base thoughts symbolized by the two sphynx like beasts. When all is in harmony, the chariot can work as a single unit. Card from the Rider-Waite-Smith Tarot Deck (1910).

are housed in different parts of the body. These three parts are the animalistic urges like fear and rage housed in the liver, the passions such as love and lust in the heart, and the rational mind housed in the brain. Plato proposed that a healthy mind was one where the rational mind was strong enough to control the two lower thoughts. He gave the example of a two-horse chariot, where the two horses were the passions and urges, and the driver was the rational brain, if the driver was weak, the horses would pull the chariot apart, but if it was strong then the horses could be controlled driving the vehicle on.

Through this theory, we see that the mind is constantly assaulted by our base thoughts. If these are not controlled than an unhealthy mindset will ensue. However, if the rational mind is strong then it can control the base thoughts and use them to achieve great things. Therefore, this kind of psychology relied on strengthening the rational mind so that it was able to control the thoughts that came to it. A healthy, rational brain would make the individual a healthy, rational person. Out of interest, patients undergoing Plato's style of psychological treatment could expect to be given philosophy to read to expand the minds thought, plays to watch to consider moral and ethical ideas, peaceful music to listen to in a method to keep calm and relax, and a regime of exercise for stress relief and a healthy body. Not a bad treatment considering alternative therapies could include drilling into the skull to release demons.

As we are specifically looking at the psychological aspect of mythology, I think we should pull examples out of the classical Greek writings to show how human emotions were displayed and explained through mythology.

It is interesting to note that emotions can be viewed as being in a position on a sliding scale. Cowardice and bravery belong on the same scale but are found in different positions of the same emotion range. Observe how certain emotional input can relate to this. If a person is presented with fear, we can see that cowardice might prevent action, yet the fear also leads to the opportunity for bravery where that panic can be overcome. This concept is the same for love and lust, happy and sad, patience and rage, etc. This scale was well known to the ancients, in the Kybalion (published by The Tree Initiates, 1908), one of the seven Hermetic laws is that of polarity where nothing is truly in opposition, only in varying degrees of being. For example, hot and cold are merely differences in temperature, where does hot begin and cold finish? There is no line in the stand to say something is hot or cold, it only becomes hotter or colder. The same applies to love and hate. Neither emotion exists as a permanent, definite state, the emotion shifts varying toward either love or hate. We will look at some examples below and see how the polarity of emotions shifts and how that shift can be at will to benefit the individual.

Athena Verses Ares - Heraclitus

The Greek scholar, Heraclitus (c. 100 A.D.) discussed the allegorical nature of classical mythology at length, paying particular attention to the stories of Homer. His work, Homeric Problems, is almost a defense made against criticisms made from Plato, Epicurus, and Xenophanes who all argued that Homer had acted impiously in his descriptions of the gods. Heraclitus sets out early in his work to show how allegory can be used to explain the workings of our world through a mythological setting. Here is what Heraclitus has to say about the battle between Athena and Ares.

> *Homer sets the virtues against vices and the corresponding elements against their opposites. Right from the start the pairing up of the gods in the battle has been philosophically devised as follows: Athena and Ares, i.e. thought and thoughtlessness. For he is, as I said, "raving, a total evil, unpredictable." (Iliad 5.831) But she is, "famous among the gods for wisdom and shrewdness."(Odyssey 13.298-9) There is an irreconcilable enmity between reason that leads to the best judgments and thoughtlessness that sees nothing. And just as reason must have been of the greatest benefit in life, so too it made good judgments in the battle. For raging and deranged insensibility is not stronger than intelligence. Athena beat Ares and sent him sprawling on the ground, inasmuch as every vice, crashing to the ground, has been cast in the lowest pits, an illness that is downtrodden and lies*

beneath all hubris. Of course, Homer lays Aphrodite (i.e. licentiousness) down next to Ares: "So the two lay on the much-nourishing earth." (Iliad 21.426) Illnesses of the mind are kin and neighbors to the emotions.
- Heraclitus' Homeric Problems, section 54
(Translation from Anthology of Classical Myth, Trzaskoma, S. M., Scott Smith, R., Brunet, S. (Hackett, USA, 2004) Pg. 118)

Emotion in Myth

Love/Lust

Love is perhaps the greatest of human emotions and is seen time and time again in all mythologies. It is a driving force for people, something that they strive to obtain. In Homer's Odyssey, we see Odysseus undergo endless trials and hardships, a lesser man would have failed but Odysseus' love for Penelope kept the fire in his heart burning. Despite being gone for twenty years, the love never faded for Odysseus, and it influenced his decisions, for example, when succumbing to the lust of Calisto, his love of Penelope broke him away from temptation.

Lust is the darker side of love, it is an uncontrolled animalistic urge that mimics its purer form and often sees people fall in to trouble and disaster. There is a story told my many classical authors called The Judgement of Paris (one version of note is by Lucian), which sees Paris influenced by the charms of Aphrodite. This resulted in his 'winning' of Helen. She was kidnapped from Sparta and brought to Troy, and despite the imminent war that would ensue, Paris' lust would not let him give her up. The consequences of this was the Trojan War and the loss of everything dear to Paris.

Patience/Rage

Patience is a virtue and always has been, the ability to stay calm and collected allows someone to make better decisions and when under hardship this could lead to the eventual gaining of freedom. During Odysseus' leave from Ithaca, his wife Penelope has to endure the persistent advances of a group of suitors trying to marry her. She hates them, but is wise enough to keep her patience, she weaves a picture on a loom every day and unpicks her work each night, biding her time until she finds the right moment to act. With the return of her love Odysseus, they manage to overcome the suitors, free themselves, and live happily ever after.

The contrast to patience is rage, a seemingly uncontrollable urge for violence and immediate action. As expected this leads to trouble as unthoughtful actions cause unexpected results. Hercules is the shining example of a man unable to control his base instincts. He is primal and animalistic and gives us great examples of rage. A simple example is when Linos struck Hercules, he killed the man in an uncontrolled retaliation. In a similar manner, he kills his wife Megara and his children in a fit of uncontrolled rage setting himself in a state of constant sorrow. The loss of control always results in the loss of loved ones and a worse condition for the hero. It can even be shown that the loss of control causes the hero to lose their humanity.

Rage is a common theme in mythology and even today it is presented in our movies, because, like then, rage is a threat to society. Storytellers write about rage as a warning of what to avoid. Homers Iliad opens with the lines,

"Rage! Goddess, sing of the rage of Peleus' son Achilles,
murderous, doomed, that cost the Achaeans countless losses."

In those opening lines, the entire epic is set up, the uncontrollable rage of Achilles is the cause of great loss. We see much later in the poem that it is only when Achilles accepts patience and understanding that he bridges his emotions and those great losses begin to heal.

Bravery/Cowardice

Fear is our inbuilt survival mechanism, it's the alarm inside out head that screams for us to run and avoid the situation, but in counter to this, we can face that fear with bravery and overcome it. Fear is presented in mythology by monsters and challenges, different monsters resemble different fears, and more often than not the hero will at first cower at the face of it. It's through discipline that bravery can be summoned, usually with the backing of a higher cause that the hero needs to live up to.

The usual case of a monster is that it is terrorizing a people who are helpless to the beast, it's only until a hero comes along who is brave enough to face monsters that the creature can be overcome. Take for example the Minotaur, a creature feared by all peoples, and who terrorizes the population of Athens. The Athenians do nothing about this beast, their fear is so great that they even allow the sacrifice of their children. Until one of them rises up and takes action. In this case, Theseus finds inspiration, he needs to prove himself to his father, and he uses this motivation to overcome his fear. As he has a reason to stand and fight, he overcomes his urge to run or cower.

It is important to keep in mind the sliding scale of emotions taught through Hermetics. Cowardice and bravery are merely two reactions to the same situation, they are not so much opposite emotions, just different aspects of it. It is natural for an individual to show both reactions, or for one to present itself only to shift to the other. These emotions are only degrees apart, the trick to emotional control is to understand this, take control of your thoughts and choose which degree you want to feel.

Joy/Grief or Happiness/Sadness

The shift from happy to sad or sad to happy is an emotional rollercoaster that people go on all too often. It is portrayed in mythology to teach the importance of control over ones emotions, and it does this by showing the consequences of losing yourself in grief, or even too much happiness. Take for example Orpheus, so in love with Eurydice that he thinks his bliss will never end. But fate has her die outside of his control, his happiness flips to a grief of unimaginable lows. He loses himself in despair, and this leads to his eventual death. The problem for Orpheus was he lost himself in the emotion of grief and losing all control of his life, he lost that too.

There is no single teaching that helps people manage these emotions, only episodes of particular situations are shared, and these mythologies give light to different possibilities. Most people agree on the old axiom written above the entrance to the oracle of Delphi, that moderation is key in all things, and moderation of emotions is included, do not be too happy, do not be too sad, all these things are transient after all.

Hatred/Delight

As we have already discussed, emotions are usually the same at different degrees, someone might do you a favor or injury and you could hate or delight in the action. These responses are again mere degrees of difference within the same emotion scale. To put this simply, we can look at a sequence of events. A woman loves a man who cheats on her, she finds out and her love changes to hate. The emotion of love/hate is the same but they sit on different ends of the scale.

Let us look at Hera and her position toward Hercules. She hates Hercules, but it is also reasonable to say that what she really hates is Zeus' infidelity from which Hercules is a product. Like the example above, her love for Zeus is morphed to hatred, but rather than placing that hatred on her husband, Hera hates the product of the infidelity, Hercules. The hate she feels drives her in an attempt to foil Hercules' every action, she sends snakes to kill him, opposes his claims to divinity, sends monster after monster and more. Hercules for his part in this is innocent, and so the dilemma of hatred

Figure 18: A 2nd Century A.D. marble statue of Hercules as a young child, strangling one of the snakes sent by Hera. Artwork housed in the Palazzo Nuovo gallery.

emerges. An innocent man is pained by hate he did not cause and cannot help to heal.

Guilt/Innocence

While we are speaking about Hercules, we can look at the psychological representation of guilt and innocence. Hercules killed his family in a fit of rage, and upon returning to a stable frame of mind felt an intense guilt for the actions. The only way for him to return to a state of innocence and remove his remorse is to pay penance. This, of course, is the origin of his twelve labors, twelve good deeds to set his conscious straight.

You will note that many myths do not attempt to give a moral teaching to its audience, instead, it is designed to show possible outcomes of these emotions. These topics give us a great understanding of our own emotions so we might find control over them and lead a balanced life.

The Story of Orpheus & Eurydice

A modernized version of the myth according to the Roman poet, Virgil.

***

Divine anger will always chase you, the man whose crimes we tell. That monster who chased innocent Eurydice through the flowing streams. That fiend, who will always be haunted by Orpheus until the day he atones for his wretched crimes.

Poor Eurydice in all her innocence fled from you, running headlong down the stream in an attempt to escape from your primal depravity. But in her terror, she did not see that fierce snake that hid along the banks long grass. In a moment, an mere flash of time, the serpent struck and the poison sank deep within her.

The Dryads filled the mountaintops with their wailing, the towers of Rhodope wept along with all the peoples of Thrace, Getae, the Hebrus, and Orythia. Orpheus strummed his lyre, singing songs of his sweet wife, and her alone as he wept on the empty shore. He consoled his broken heart, day and night singing only of his love, Eurydice.

Orpheus picked himself up and entered the jaws of Taenarus. He passed through the high gates of Hades, through the groves that are dimmed by fear. He came upon the spirits and their dread kings, playing his song of sorrow. The shadows and phantoms were drawn to him as light in the darkness, crawling out from the depths of Erebus to see the source of such heartache. Orpheus traveled down and down, playing his melody of despair, passing between fallen mothers and fathers, and the bodies of noble heroes. He pressed on through the crowd of lifeless souls, past boys and girls who had met the pyre before their fathers eyes, through the black mud and foul reeds clinging to the vile marsh of Cocytus and its sluggish waters.

The house of the Dead was stupefied, the Furies with their snake entwined hair, Cerberus with his three jaws gaping, and the halls of Tartarus all stood silent at the pain pouring from one poor man. Ixion's wheel stopped in the wind and all listened in to the tragedy. Orpheus' pain moved Proserpine, and that queen ordained a second chance. She declared that he was to guide her back to the light of Helios but to never lay eyes on her until she had returned. Retracing his steps, he evaded all mischance, and loyal Eurydice followed in his steps. But as they approached the upper air a sudden madness seized the incautious lover. A moment that could be forgiven, if the wretched spirits knew of the term. He stopped in doubt, at the edge of the light, his will conquered and looked back to see his beloved Eurydice.

In that moment, Proserpine's pact was broken, the waters of Avernus crashed thrice, and all his efforts were wasted.

"Orpheus," she cried, "what madness has destroyed my wretched self, and you? The cruel Fates now recall me, and sleep hides my swimming eyes. Farewell my love, for I am taken."

She reached out her arms, but they were no longer his, and wrapped around in vast night she was taken, and in an instant fled far from his eyes, like smoke vanishing in thin air, and never again did the lovers meet.

Orpheus grasped out at the shadows, but all was in vain, he longed to speak with her but was not permitted to pass the barrier of that marsh again. Denied by Charon, ferryman of the dead, what could he do? Where could he turn now robbed twice of his wife?

He wept below the airy cliffs of Strymon for seven months, telling his tale in icy cliffs, and bringing the wild spirits to tears with his song. Orpheus heart could not be healed, no love or wedding song could bring him to smile. He wandered the northern wastes, through snowy Tanais and frosty Rhipaean, mourning his lost Eurydice.

It was in Ciconia that Orpheus met his end. Full of sorrow he came upon Bacchic women, spurred on by their devotion. They tore the youth apart in their divine rites and midnight revels and scattered him throughout the field. But as his head rolled through an icy stream, the

whispers of a voice alone, an ice-cold tongue, with ebbing
breath cried out,
  "Eurydice, my poor Eurydice."

***

Heavenly Spheres & Astro-Mythology

Myths In The Sky

Where did mythology come from and how did mankind become religious? Did we just wake up one day and decide to tell fanciful stories to one another? Did a god come down from the heavens to reveal hidden mysteries to the people populating the earth? How is it that civilizations and cultures separated by time and space all share the same fundamental beliefs? Surely this was not an accident, there must have been a common link to all people, a common source of inspiration and truth.

To our ancestors, there could be no greater mystery than that of the life-giving sun. To watch the celestial body rise in the morning sky, arching its way slowly through the day before setting over the horizon would have been like staring into the face of God. The sun may well have been the birthing place for humanities spirituality as we asked the first philosophical questions to ourselves, where does the sun go each night, and from where does it rise each morning?

The suns deification is common to all people around the globe and can be found in countless pantheons, just look at Ra (Egyptian), Helios (Greek), Huitzilopochtli (Aztec), Amaterasu (Japanese), or Belenus (Celtic). Though these gods may vary in specific details, they all broadly represent the sun and are from cultures divided by space and time, suggesting that the rise of sun worship was natural to humanity and occurred without external cultural influences.

A plethora of solar myths sprang up around the world and it did not take long before the primary actions of the sun took on symbolic meaning. The sun's daily setting and rising was likened to death and rebirth. Each morning the great orb would rise again, chasing away the darkness of night and this was symbolically seen as light conquering darkness, or good defeating evil. The solar deity was soon seen to represent all things good in the world, and this is exemplified perfectly through the belief of the Greek god, Apollo, being the bringer of light and honesty.

The symbolic importance of the solar deity took an uncontrolled leap during the Amarna Period of Ancient Egyptian history. Pharaoh Akhenaten (1353 - 1336 B.C.) brought into existence the earliest form of monotheism through the sole worship of the solar disc, Aten. The details are still debated in academia, but it appears that Akhenaten banned (or at least severely limited) the worship of all other gods in Egypt, and eventually promoted the Aten to the status of universal deity, showing us that solar worship was seen as the highest form of divinity.

However, humanity's first leap into monotheism was ultimately a failure as we see Atenism collapse immediately with the death of Akhenaten. The old gods were reinstated and it is clear that a single solar deity could not fill the numerous roles found within a pantheon.

Astrology As A Science

It is clear that the study of the stars has always been close to the human heart as we have been observing and measuring the heavenly movements from before we could record written history. The greater majority of prehistoric monuments that still stand around the world today show precise astrological significance, perfectly lining up with specific celestial events. For examples, look at Stonehenge (England, c.8000-1600 B.C.), Gobekli Tepe (Turkey, c.9130-7370 B.C.), or Napta Playa (Egypt, c.6400-4900 B.C.). The age of these constructions show how important the movement of the heavens really were to early man and is a testament to our ancestors extensive knowledge of the heavenly movements.

But why was there so much time and energy invested into measuring the movements of celestial bodies? The answer is evolutionary, in that the reason changed over time. It did not take long for early humanity to realize that particular celestial phenomena occurred at the same time as significant changes on the earth, like the coming of spring, or the annual flooding of the Nile. The implication of this, of course, is that by knowing the events that occur in the night sky, one can predict what will happen on earth.

As time went on, humans began to associate their gods with the orbiting planets and stars, believing that they were the physical emanations of the gods themselves. From this point on, humans could predict an even deeper understanding of the future by understanding the varying nature of the celestial bodies, for these were seen as signs from the gods. Now, having insight into what the future holds is a powerful tool, and the need for constant observation and interpretation of the night sky makes sense when considering this translation from the State Archives of Assyria (Koch-Westenholz, 1995, p.12) where a tablet from an astronomer to the Babylonian king Esarhaddon voices the concern of a lunar eclipse in 673 B.C.

In the beginning of the year, a flood will come and break the dikes. When the Moon has made the eclipse, the king, my lord, should write to me. As a substitute for the king, I will cut through a dike, here in Babylonia, in the middle of the night. No one will know about it.

Clearly, we see that to understand the celestial spheres was to comprehend the future, and this knowledge was vitally important in the protection of the royal house and the entire nation. To read the skies was to predict the future, to know the future was a source of unprecedented power.

Figure 19: A photograph of a Babylonian ziggurat from which early Mesopotamian astronomers would take readings of the night sky. Herodotus writes that atop each of these ziggurats was a shrine where priests would maintain religious rituals and initiation ceremonies. This Ziggurat is located in Ali Air Base, Iraq.

We have now come to a point where we must discern between astrology and astronomy for there is a great amount of assumed knowledge and preconceived ideas on the subject. Astrology and astronomy both work to study the phenomena seen in the sky, and they work together to do this. They came into existence as a single subject, working together for an end result which is best described as this, astronomy is the study of the physical movement of objects in space, and astrology is the study of the impact these variable movements have on earth. There is a common misconception that early astrology was an illegitimate science as many believe it to be based on magic and superstition. This, however, is entirely untrue, as the Babylonians developed their system mundanely through observation and inquiry. Their astrology is based on rules formulated from the data they collected which was set in tables that could not be changed. This, of course, meant that the oracles they produced could not be objective as they came from set laws.

In other words, astrology, at least to the Babylonians, was developed through careful observation of what transpired on earth when varying celestial phenomena occurred. These observations were noted and studied, the patterns were formulated into tables allowing for future observation and study. After enough tangible evidence was produced, these tables were set as laws, allowing for future predictions based on heavenly events.

The Wandering Planets

Each of the known planets was likened to a specific divinity, and the divinity's action in the skies could help man predict the future, or elaborate on divine messages.

These planets interacted with each other and the stars around them through their wanderings and all of this was measured and theorized on. Below is a list of the planets as known by the ancients, ordered in the traditional way of the Babylonians. Their meanings and interpretations are limited as they will be discussed at length in Chapter 10.

I - Jupiter / Marduk / Zeus

Jupiter corresponds to the great sky-god, the chief god of nearly every pantheon. He symbolizes growth and expansion, luck and wealth, and is studied to interpret success. The planet corresponds to a range of life activities, but above all represents the freedom that humanity longs for, and hopes to secure through success in the various spheres of life.

II - Venus / Ishtar / Aphrodite

The goddess of love and lust, it's not surprising to see the planets association with sensuality and relationships. The planets movement have long governed harmony, resilience, beauty, and the desire for pleasure. Obviously, the study of Venus in the night sky corresponds with that of relationships above all else.

III - Saturn / Ninurta / Kronos

Saturn deals with reality and time, and with that the possibilities and limitations in one's own ability. With this, it is common to interpret Saturn's influence on mankind with the ability to make and succeed in long-term goals.

IV - Mercury / Nabu / Hermes

Mercury is the intermediate messenger between humanity and the gods. Communication, reason, and rationality are hallmarks of the planets interpretation and it was vitally important in interpreting timing of transport and messages.

V - Mars / Nergal / Ares

Blood red Mars is associated with warfare, violence, and bloodshed, leaving its study crucial for courses of war. Controlling an individual's aggression, sexuality, self-assertion, energy, strength, and ambition. Mars is the archetypal impersonation of the warrior.

VI - Luna (Moon) / Sin / Selene & Artemis

The moon has always been interpreted as a feminine deity, representative of the unconscious psyche. In this, it is associated with maternal instincts, especially internal rhythm, memory, emotions, and mood. The 28-day moon cycle should not be forgotten in its association with the feminine.

VII - Sol (Sun) / Shamash / Helios & Apollo

Represented by the solar deities, the sun is representative of the conscious ego and therefore the expression of one's self. This is why we see these gods symbolically standing for truth as the ego reveals itself. The sun itself is the life force of earth, and this was not lost in ancient interpretations where it symbolized health and vitality, and most importantly - creation.

The Curious Case of the Dogon People

The sub-Saharan tribe known as the Dogon are a curious people for the great wealth of astronomical knowledge that they hold on account of the fact they are seemingly unadvanced in relation to the western world. They occupy the rocky plateau's of Mali, making a living from rudimentary agriculture, taking to the caves and outcrops for shelter. The inhospitable location of their dwelling has kept the Dogon people out of contact from the rest of the world, and they were only encountered by European explorers in the early 20th century. A three-decade-long study ensued by French anthropologists Dr. Marcel Griaule and Germaine Dieterlen who had made some astonishing findings from these people. Firstly, they believed their origins to be that from Egypt, where they migrated from the Nile around 3200 B.C. From here the Dogons moved through Libya and eventually to their homeland in Mali. However, it was the extensive knowledge of astronomy that was traditionally kept in the mythological accounts of the Dogon people that surprised the anthropologists.

Their myths told of a race of beings that had come to earth for the betterment of humanity from the distant star, Sirius. The Dogon priests told Griale and Dieterlen that this star did not exist alone but has a companion star that moved in a 50-year elliptical orbit around Sirius. What is astonishing about this belief is that it is true, modern astronomy found the second star (Sirius B) in 1862 but it is far too small for the naked eye to see and was only able to be photographed in 1970. Artifacts dating well over 400 years from the Dogon culture show Sirius B and its orbit to within an orbital error of 0.09 years, an incredible accurate model.

The Dogons gave the anthropologist further information including the density difference of the stars and earth, descriptions of the rings surrounding Saturn, and a third star in the Sirius system (which is currently undiscovered) but it was the mythological account of the beings that are of interest. The legend of The Nommos describes these creatures as awful-looking beings that came in a vessel with fire and thunder. The creatures were amphibious, the Dogons calling them 'Masters of the Water', 'the Monitors', and, 'the Teachers'. Their parallels to water beings should not escape our attention that the Babylonian fish-god shares an uncanny similarity in name to these people - Dagon and that the Babylonian myths speak of an amphibious race called the Annedoti that teaches mankind and are also described as 'repulsive'. This may link back to the Dogon peoples origins in Egypt, a cultural neighbor of Mesopotamia.

The myth of The Nommos continues, telling of the self-sacrifice of these amphibious beings, how they fed the earth and humanity with their own bodies before dying and being resurrected. Finally, it is prophesized that the Nommos will return to the earth in the form of people, and take us into the next phase of evolution where we will be amphibious and rule the world from the oceans.

A plethora of theories surround this peculiar knowledge of the Dogons. Contact with extraterrestrial civilizations is common, and though it should not be discounted, Carl Sagan also voices a rational alternative. He suggests that the Dogons may have been in contact with advanced civilizations prior to the first anthropological studies. Such contact would naturally have turned to the sky and to the star system Sirius in particular as the Dogons had an interest in the brightest speck in their night sky. The civilizations Sagan speaks of are human of course, but undocumented contacts. This does not explain the age of the Dogon knowledge though, and it does not incorporate the link to Egypt and Mesopotamia. The study into this phenomenal culture continues.

Celestial Studies & The Birth Of The Zodiac

As the Babylonians studied the night sky, they began to record and categorize their observations with a staggering degree of detail and precision. Dividing the sky above them into 360 segments, or degrees, they were able to record phenomena in individual segments with such clarity that we can still use the information they recorded today. These 360 segments were again divided into 12 houses, to which the star systems within became the Zodiac.

The precise calculations and observations of the Babylonians were handed down and further worked on through generations. Through trade and cultural exchanges, their information found its way to all the great nations of earth, seen directly and indirectly in India, Egypt, Greece, and Rome to name but a few.

After nearly a thousand years of research, Claudius Ptolemy (c. 100 - 170 B.C.), a Hellenistic scientist from Egypt, compiled all that had been observed into his great work the Almagest. His geocentric model put the earth in the center of the universe with a series of crystalline spheres surrounding it. Each sphere was the abode of a separate planet with the stars painted onto the outer most sphere.

It is in Mesopotamia that we see the first written records of the detailed study of the night sky thanks to the Babylonian Chaldeans. They categorized what they saw in the night sky, and created the first zodiac. This knowledge was huge, and it did not take long before the other great culture of the time, Egypt, took up the information for their own use. From Mesopotamia and Egypt, the zodiac exploded into popular culture, passing from one people to the next, all the way down to us today. Though this theory has now been disproved, Ptolemy's geocentric theory is completely rational and is a perfect explanation for the phenomena he could observe.

It was theorized that each sign of the zodiac ruled earth for a certain amount of time, sending its specific characteristics from the heavens to divinely alter the fate of humanity. However, the symbols of the zodiac represent more than this. Each symbol is an archetypal representation of a specific personality. This, of course, gave birth to the idea that an individual born in the time of a certain sign will inherit its traits. Whether this is true or not is of no concern to us though. The simple fact is that these beliefs were true to many cultures, and that the archetypes they represent do exist and that they form the basis of characters commonly found in mythical stories throughout the world.

The Zodiac & Archetypes

I - Aries

The constellation Aries has not always been that of the Ram. It is believed that the original interpretation of the sign was that of an agrarian worker. It was the Mesopotamians that altered this due to their beliefs. They likened the constellation to Damuzid the shepherd, and through his association with the sheep he herded and this evolved the symbolism of Aries to that of a Ram we know today. In their mythology, the goddess Innana sacrifices Damuzid to the demons to save herself and this interpretation is still associated with the star sign through the Abrahamic tradition of the Sacrificial Lamb.

Figure 20: A first century A.D. Roman cast terracotta of the ram-horned Jupiter Ammon. Located in the Museo Barracco, Rome.

In Egyptian mythology, Aries is associated with Amun-Ra, often depicted as a man with a rams head forming the figure of a strong warrior. This symbology continues in other cultures, such as Greece, where even Zeus is occasionally shown with rams horns to indicate his prowess as a warrior. It is through this more modern symbolism that we know Aries as the leader, strong and bold, an initiator, the first, and the mighty ruler.

II - Taurus

Taurus is Latin for the Bull. It is possibly the oldest constellation recorded, dating back to the Upper Palaeolithic where it is depicted in cave paintings symbolizing the Spring equinox from around 4000 -1700

B.C. From the early bronze age, we see specific depictions of Taurus in the Minoan culture and depictions of the constellation moving into Aries through Mesopotamian reliefs and mythology depicting the death of the "Bull of Heaven", such as in the Epic of Gilgamesh.

In Egypt, Taurus was symbolized by the goddess, Hathor, who represented fertility, music, and dance, and is depicted with the bullhorns enshrining the life-giving sun. The sacred bull brought Spring's fertility and its feminine counterpart, Hathor, is often seen giving life and nutrients in relief through suckling rulers such as Hatshepsut. Taurus is depicted later in Greek mythology through the stories of Zeus and Europa, Theseus and the Minotaur, and many others. The key characteristics which Taurus represent include stubbornness, links to the earth, sensuality, the arts, beauty, and the possessions of wealth.

III - Gemini

Gemini is Latin for The Twins and appeared in Roman astronomy as Castor and Pollux. Both Roman and Greek people Castor and Pollux as patrons of sailors and travelers due to their guiding light, Saint Elmo's Fire.

The ruling planet for Gemini is the Latin god Mercury (Hermes in Greece and Thoth or Anubis in Egypt). Mercury, Hermes, Anubis, and Thoth all share the same qualities in being messengers between humanity, the gods, and the underworld, and it is in this that Gemini is supposed to be a great helper to mankind. Due to the association with the messenger, it is a typical trait of Gemini to show strong communication skills through oration, writing, education, and art.

Due to their nature as twins, there is a duality found in Gemini that gives them polarising traits. They have two minds making them stubborn yet open to change, helpful and mischievous, hungry for knowledge and restless.

IV - Cancer

Governed by the moon, Cancer is symbolized as The Crab and is known in Mesopotamian astronomy as the Northern Gate of the Sun due to its association with the summer solstice. Egyptian society symbolized Cancer as the scarab beetle holding its egg, the solar disc. Carrying its egg for 28 days, linking it to the moons cycle, the scarab rolls its egg into the water where its hatchlings are born on the 29th day, representing rebirth and creation (creation being associated with the egg symbolizing the solar disc). Through this, birth, rebirth, baptism, and immortality are all associated with Cancer.

Babylonian mythology associates Cancer with the underworld, this representation can be seen influencing later Greek mythology through the Labours of Hercules, where a chthonic crab assaults the hero. All of this symbolism leaves Cancer to represent bearing, birthing, nurturing and protecting, all of which can be understood by the feminine moon, through which Cancer is governed.

V - Leo

The greatest monument to the constellation Leo may be that of the Sphynx in Egypt. There is a popular theory that the Sphynx was built in the Age of Leo, around 10,000 B.C. due to it aligning perfectly with the Leo constellation with the addition of the Great Pyramids of Giza and the River Nile. Together, the earthly monuments line up with the celestial stars to form a kind of ground map of the heavens.

The constellation of Leo, The Lion, is governed by the sun and this is most obvious in Egyptian mythology the feline god Sekh-Met. Sekh-Met was seen as a solar deity and wore the Uraeus crown associating her with royalty. In Babylonian mythology, Leo is symbolized through the monster, Humbaba, who was slain by Gilgamesh.

It is in Greece that we see the alter ego of Leo through the Nemean Lion, a primal beast who has an impenetrable hide. Hercules defeats the Nemean Lion and wears its hide for protection, symbolizing the ability to overcome ones darker characteristics and to wear them for protection. In this, we see Leo as a royal character exhibiting pride, courage and full of life.

VI - Virgo

Virgo, The Virgin, is associated with health and the harvest. She is the only portrayal of a feminine figure in the zodiac and is always associated with wheat. There are Mesopotamian representations of Virgo from around 1000 B.C. representing her as a furrow and grain. In Egypt, the virgin Isis is the portrayal of Virgo. She is the "world mother" symbolizing health and knowledge, bearing a sheaf of grain, or alternatively, her son, the baby sun god, Horus. In Greek mythology, Virgo is represented with the constellation of Demeter, the mother of Persephone, both of which are goddesses of fertility and the harvest. The Christian, Virgin Mary, has been likened to Virgo, and in astrology, Virgo is associated with specific tastes, attention to detail, and the bodies health.

VII - Libra

Known in Babylonian mythology as the Claws of the Scorpion, Libra is associated with the Mesopotamian god, Shamash, representative of truth and justice, giving it the symbolic sign of the scales. The symbolism of the Claws of the Scorpion lived on in Arabic and Greek astronomy, and its association with law and justice continued there as well. The Egyptians symbolized Libra as Khonsu, the divine child, representing birth and renewal. In the Egyptian book of the Dead, the scales are used to judge the dead, where tipping the scales resulted in reincarnation.

VIII - Scorpio

The house of Scorpio, The Scorpion, rule the qualities of life, death, sexuality and the mysteries. Modern astrology see's Scorpio as governed by Pluto, however, this planet was only recently discovered, and in antiquity, Scorpio was in fact ruled by Mars. In Greek mythology, Scorpio is nearly always linked with Orion the Hunter, for when Orion threatened to kill all the beasts of the earth, it was the goddess Gaia who sent the scorpion to stop him. The great scorpion stung Orion on the heel, and this can be seen in the interpretation of the constellations.

Scorpio was recognized in Mesopotamian astrology and is represented in their mythology by the scorpion-men who guard the passageway of the sun, opening the gates each morning as Shamash passed through the sky, and locking them closed each night as the solar deity returned to the underworld.

In Egyptian mythology, Scorpio was originally portrayed as Serekhet who had power over venomous snakes and scorpions. Sekhmet was also a kind of patron for midwives, helping women in childbirth and nursing.

Through interpreting these stories, one can see Scorpio exhibiting three prime characteristics - passion, secrets, and legacy.

IX - Sagittarius

The Babylonians first likened Sagittarius to their monstrous god Nergal. This may be the origin for the mythical Greek centaur, to which the constellation is now associated with. We interpret the constellation of Sagittarius as a centaur charging forward whilst pulling back a bow to it full capacity and aiming it high into the sky.

It is in the Greek mythology that we see the centaur Chiron, famous for his abilities as a healer. Greek tradition also gives us Chroitos, the centaur archer who lived among the muses whom placated Zeus to set him into the night sky. Through this tale we see why Jupiter (Zeus) is the planet governing the constellation, characterizing Sagittarius with wanderlust, higher learning, and culture.

In the heavens, the stars aligning Sagittarius' arrow aim for the star, Antaries, which is the heart of the Scorpio constellation. This is deeply symbolic of the centaurs protection for the nearby Orion. Sagittarius is Latin for arrow which perfectly encapsulates the sign, it is typical for those of Sagittarius to aim high, wander far and to be fiercely protective over those they love.

X - Capricorn

Capricorn is Latin for the horned goat as it is commonly represented as a sea-goat where its lower half is that of a fish. The sign is based on the Sumerian god Enki, primordial god of waters and wisdom, who was commonly shown as bearing the upper half of a mountain goat and the lower half of a fish. Enki was commonly attributed as the patron of intelligence, creation, crafts, magic, water, and the sea. Capricorn is seen in Greek mythology as the goat that suckled the infant Zeus during his hiding from Kronos. The Goats broken horn was later turned into the cornucopia, or, horn of plenty. As the constellation is ruled over by Saturn, Capricorn displays strength, tenacity, and overcomes obstacles to reach mastery.

XI - *Aquarius*

Aquarius is found in the Babylonian star catalogs where they call it, Gu-La, the Great One, and represented the chief god, Ea. Ea is commonly depicted as holding an overflowing vase, and this may be Aquarius' origin as The Water-Bearer. The Aquarius constellation is ruled by Uranus, symbolic of higher consciousness, and the overflowing water is representative of an abundance of fluid understanding.

In the Early Bronze Age, Aquarius was linked with the Winter Solstice, which in Ancient Egypt, was associated with the annual flooding of the Nile. They believed that the Water-Bearer would pour the jugs into the river, flooding the banks and bringing Spring to the land. Egypt also associated Aquarius with the God of inundation, Hapi, who joined the Papyri and Lotus plants of Upper and Lower Egypt into a symbolic union of the entire land.

In Islamic astrology, Aquarius is depicted as drawing water for humanity from the well of knowledge. It is in all this symbolism that Aquarius can be seen as the bringer of knowledge and wisdom, uniting differences and expanding consciousness.

The Egyptian Zodiac from the Ceiling of the Grand Portico
in the Temple of Isis at Dendera.

Figure 21: A sketch taken from the ceiling of the Grand Portico in the Temple of Isis at Dendera shows the twelve zodiac symbols of ancient Egypt. From top left to right we see Cancer, Leo, Virgo, Libra, Scorpio, Sagittarius, Gemini, Taurus, Aries, Pisces, Aquarius, and Capricorn.

XII - Pisces

Pisces, Latin for the Fish, is the final symbol of the zodiac and draws characteristics from each of its predecessors. Ruled by Neptune, Pisces is commonly associated with spirituality and surrender.

The glyph of Pisces originates from Egypt, where two separate circular cycles are joined by a line, symbolizing the meeting point of two worlds - the mundane and the spiritual.

In Greek mythology, Pisces is seen aiding Aphrodite and Eros' fleeing from the monster Typhon. In their mythology, it becomes clear that Pisces is, in fact, two beings, but joined forever by the rope they tied to each other. The fact that they are two separate entities that are inseparable is further symbolism to their ultimate meaning of two connecting realities.

In modern astrology, it is believed that the world entered the age of Pisces around 1 A.D. and that Christian iconography through the fish symbolizes this, and that Christ himself is the archetype of a Piscean. It is in this that Pisces represents the death of ego, and its merging completely with spirit.

It has not been decisively shown how mythology emerged from the stars but a good inference can be set out. As man studied the heavens, monitoring the regular movement of the planets and stars, he also noted the general effect that they had on earthly events. This scientific inquiry eventually drew people to conclusions on what effects the variables in the sky had for humanity. The early scientists had two ways in which to explain their discoveries, either through logos (logical explanation) or muthos (a fable-like explanation). As the greater population would have been uneducated, it makes sense to explain the discoveries through allegory and mythology. So, our astrological myths were created, told, distilled, recreated, and told again until they reached our modern readership.

The Celestial Significance Of Saviour Mythology

The story of the son of god returning to earth to save humanity is not solely a Christian one. Indeed Christian theology is at the end of a long list of other cultures that built very similar stories long before it. From the Persian god Mithras to the Egyptian Horus, Dionysus of Greece and the Lord Krishna of Indian Hinduism, all these mythologies share uncanny qualities to that of the Christian savior, Jesus Christ. Some notable similarities across these mythologies include the virgin birth, usually occurring on the 25th of December, the god as a child protégé in youth, a divine ministry later in life (around the age of 30 years) while being joined with 12 disciples, and finally the resurrection that always occurs after three days of death.

But what does it mean to have all these mythologies nearly identical? It is almost certain that they impacted on each other through cultural exchanges, but there is more to it than that. These mythologies are based on astrological symbolism.

Take the birth date of December 25th. On the 24th of December, the Star of the East, Sirius, aligns perfectly with the three brightest stars in the night sky, those of Orion's Belt. In ancient times, these three stars were called the Three Kings. But there is more to it than that, for when the Three Kings "follow" the Star of the East, they align to point directly at the place on the horizon where the Sun will rise on the following morning, December 25th. This is the place of birth for sun god.

For the northern hemisphere, the winter solstice, or the shortest day of the year, will occur somewhere between December 20-24th. So between June (summer solstice, longest day of the year) and December, the sun appears to be dying in the sky, slowly dropping in the horizon until it reaches its solstice and optically appears to remain in its lowest point for three days. During these three days of death, the sun sits in the vicinity of the Southern Cross constellation, and so has been crucified, killed, and lays dormant for three days. After the three days, the sun is gloriously reborn and begins to rise in the sky once more, traveling back toward its zenith, bringing spring and fertility with it.

It is at the spring equinox when day becomes longer than night, and therefore goodness has overcome evil, that the resurrection is celebrated. For the northern hemisphere, the spring equinox occurs roughly at the same time Easter is celebrated, somewhere in late March to early April.

But how do the 12 disciples fall in to an astrological assessment of the savior mythology? They are simply the 12 constellations of the zodiac in which the sun travels through during its journey. This explains why 12 is a reoccurring number of importance in holy texts and mythologies throughout the world, the 12 Tribes of Judah in Judaism, the 12 Disciples of Jesus in Christianity, there are 12 legitimate Imams in Shi'a Islam, there are 12 Olympians in Greek mythology, the Norse god Odin had 12 sons, King Arthur won 12 great battles, Hercules overcame 12 great labors. In each of these examples, we see a central figure revolving around 12 lesser which is a direct symbolic interpretation of the suns celestial orbit through the zodiac.

Assuming that the central figures of these great religions and mythologies represents the sun, we can look with fresh eyes on some of the titles given to them. "The Son of God", "The light of the world", "The Risen Savior who will Come Again", "The Glory of God", " Defender Against Darkness", etc.

The Abrahamic religions have left us further clues to their astrological understanding and teaching within their Holy Scriptures. But to understand what is next, we have to quickly discuss the precession of the equinox. Put most simply, the earth wobbles very slightly on its axis, this causes an optical phenomenon where the constellations of the zodiac seem to move back across the night sky incredibly slowly. While we occupy a certain zodiac sign, it is called an "Age" and lasts for approximately 2150 years. It is common to see the shifting of ages in mythology, for example, the Persian Mithras is the great Bull slayer, taking us out of the Age of Taurus. Moses does this too, showing utter disgust at the Israelite worship of the Golden Calf (Taurus) at Mt. Sinai. Moses demanded the people to relinquish their belief in the idol, effectively ushering in the age of Aries the Ram. Around 2150 years after this the next great savior, Jesus, brought in the Age of Pisces, easily noted by his widespread association with the fish.

How does this effect Christianity and all the other savior based religions though? Are they to be summed up as copies of older pagan beliefs, or dismissed as outdated superstitious astrology? I do not think so. Cultural exchanges and influence is seen on all levels and religion is far from immune to it. It makes perfect sense to understand some of the theology, rituals, and significance in modern religion as having been carried over from older religions and cultures. This is especially true when forcing a new religion on people, the most effective path to successful indoctrination is to bring the old beliefs into the new ones. This explains the Christian festivals that fall on the dates of older Pagan ones. There are universal truths and meanings behind the old astrological customs, and they should be understood for what they are. They obviously still exist in our belief systems today, but this only adds depth beauty to the religion, not detract from it.

Archetypes & The Collective Unconscious

Archetypes

What if I told you that all things in this world have a perfect representative that exists outside of time and space? That our perception of everything, from people, places, experiences, and imaginings come from a stencil-like source found somewhere in the subconscious of everyone? This is Carl Gustav Jung's theory of archetypes and it is vitally important in the understanding of mythology and the world around us.

It is first useful to look at the word archetype as this will give us insight into its proper meaning. Etymologically, archetype stems from two Greek nouns, arche, meaning "first, origin, or beginning", and tupos, meaning "pattern, model, or type". From this, we derive archetype, the first pattern, the original mold, the model at the beginning. And so, we can quickly conclude that an archetype is the original mold of an idea or thing, from which other varieties can be created from.

To put this theory more directly, an archetype is the perfect representation of anything found on earth. By its nature, the archetype doesn't exist in any material reality, but transcends time and space, existing of itself. In this, it is a perfect stencil or mold. From this perfect mold, similar patterns, people, places, personalities, objects, or concepts are modeled or created. For an example, the mother is a generic archetype and is immediately recognized by all people across the earth. However, each mother on earth is unique, yet they are still recognizable and hold certain traits and expectations that are generic. The instantly recognizable feature that a woman is a mother come from the archetype, however, the individual herself is a unique variety from the original mold.

Plato's Forms

This theory of original forms does not actually originate from Jung himself but was developed over millennia. Jung actually worked from the theories and philosophies of his predecessors, and a useful point for us to start from is Plato. Plato developed his Theory of Forms in an attempt to answer the philosophical problem of universals. The problem is whether qualities exist and if they do, where? So take for example the quality of beauty.

1.   Is beauty a quality that exists in a perfect form independent from description, thought, or personal preference? (Platonic Realism)
2.   Does beauty only exist when there are beautiful things in existence? (Aristotelian Realism)
3.   Or, is beauty only a construct of the mind, existing only in description? (Idealism)

Plato's Theory of Forms states that qualities exist independent of the mind and description and argues that it is these non-physical, but substantial forms and ideas that give us the closest representation of reality. For in our observation, all things are variable and subject to change, take for example a dog, is the dog at birth the same dog in

Figure 22: In his work The Republic (380 B.C.), Plato writes the allegory of the cave. Here he describes, through allegory, how the reality we perceive is only a 'shadow' of divine reality. He likens humanity as people sitting in a cave looking at the back wall. They see shadows of objects on the wall, but because they cannot turn around, perceive the shadows as the real objects. The source of the shadows can be viewed as archetypes, mediators between our world and the divine.

old age? The dog itself has changed so much that it is not the same thing, however, it is still a dog, and so Plato tells us that the universal Form is the dog, despite its variable changes.

The Form is the essence of the thing, and without the universal Form, the thing would not be the thing it is. So, the dog would not be a dog, unless its essence was derived from the universal dog Form. The Form itself can be seen as the perfect blueprint, from which an unlimited number of things can come from. There are an uncountable number of dogs that have existed, but they have all spawned from the original Form blueprint.

Jung's Archetypes

Plato's Theory of Forms was criticized and built on by many great philosophers, but we are going to skip ahead to Carl Gustav Jung who truly modernized the theory and adopted it into contemporary psychology.

Jung developed his theory of archetypes as an alternative response the psychological theory of tabula rasa, the theory of a human mind being born as a blank slate with no prefilled knowledge. Jung believed that the mind inherited knowledge in the form of primordial images, or archetypes themselves and that they belonged to the subconscious at least by the time of birth. He described these thoughts as a kind of state of knowledge a priori (from before) the period of psychic orderedness. In other words, Jung believed that the knowledge or recognition of archetypes was housed in the subconscious before the mind developed any kind of order, and it was from these archetypes that the conscious mind could sort out and categorize the world around it. In a way, the archetypes act as categories with which the mind can find order in the world and make sense of it.

This a priori knowledge in all humans comes from what Jung called the "collective unconscious", a kind of structure for the psyche which is inherent in all people. The collective unconscious is filled with instincts and archetypes and is hugely influential on an individual's life, as they live out the experiences and dress the symbols based on the influences of their own lives. This is what we see in mythology, where the details of a story differ from culture to culture, yet the underlying principles remain the same.

The archetype itself resides in the subconscious and can never be understood by the conscious mind. A single subconscious archetype may give rise to an infinite amount of symbols, images, and patterns of behavior and this is why we see many varying mythological stories that all break down to common ideas in their interpretation. Jung likened this idea to the crystallization process of minerals. For you see a mineral begins its life from a liquid form of itself, the liquid has no crystalline structure, but as it cools, the crystal will always form by the constraints of its predetermined axial system. The axial system is the archetype of the crystal, and even though every crystal is different in its specifics, they all follow the predetermined axial system. In the same way, a phenomena will have its own characteristics, but be constrained by its predetermined archetype.

Jung explained the existence of archetypes in our reality by example of the light spectrum. Visible light is only a slight section of the spectrum bordered by the lower red (representing basic urges) and the higher ultra-violet (representing the spiritual). It is from this higher end of the spectrum, the ultra-violet, that Jung puts archetypes, from which they govern all that is below them, both living and inorganic. With this analogy, Jung tries to answer the problem of a unus mundus, a unified reality where everything comes from a single source, and will eventually return to it. In his theory, the archetypes work as a mediator between the higher single source and the lower numerous products of this source. In other words, archetypes work as a kind of "sorter", where everything in our reality has come from a single source, the unus mundus, the archetypes dictate how the single source is dispersed into the infinite amount of products that shape the world we know. They organize everything from the ideas in our mind, to the way energy and matter behave in our world.

However, we are only interested in the psychological aspect of archetypes and how they can help us understand and interpret mythology and the way in which we see the world around us. It is helpful for us to categorize archetypes found in mythology in three distinct branches, archetypal events, archetypal characters, and archetypal motifs. What is important to understand in this exercise is that we do not know what the original archetypes are, they are hidden in the depths of the subconscious, so our categorizing must be flawed. Where we might see three separate figures in a myth conveying three separate meanings, we may easily conclude that there are three separate archetypes at play, where in reality they may be three aspects of one archetype. The lines blur and it is your interpretation and open-mindedness that will lead you to truth.

Archetypal Events

Archetypal events are the moments in the experience of life that are common to all people and that have a significance that take you from one state of being to another. For example, a wedding is an archetypal event. There are preparations in the physical, mental, and spiritual realm followed by a ceremony which ultimately leads to two separate individual people uniting as one coherent unit. At the climactic moment, the lives of both people are changed forever and the dynamics of their inclusion within society and their own minds has been morphed into something new. Take for example ritual and initiation, through this archetypal event an individual passes through a process that changes them to a new role with new understanding, this is easily understood by a rite of passage that child undergoes to become an adult. Common archetypal events include birth and death, transcendence, the battle of good and evil, initiation ceremonies, puberty, and many more.

Archetypal Motifs

A motif is a reoccurring idea that is presented in art, including mythology. Archetypal motifs and patterns, therefore, are the primordial source of these ideas and they underlie mythologies across the world. The Creation is a prime example of this, where every culture has at some point attempted to explain the existence of the world. Immortality is a reoccurring theme probably derived from the human fear of death, it often crops up in one of two forms, either a return to paradise or heaven or the reincarnation of the soul. The scapegoat is a common motif, where a sacrifice is made by the people in an act of spiritual cleansing. By conferring the sins of the population onto the victim, a ritual cleansing can take place which effectively keeps the health of the group. This, of course, is seen in the Hebrew Bible, but is common throughout the world, being a throwback to the ritual killing of the "Divine King".

Motifs differ to symbols, in that a motif will occur many times through a work, whereas a symbol may not. In Steinbeck's Of Mice & Men, there is the reoccurring sentence "we got a future", this is a motif representing the archetype of hope as George and Lenny share the desire for better circumstances.

Archetypal Characters

Individuals within mythological tales almost always fall into the category of an archetypal character. There are a plethora of these character types and they have been represented by everything from the tarot's major arcana to the symbols of the zodiac.

Now Jung did not believe that each archetypal character was equal. As they represent the psyche of a person, it makes sense that a certain archetype will be present at a certain time in an individual's life. As the individual grows and learns, the psyche evolves or devolves too, so a hierarchy develops where archetypes like the wise old man or woman (exhibiting maturity and understanding) outrank those of lower psychological development such as the shadow.

However, Jung also understood the reality of polarity, and any aspect of a certain archetype had its opposite attributes as well. This polarity was vitally important, and the darker side of consciousness is as equally important as the side of goodness. This is because enlightenment of the self can only occur through the union of opposites. Once this is achieved the self-understands it is both light, and dark, and neither at the same time. As Jung put it in his work, Alchemical Studies (London, 1978, p.265),

'One does not become enlightened by imagining figures of light, but by making the darkness conscious.'

Self & Persona

The self is the most important archetype as it is the midpoint between conscious and unconscious thought. It is the psyche in equilibrium, bringing harmony and balance to the light and dark aspects of the psyche, creating a perfect unity within the mind.

Where the self is the perfect representation of the mind, the persona becomes a mask which an individual uses to identify themselves (when the perfect self-has not been realized). Because of this, the persona compromises the identity of the true self. It is a product of the struggle between society's expectations and our internal desires, as they are usually in conflict, the persona mask is created to find a kind of middle ground between the two. However, the persona is far from a perfect state of mind.

Mother

The mother archetype is exactly what you think, the typically feminine, caring mother. She is seen as the bringer of life and nurturer of health. Primordially depicted as Mother Earth but also given detail like the Virgin Mary, the comforter of souls. The mother often overlays with the anima archetype, and like with all archetypes, she bears a darker side. Look for the devouring mother in mythology, the woman who must be obeyed, watch for the gorgons and Medusa.

Father

The father represents the law, he is the great defender, the king, and god. Where the mother is concerned with nurture and care, the father stands for knowledge and learning, he is concerned with event in the physical world, within the confines of space and time. The individual relies on the father archetype to bridge the gap between family life and life within society, this is clear in the Theseus mythology, where he's coming to Aegeas is representative of him leaving home and entering society. The role of the father as an intermediary between worlds is brought through the fact that unlike a mother's love, which is unconditional, the father's love must be earned. To win the fathers love, the individual must assert dominance and stick their neck out in situations, ultimately preparing them for a life separated from the protection of parents. Looking again at Theseus, this is clear by Aegeas setting up the initial challenge for his son, once the prized sword was won, Theseus could use it as a token to gain respect from his father, and begin his own individuation process.

Like all archetypes, the father has a darker equivalent, the overbearing parent that controls the child, such as Kronos who eats his children, or Ysbathaden (Celtic mythology) who never allows his daughter, Olwen, the freedom to marry. These examples show the dangers of a father likened to god, who can use his position to defend his power and title rather than to prepare his children to exemplify the next generation.

Shadow

The shadow is the unknown side of the personality, usually representative of the darker aspects of the unconscious that the individual is either unaware of, or unable to accept as part of them. It is the part of the psyche that the conscious mind does not identify with, which also allows the shadow to bear good qualities (such as the good qualities a person of low self-esteem does not identify with). Jung explains that if a person identifies a weakness in them self then they will project this onto others as a moral deficiency. This is obvious in mythology and the shadow character can be understood as the weakness of the hero. In fighting the shadow, the hero is effectively fighting himself. Jung believes that confronting and overcoming the shadow is the only way forward for a developing psyche. He liken the confrontation to descending into the abyss, and it is at the lowest point of the fall that one is in most danger of being possessed by the shadow making it the dominant archetype of the individuals mind. However, in the abyss, the individual can also confront the shadow for what it is, accept it, and assimilate it into himself. From here, the individual can begin the ascent into light once more, being always aware of the shadows existence, but no longer associating the self with it. By assimilating the shadow, the individual widens their consciousness, and with this obstacle overcome, further development of the psyche can occur.

The shadow is obvious in mythology, usually represented by the evil character that is in direct opposition of the hero. In star wars we see the process above with both outcomes presenting them self. In Episodes I-III we see Anakin Skywalker confront the shadow and fail to assimilate it, his darker side possesses him and he becomes Darth Vader. In Episodes IV-VI we see Luke Skywalker confront the shadow, Darth Vader, accept it for what it is and successfully assimilate it. Through these episodes, we see the temptation, confusion of morals, and hardship involved in confronting the shadow. In classical mythology, the shadow presents itself as the Minotaur (Theseus), Kronos (Theogony), and Set (Egyptian Book Of The Dead) to name but a few.

Threshold Guardians

The threshold guardians are those that present themselves at the crucial points of change within the hero's psychic development. At the precipice of change, a challenger will emerge, a being whose sole purpose is to be overcome to discern those of readiness. The Threshold Guardian comes in many guises and are often stepping stones for the hero to navigate until the final confrontation with the shadow. They can be seen as jealous enemies or monsters in league with the shadow or standing alone. In any case, they symbolize the inner fears and doubts of the hero which he must come to terms with and overcome. To use examples from classical mythology, the Threshold Guardians to Theseus are the five challenges he met on the road to Athens. In the tales of Hercules, they are his twelve labors.

Anima/Animus

The anima/animus resides in the unconscious, representing the inner feminine of a man (anima) or the inner masculinity of a woman (animus). It is the totality of the opposing sex's psychological qualities residing in the individual's unconscious, and in this shapes the way an individual views and interacts with the opposite sex.

Jung described the encounter with the shadow as an "apprentice piece" in the development of the psyche, whereas a confrontation of the anima/animus is the "masterpiece". To come to terms with the anima/animus puts the individual in position of power where they have a mediator between the conscious and unconscious mind. This is likened best by a god like Hermes, a messenger between two worlds.

Understanding and assimilating the anima/animus is a complex affair that Jung attempts to describe into four sections that differ for men and women. Time does not allow us to go into detail on the matter, but it is (in very simple terms), acknowledging the existence of the opposite sex in the psyche of the individual, understanding the abilities and disabilities of the anima/animus, and realizing that the positive and negative aspects exist in perfect equilibrium.

With regards to Demeter in the Homeric Hymn to her, we see two aspects of the animus archetype. In Hades, we see the negative aspects of the animus in his brutality of taking Persephone away. In Helios we see the positive animus by his role as a helper, offering Demeter knowledge and aid.

Wise Old Man

Sage, Senex, Hermit, Mentor, or Wizard, the wise old man is seen in many lights but is always characterized as an older gentlemen full of patience and wisdom. Jung believed this archetype to be a later development of a mind who has struggled with and overcome his own animus. The wise old man is often see as a philosopher bearing wisdom and knowledge that he uses to guide those in need. Due to his advanced understanding of the world, it is common to see the wise old man as a foreigner, or a liminal character only half inhabiting the world. This is most obvious in characters like Gandalf, Yoda, or Dumbledore from modern stories, or Mentor (Odyssey), Tiresias (Greek Myth), Utnapishtim (Epic of Gilgamesh), and Zarathustra (Zoroastrianism) from classical mythology.

Wise Old Woman

The wise old woman is the feminine counterpart of the wise old man and encapsulates the wisdom of the eternal feminine nature. Like the wise old man, the wise old woman is a higher development of the psyche, often described as a "subordinate" personality due to the individual's "wholeness" of self. The wise old woman is formed in the psyche when the self is realized for what it is and there are no other internal doubts, Jung suggests that it is this moment that the woman successfully divides herself entirely from the mother, and becomes the great mother herself. Mythology see's the wise old woman in various guises, from the old crone to the mother goddess herself, her darker side exhibited as the witch or the evil mother.

Trickster

The trickster can be represented by any being, whether it be a god, person, animal, or spirit, but is often characterized by its possession of secret knowledge or high intellect. Through its knowledge, the trickster is able to disobey conventional rules or expected behavior, and as its name suggests, plays tricks on people. The trickster's abnormal behavior makes it a "boundary-crosser" where it can be artistically employed to question society, break down norms, and reestablish new natural orders. It does this by acting as a catalyst for the hero, often leading him to ridiculous and sometimes self-destructive actions.

In mythology the trickster is easy to spot, he (almost always male) is often employed for comic purpose but despite his foolish exterior is actually quite cunning. Breaking social boundaries, the trickster fools both gods and people, using his wit to outsmart, steal, and wreak havoc. Some trickster characters from classical mythology include Mercury (Roman), Hermes (Greek), and Loki (Scandinavia) among many others.

There are of course an endless list of archetypes that simply cannot be listed in detail here. There is the amazon, a woman warrior who society shunned until modern times, effectively cutting off the acceptance of feminine aggression. The teacher, the lover, the victim, and countless others which are more or less self-explanatory. All it requires is thought on your behalf, meditate on the figures you see and try and find what they represent.

Archetypes In The Tarot

The Major Arcana of the Tarot is of great importance to us as it maps out the development of the human psyche with astonishing accuracy. The cards have been given many names, but above all The Book of Life should scream out that there is deep psychological knowledge held within. However, the book is unlike any you will have ever encountered, for aside from the titles, there are no words, only pictures. Remembering our discussion on symbolism will be imperative for your understanding of what follows, for the meanings of the cards differ from reader to reader as it is intuitive interpretation that teaches the lesson.

Of course, the Tarot is shrouded in mystery. Historically we can only track the cards back 500 odd years when they became popular in Italy, but it is common knowledge that they most likely developed in Ancient Egypt. It is from here that we see its name The Book of Thoth become apparent, but it should not be forgotten that this isn't proven and that the birth of the Tarot is unknown. The mysterious origins are of no concern to us though, in fact, they are fitting, for we are looking at the cards through the eyes of archetypal psychology, and as we now know, this exists outside the limits of time and space.

Now, the Major Arcana are the trump cards of the deck, numbering 22 cards (21 numbered cards plus 1 unnumbered). Each of these cards is a symbolic step in the development of the psyche, but its meaning is only found within the symbols depicted and the oral tradition surrounding it. When put together, the 22 cards tell a story, and that is what we are going to look at now.

I - The Magician

In early life, the child comes to grips with his physical body and realizes that tasks that seem impossible are actually well within his grasp. By using the right tools, having motivation, managing time, and being in the right place, the child can manipulate circumstance to reach achievement. However, despite his newfound ability to achieve, the power to do so does not come from within himself but is dictated by the forces outside of his control.

II - The High Priestess

Where the magician represent the child's learning and developing in the physical world, The High Priestess symbolizes the development of the sub- and unconscious mind, occurring through sleep and dreams. Through this, the child develops his passive intuitive assets and becomes receptive to the psychic world.

III - The Empress

The Empress represents the Mother archetype, and as the child is developing she provides unconditional love through nurturing. She offers the child practical support and pours love and care in abundance. Through this, the child can express himself to her and she is open to the passions that he exhibits.

IV - The Emperor

The Father archetype is seen in The Emperor and he develops the child's view of society by teaching him what will be expected when he comes of age. The Emperor teaches the child to finish what he starts and shows the limitations of a physical world. It is not surprising that the child will fight back at the father, resenting the limits imposed on him.

V - The Hierophant

The Hierophant teaches the spiritual world to the child and is representative of priests, holy men and women, and books of spirituality. Where the Emperor and Empress guide the child in the ways of emotion and the physical world, the Hierophant shows the child where they fit into the bigger picture of the universe.

VI - The Lovers

Up until this point, relationships to the child have been unidirectional, with information and emotion always traveling to him. The Lovers represent the awakening of the sexual urge within the individual, leading the young man to a new kind of relationship. Finding a partner, the young man becomes involved in a relationship of dual direction, both giving and receiving love as an equal for the first time.

VII - The Chariot

Pulled by two wild beasts, the young man is represented as the driver within the Chariot. The beasts are his untamed emotions, sparked by his encounter with the lover, and through discipline, he can learn to tame these emotions. Once under control, he can drive the chariot of his life with purposeful direction.

VIII - Strength

The Strength card symbolizes the man's acknowledgment of the beast within. Taking time to meditate and focus his energies internally, he finds that he still cannot control life and that it will guide his emotions. In the quiet, he finds his inner beast, acknowledges its existence, and finds strength in it. However, he still must develop, as merely acknowledging the beast means that the strength is still not sourced from himself.

IX - The Hermit

Having acknowledged the beast, the man can turn to inward reflection. He studies his own mind, observing and learning from the symbols that surround him. He does so in silent solitude for there is no one else who can aid his task. He discovers his inner voice and learns to be alone without being lonely.

X - The Wheel Of Fortune

Spending time in solitude, the man becomes aware of the polarity in all things. The opposing seasons, the forces of nature, and the differences between a non-linear universal time, and the man-made construct of it. He learns that all things in life have their time and place and of how much he has still to learn.

XI - Justice

The man now learns of cause and effect, that the universe has laws which simply cannot be broken, and he is subject to them like everything else. From this, he concludes that the events in his life that he had quickly judged were not as simple as they seem and that lessons in life are learned through the hardships and challenges it offers.

XII - The Hanged Man

The man now hits a period of stagnation in life and must wait patiently like a tree barren in the winter awaits for the new life in spring. He knows all things are cyclical and uses the time to meditate on his life thus far. Learning from his past he comes to a realization of what he is holding onto that is no longer needed.

XIII - Death

As life leads to death, death also clears the path for life. The man leaves behind the parts of himself that are no longer needed, and cleanses himself physically, mentally, and spiritually. He learns that surrender is strength and prepares for what is to come.

XIV - Temperance

As the old self is stripped away, the man finds harmony within himself again. A deeper awareness and sense of purpose arises within himself, but he is no longer quick to act, knowing that all action has its proper time. He awaits the time to act and learns that harmony within leads to harmony without.

XV - The Devil

With his new sense of self, the man again faces the beast within. He must remind himself that there is more to life than the material and rise above the temptation of earthly desire that the Devil offers.

XVI - The Tower

Releasing the ingrained belief and safety of the material world is not always easy to give up, and the man may struggle with the Devil. Life, however, will bring about change, and the beliefs he held onto, represented by the tower itself, will topple and collapse. The sudden change causes him to relinquish his old ideals allowing him to move forward.

XVII - The Star

The sudden collapse of beliefs teaches the man to live in the present moment. He regains his creative senses and remembers that he can bring unconscious energy into physical results. This is symbolized by the water and land. He regains faith in what life has to offer.

XVIII - The Moon

The man must reenter his mind to confront his inner demons. This time the path is deeper and more dangerous, he must use his subconscious as a tool to reach the unconscious, facilitated through dreams where he will face terrifying monsters. This is the final battle in confronting the beast within.

XIX - The Sun

Having overcome the beast, the man finds a new outlook on life where he is as free as a child but as wise as a man. After exploring the unconscious in the moon, he has free range of his full imagination and finds happiness not only on the surface of his being but deep within him.

XX - Judgement

The man becomes old with time and can feel the call of the divine. His old beliefs turn to understanding, and the interconnectedness of the world reveals itself. He realizes that he is the accumulation of his past deeds and beliefs and that these shape his future.

XXI - The World

Inner peace and fulfillment are the man's rewards for mastering his lessons in this lifetime. He learns that the entire universe is in a constant state of motion, speeding up and slowing down, and has balanced the elements within himself. The man is at one with the world and has become his own master.

0 - The Fool

A soul enters the physical world and a child is born. As she enters the world she chooses to forget the accumulated knowledge she holds from her past lives in an effort to learn the lessons of this life properly. She will come with innocence and love, the innocence will evolve to understanding, and with strength, the love will not succumb to fear. Life will give her the opportunity to learn

through challenges, and it will reward her for her
successes.

Odin & The Well Of Knowledge

This narrative has been re-written for a modern audience
but comes from the Icelandic Eddas as part of the sagas
involving the mythology of Odin, chief of the Norse gods.

***

His eyes scorned the world around him, hidden deep in
the enveloping folds of his dark cloak, a white beard
bristled down his neck, and he clutched his craggy staff for
support. No longer did he bear the glistening golden
armor, nor wield his fearsome spear, his great steed had
deserted his side, no longer was he Odin All-Father, but
Vegtam the Wanderer. The old man walked the land of
Midgard, realm of men, journeying to that dreaded
kingdom of giants, Jotunheim.

But not all is as it seems, and the wanderer appeared as
man to men, and a giant to giants. And this is how he took
his advantage. For during his travels, Odin came upon
Vafthrudner, the wisest of the giants. His infamy was
widespread, for many men had sought the giant for the
questions they wished answered. But Vafthrudner's
bargain was a double-edged blade, to seek his answer, one
must first answer his questions thrice. The price for failure
was your head!

But Odin had no fear, and he asked the wisest of giants
to answer his question.

"I am Vegtam the Wanderer," Odin said, "and I know who you are, O Vafthrudner. I would strive to learn something from you."

The giant burst into laughter, heaving his chest like bellows and showing his teeth.

"Ha, ha," he laughed, "I am ready for a game with you. Do you know the stakes? My head is yours if I cannot answer any question that you ask. And if you cannot answer any of my questions, then your head goes to me. Ha, ha, ha, let us begin!"

"I am ready," Odin said.

"Then tell me," began Vafthrudner, "what is the name of the river that splits Asgard from Jötunheim?"

"It is the river Ifling," said Odin. "which is as cold as the dead, yet never frozen."

"You are correct, O Wanderer," said the giant. "But you must still answer my other questions. What are the names of the horses that Day and Night drive across the sky?"

"Skinfaxe and Hrimfaxe," Odin answered. This startled Vafthrudner, the names of these horses were only known by the gods and the wisest of the giants. He had only one last question to ask before his turn was over.

"Tell me," said Vafthrudner, "what is the name of the plain on which the last battle will be fought?"

"The Plain of Vigard," said Odin, "the plain that is a hundred miles long and a hundred miles across."

Odin faced Vafthrudner and prepared his own questions. "Tell me, Vafthrudner," He said, "What will be the last words that Odin will whisper into the ear of his dear son, Baldur?"

The giant roared as the question startled him. He sprang to his feet and looked at the stranger keenly.

"Only Odin knows what his last words to Baldur will be," he hissed, "and only Odin would have asked that question. You are Odin, O Wanderer, and I cannot answer!"

"Then," said Odin, "if you want to keep your head, answer me this: what price will Mimir ask for a draught from the Well of Wisdom that he guards?"

"He will ask for your right eye as a price, O Odin," said Vafthrudner.

"Will he ask no less a price than that?" said Odin.

"He will ask no less a price. Many have come to him for a draught from the Well of Wisdom, but no one yet has given the price Mimir asks. Now, I have answered your question, Odin, give up your claim to my head and let me go on my way."

Odin gave up his claim to Vafthrudner's head, and the giant went on his way. However, things did not become easier for the knowledge Odin had gained deeply disturbed the god. He contemplated a return home, to surrender his quest, but decided against it, yet he could not bring himself to Mimir's well either. To lose the sight of his right eye for all eternity was a high price to pay, and in his despair, he continued his wandering.

He traveled south to Muspelheim, and standing there he saw Surtur with the Flaming Sword, a terrible figure, who was destined to join the giants in their war against the gods. Then he turned north where he heard the thunderous cauldron of Hvergelmer as it poured itself out of Niflheim, the place of darkness and dread. This troubled Odin and he knew that the world must not be left between Surtur, who would destroy it with fire, and Niflheim, that would gather it back to darkness of nothing.

As he was the eldest of the Gods, Odin knew it was up to him to win the wisdom that would help to save the world.

Odin turned to Mimir's well, his face hardened for the pain to come. And as he approached, Mimir hailed him, for he had drunk every day from the Well of Wisdom and knew who it was that stood before him.

"Hello, Odin." He smirked.

Odin paid his respect the wisest of the world's beings. "I would like to drink from your well, Mimir," he said.

"You know that there is a price to be paid for this? All who have come here to drink have shrunk from paying that price. Will you, eldest of the gods, pay it?"

"I will not shrink from the price that has to be paid, Mimir," said Odin All-Father.

"Then drink," said Mimir. He filled up a great horn with water from the well and gave it to Odin.

Odin took the horn in both his hands and gazed into the deep water with his dark eyes, he lifted the horn and drank and drank. And as he drank all the future became clear to him. He saw all the sorrows and troubles that would fall upon men and gods. But he also saw why the sorrows and troubles had to fall. As he drank he saw how these sorrows might be borne so that gods and men, by being noble in their darkest days, would leave a force in the world that would eventually destroy the evil that had brought the terror and despair into the world in the first place.

As his cup was drained, Odin stepped back, he put his hand to his face and forced his fingers deep into his eye socket. He grasped his eye and wrenched it forward, the pain was terrible, but Odin never groaned. He bowed his head and put cloak about his face. Mimir took the god's eye, and dropped it into his well, letting it sink deep into the water of the Well of Wisdom. From there the eye of

Odin remains, shining up through the water, reminding all of the price that the All-Father paid for his wisdom that would save the world.

***

The Odinic Wanderer

Now, as we are discussing archetypes it might be useful to look at Odin's form as Vegram the Wanderer under this lens of study. A clear parallel can be made to the Wise Old Man, physically we see Odin take on this persona with his aged vessel, wise beard, and staff for support. However, he is not quite at a final point of being all knowledgeable. What we are seeing in this myth is a point of transition for Odin, he is literally journeying between archetypal states, and is hoping to achieve the enlightenment from Mimir's well to achieve a higher state of being that will elevate his psyche to that of the Wise Old Man.

It is interesting now to consider the cards of the Tarot, which are archetypal representatives themselves. Immediately Odin stands out as the ninth card called, The Hermit. The card's image depicts an old man wearing a cloak with his shaggy beard poking through, not at all, unlike Odin. But the parallels to Odin as wanderer are also revealed through the interpretation of the card. The Hermit seeks solitude and surrenders material wealth in an attempt to find himself which will inevitably lead to wisdom. This is the story of Odin's search for the Well of Knowledge. He no longer travels in the finery fit for the king of the gods, but wanders the earth in rags, on foot and on his own. The path to wisdom is the same for all, an arduous journey that even gods must take.

Figure 23: Odin in his wandering form displays the qualities of the Wise Old Man archetype. Painting is Odin the Wanderer by Georg von Rosen (1895).

What we can infer from this is that The Hermit card is not an archetypal character, but rather an archetypal path that leads to a character. This is alluded to in the Jewish mystical tradition of Kabbala, where there are 10 sephiroth (each representing an archetypal state of being) in the tree of knowledge, and a total of 22 pathways between each sephiroth. The 22 pathways have been likened to the 22 cards of the Tarot's major arcana by scholars throughout the ages which seems to add weight to them being the representatives of the psyche's transitional periods between steady archetypal states. Hence the Tarot is the journey of minds development.

So what we are seeing in this myth is Odin's need to evolve. This need is explicitly described in his responsibility to save the world, a task only achievable through the attainment of wisdom. To achieve this wisdom, Odin must strip himself back to modesty, symbolic of ego death, and represented by The Hermit archetype. Through modesty and self-sacrifice (his right eye) he gains insight into universal wisdom (the Well of Knowledge) and evolves to a new state of being, that of The Old Man archetype.

Gods, Lesser Gods, & Monsters

What Is A God?

The definition of a god is a complex and futile discussion. What God is to a Christian is completely different to what a god is too a Buddhist, a Pagan, a Pantheist or anyone else. God or gods are very personal things, but, for our purpose, we will ignore our own beliefs or preferences and look at what gods are in mythology and what purpose they serve.

As we are concerned with mythology and stories, we will accept that a god is a being or spirit that holds significant power of nature and humanity. A god will usually be associated with some force of nature, either a physical force, like Poseidon and the sea, or a psychological force such as Eros and love, and in many cases, a single god will occupy various stations simultaneously, like Zeus who controls lightning, justice, and hospitality to name a few. Gods are also personalities, there are characteristics which are individual to each one, and with this, the gods have relationships amongst themselves and other sentient beings, like humans.

Once a realization of what the gods represent occurs, the true teachings of these stories begin to unravel. For example, Kronos (time) consumed his children (each representing an aspect of humanity and civilization) suggesting that time destroys all things. However, Zeus (justice) manages to overcome Kronos and reinstates the other gods. This teaches the audience that it is justice or goodness that will ultimately save humanity from the decays of time.

The backgrounds of gods give us similar teachings. Apollo and Artemis were born on Delos, an island that didn't see the sun, and didn't touch the Earth. From the outset, these gods were distant from the rest of creation which is backed up by their personalities and actions in stories - one example is their weapon of choice, the bow. They keep their distance from their business.

A note on all divinities of all cultures is that their character is evolutionary. They were always being updated and changed, ever so slightly, to fit the needs of the poet or author whose tale they inhabited. In that, the traits of gods change, and over time they might even conflict. For example, Zeus is the god of justice, but his stories are abound with injustice, especially against his wife. A typical explanation for this is that as humanity advanced and became more complex, its understandings also progressed, and what they found to be beautiful concepts become refined. In Zeus' case, this would imply early man thought it was fine to take many wives or that polygamy was acceptable, where later in history man decided that this was wrong and that fidelity and monogamy was the truly righteous path. Another reasoning for contradictions is that, as cultures spread and mingled, gods merged and took each other's forms. For example, the Greeks might settle a new land where the local head god is merged with Zeus, the tales of both become intertwined, and the Greek Zeus is changed slightly. This theory for Zeus implies that his multiple love affairs are merely a product of the old head gods wife becoming a new lover of Zeus to keep the foreign populace happy. In any case, be aware that the roles of gods conflict.

The Major Greek Deities

Zeus

The King of Olympus, leader of the gods, lord of the sky, god of thunder, weather, oaths and addressed by all as father. His actions through the Titanomachy show him as a fair ruler, dispensing punishment and reward as befitting his subjects and generally installing order over creation. His constant infidelity against his wife Hera reveal his darker persona, yet he is still respected above all. His role of sky father and head of the pantheon is common to nearly all early belief systems. It is interesting to note, he is the youngest son of Kronos, yet he is the wisest, this theme is reoccurring in mythology where the youngest sibling is usually the most cunning.

Hera

Hera is the sister and wife of Zeus and the Queen of Olympus. She is ideally portrayed as a majestic woman in power, however, she is often taken by her jealousy and vengefulness to take on less than majestic acts. She spends a great deal of time punishing the women of Zeus' infidelity and attempting to take her revenge even to his bastard children. Fittingly, Hera was the protector of marriage and in particular of married women. Hera was the ultimate matriarch, female head of the family, strong enough to defend her position and those she loves.

Poseidon

The great god of the sea, Poseidon was venerated throughout Greece as their seafaring culture relied on their control of the ocean. He was brother to Zeus and nearly held just as much power over mortal events as him - in Homers Odyssey, it is Poseidon who is the great protagonist, and in countless other tales, he is the father of heroes and monsters. It is theorized that Poseidon was originally an inland god, this is suggested by his association with horses and his title of 'Earth-Shaker'. As cultures spread to coasts, his role evolved to that of the sea.

Hades

Also a brother of Zeus, Hades ruled the underworld. He was a just, pitiless god whom all souls faced after death, he was however not evil, and he was not death personified. Hades was also given the name Pluto (Dis in Latin) which meant wealthy, some believe this name is given due to his control of the Earths minerals, however, true wealth is not in material goods but intellect. As his realm is of a luminal nature, it could be viewed that the wealth he holds is in the wisdom he gives through those that face him to get it.

Athena

Daughter of Zeus, and bearing no mother, Athena was born from Zeus head. She is therefore symbolically associated with being the masculine offspring of justice and order. She is the protector of the city and civilization. She is Zeus' favorite offspring and is trusted with his thunderbolts and shield, the

Aegis. Often associated with war, she is not violent but upholds planning and battle tactics. As she has no ties with the feminine, she is almost the perfect son, save she is a daughter. She holds no feminine qualities and as such has no feminine wishes, she is a virgin warrior and patronizes heroes.

Figure 24: The Athena Giustiniani is a Roman copy of the Greek statue of Pallas Athena (late fifth century B.C.). Note the way in which she has been represented. Gods are usually depicted naked, as they are seen as perfect in their being and need no clothes to cover themselves. Here Athena is garbed from head to foot possibly to conceal her femininity. Should she have been born a male she would have been the perfect son. She bears armour, spear and helmet signifying her importance to warfare and Medusa's head can be seen adorned on her chest (though it would usually be found on the Aegis shield).

Apollo

The product of one of Zeus' infidelities (with Leto), Apollo was born on the island of Delos where he came into existence without being of the Earth, nor seeing the sun. Apollo's psyche meets his birth in his cold and distant manner, further suggested by his prevalent use of the bow. He is the god of light, associated with the sun, and is the truth teller, unable to speak lies. The Oracle at Delphi is the medium from which he speaks with humanity on matters they want answered, and through him, people could be cleansed and healed. Often described as beautiful, and an authority on music, Apollo's cold nature found him luckless with love, and dangerously insecure. Despite his good powers, tales of Apollo show him as a dangerous, vengeful, calculating character.

Artemis

Twin sister of Apollo, her shared birth gave her similar traits in her cold and distant manner, similarly portrayed through the use of the bow. She is the goddess of the hunt, her realm is the untamed wilderness far from civilization. She is protector of the young, and deathly protects her chastity and the chastity of those devoted to her. Countering her twins association with the sun, Artemis is associated with the moon and with it, the eerie energy and power it holds in the night. She was later confused with Hecate and was an authority on dark magic.

Aphrodite

The goddess of love and beauty was the product of a castrated Kronos' manhood crashing into the sea, from the foam washed up Aphrodite to the shores of Cythera or Cyprus. She is often described by her divine beauty, and in it lies her powers to bring, or force, love to deities and humans alike. It is said that without her, no joy could exist and many prayed to her for help with love. It is not hard to imagine Aphrodite's wretchedness in her power to create love where it should not be. She was more than capable of creating devastation through manipulating the emotions and desire of anyone she pleased, which was often her chosen path when working toward her own goals. Her marriage to the hideous and lame god Hephaestus is telling of the truth of love and where its qualities are truly found.

Hermes

The fleet-footed messenger god, son of Zeus and Maia. He is often depicted as handsomely youthful, wearing winged shoes and a winged hat, wielding a magical rod that bore the caduceus. His speed and grace has him relay messages from and between the divine. He leads the dead to the underworld. His role as a messenger see's him as a guide who can transcend boundaries between the divine and mortal realms. Psychologically, Hermes could be seen to help guide people through stages of mental transition. In other mythologies, he is likened to Thoth (Egypt) and the esoteric teacher Hermes Trismegistus who brought a plethora of innovations from the divine to humanity including writing.

Ares

The detested son of Zeus and Hera, Ares was the god of war. He is not often depicted in mythology, and when he appears, he is hated - by the Greeks that is. The Romans on the other hand, to whom he is known as Mars, revered him, revealing their warrior culture. Ares does not hold a personality like the other gods, he is rather a symbol for the chaotic carnage of war. When he strides across the battlefield, he is accompanied by his sister Eris (discord) and her son Strife, as well as his wife Enyo and the lesser gods Terror, Trembling and Panic. Greek society shunned Ares due to the destructiveness associated with him, with this, he is not associated with any Greek city and is said to inhabit barbarous Thrace.

Hephaestus

The god of fire and the forge, he is the son of Zeus and Hera. Hephaestus is the only god described as ugly, and along with this, he is lame too. Though often reminded of his imperfections, Hephaestus is portrayed as a kind god, loved by mortals and immortals alike. Along with Athena, he is a protector of civilization and an authority on handicrafts, in particular trades and metal work. Early tales tell of Zeus flinging the infant Hephaestus off of Mount Olympus' peaks due to his birth defects, however, with maturity, Hephaestus proved his place with the gods through his divine workmanship.

Hestia

The sister of Zeus, Hestia was the virgin goddess of the hearth. Like Ares, she is not often seen in myth's and holds no real personality. Her role was the symbolic representation of the home and was worshipped by all people in Greece because of it. The coals of her hearth fire would be taken by colonists to new cities being established to kindle her homely spirit wherever the Greeks traveled.

Demeter

In the literal world, Demeter would have been a very early deity to humanity, she is the goddess of corn or grain and her worship would have risen through early agricultural society. She is feminine because originally, the work of the field was that of women when men would of still held a hunting role. She is also feminine in that the miracle of the crop cycle mimics the fertility of woman, and this was very apparent to early people. In Greek myth, Demeter is associated with the loss of her only daughter Persephone and thus grief. She is a good goddess, good to people and to other divinities, however, her power to stop the crop from rising was never forgotten.

Dionysus/Bacchus

Dionysus was the demigod of the vine, drink, and ecstasy. He is deemed a demi-god as he was born through Zeus' relationship with the mortal Semele, but due to her untimely death, Dionysus was birthed via Zeus' thigh. His myths are abound with his attempts to persuade mortals of his divinity, and the challenges he sets those that disbelieve. He is a kind, loving god to those that worship him, and a horribly cruel force to those that disbelieve. This bipolar force of Dionysus mimics his patronage of the vine and wine, he is capable of lifting his followers, the maenads, to greatness or devastating cruelty, much like the powers of alcohol. However, Dionysus concern is with having his followers experience the divine like state of ecstasy. Ecstasy in its original term being a state outside of the normal self, and therefore teaching people that they can be more than they believe and that there is more to reality then they know.

Lesser Gods

Along with the principle deities, mythology is alive with lesser immortals and fierce monsters. The deities in these cases are often symbolic of some force of nature, much like the greater gods discussed above, but they play a much lesser role. For example, Zephyr, the west wind, often appears in stories as a force to fill ships sails or carry people away into heaven. Monsters play a different role, they are usually set as challenges for mortals to face, and as such their physical description is usually symbolic of the psychological problem faced by the hero. Many monsters are of a luminal nature, where they stand on the threshold between a civilized/wild nature, the balance allows them flexibility to be recognizable yet unpredictable. The civilized against non-civilised dichotomy presented in mythology is telling of the culture the stories come from, it gives a sense of where the cultural boundaries are, what is and what is not acceptable, and the heroic interaction with these creatures appeals to the urge to confront and conquer the uncivilized.

Muses

The Muses are the daughters of Zeus and Mnemosyne (the deity representing memory) and so represent what is passed down or remembered from each generation, which in turn is the attributes that create culture. So the Muses can be seen as characterizing literature, arts, music etc. There are various versions of how many Muses exist, but nine seems to be prevalent. They are Calliope (epic poetry), Clio (history), Euterpe (flutes and lyric poetry), Thalia (comedy and pastoral poetry), Melpomene (tragedy), Terpsichore (dance), Erato (love poetry), Polyhymnia (sacred poetry), and Urania (astronomy). As they represent these qualities, the Muses become their symbolic patronesses and are often called upon by poets and artists to inspire or work through them to deliver great works to mankind.

Fates

The Fates, or Moirai, are a complex form of being that is neither mortal nor deity. They are outside of that dichotomy as they are the controllers of destiny for all things in our universe, divine and mundane. There are some traditions that hold them as Zeus' children, however, these stories are usually contradictory to what the Fates are in essence so we will focus on what is important and what was generally believed by the people of these tales. The fates are seen as controlling the thread of life, weaving every beings destiny and watching them live out their pre-destined lives. They number three personages, Clotho spins the thread determining the individuals life, Lachesis measures out the length of thread

198

and hence the length of life and Atropos cuts the thread determining the individuals death. The Fates are always associated with death, but in that they are also seen as seers to the future, knowing what events are still to be played out which gives them special attention in many cultures that also links a common belief in that the dead can tell the future. They were depicted as old hags, usually misshapen yet mentally stern and unchangeable in their decision.

Nymphs

These are all lesser goddesses, always depicted as lovely maidens. Their existence was to be the spirits that animated particular parts of nature. Dryads and hamadryads were the nymphs of the forest, often tied to their own particular tree. Oreads were the nymphs of the mountains. Associated with water were the naiads, occupying rivers, creeks, springs and the like.

Pan & Satyrs

Pan was the natural chief of the wild, he was part man, part goat, bearing hoofed feet and horns. Pan is often described as a merry and joyous god playing his reed pipes as he traversed the fields, groves and wooded glens. However, he also struck fear into travelers arousing the term panic into the tongues of man. Pan's horned exterior eludes him to a sexual nature which unfortunately for him is often left unreciprocated due to his ugly nature. Regardless, Pan is associated with sexuality and the associated coming fertility of spring. The satyrs were more or less lesser Pan's, half goat-half men lesser immortals.

Pan can also be seen outside of these roles as the raw power of nature. In this way he is neither good nor evil in his intentions, he just is, his actions are powerful yet neutral, like that of nature.

Monsters & Creatures

Monsters are present in all stories, they are the gatekeepers protecting the wisdom that is revealed from overcoming them. More often than not, these monsters are representatives of deep psychological issues which is why they are relatable across cultures and time. The mere physical attributes of the beasts usually give away their hidden psychological attributes. It is also important to note how they are defeated or overcome, is it brute strength or cunning wisdom that see's the hero through? Or does he find help through friends or the divine? Continuously question yourself this and note it down, what does it mean to ask for help and through whom? Is that even possible in some situations and why not? Perhaps at times, it is up to the individual alone to overcome his monsters, sometimes the test is to acknowledge your own limitations and seek that help. The monsters faced are the monsters within yourself, but be warned... it is a universal theme that you will inevitably take on some of the qualities of the beast you fight.

> *"Beware that, when fighting monsters, you yourself do not become a monster... for when you gaze long into the abyss. The abyss gazes also into you."*
> *- Friedrich Nietzsche, Beyond Good, and Evil, Aphorism 146*

Centaurs

How centaurs came into mankind's imagination is a mystery, one theory is it is the result of mounted raiders attacking people whom had never seen horses, this is how the Native American peoples adopted the creature, but for Greece, we simply do not know. However, they were a significant creature in mythology described as a bottom-half horse, top-half man-beast. The centaur is not itself a monster, but being on the threshold of civilization, they were capable of monstrous deeds - often unpredictably. They eat raw meat and arm themselves with natural weaponry - sticks, stones etc. They inhabit the wilderness close to towns and are particularly susceptible to wine, and though friendly to humanity, their unpredictability makes them dangerous.

Amazonians

Warrior women of the apparent Scythian lands, they were the feminine counterpart to the centaurs in Greek mythology. Where the centaurs are the male aspect living on the fringes of civilization, the Amazonians were a totally female society living without male rule. This itself challenges social norms making these women dangerous. The Amazonians express their independence in a number of ways, they cut off their right breast to renounce their femininity and to challenge male conceptions of beauty. Like their patron goddess Artemis, they are adept huntresses and are well versed in war. The conception of these warrior women most likely spawned from a fascination with foreign, barbarous tribes and their customs.

Minotaur

The Minotaur is the half-man half-bull monster central to the mythology of Theseus. Properly named Asterion, he was the shameful son of the Cretan King Minos, he was actually conceived by Minos' wife and Poseidon's sacred bull. The Minotaur was hidden away in the labyrinth maze, which psychologically looks like hiding ones shames in the depth of the mind. In this way, the man and beast parts of the minotaur become apparent as one looks at their own shames and shortcomings. It is human to fail yet these shortcomings can still seem monstrous. The Minotaur may seem terrifying, yet once confronted is easily overcome as Theseus finds out. The Minotaur is the fear of our own failures, often hidden and forcibly forgotten.

Medusa

The all famous Medusa is a mortal woman punished by Athena to bear living snakes for hair and whose gaze turns all who meet it to stone. She is overcome by Perseus who uses gifts from the gods to kill her, refusing to meet her gaze, he uses his polished shield as a mirror to look through rendering Medusa's gaze as useless enabling him to

Figure 25: Testa di Medusa by Caravaggio (1595) depicts the classic monster moments after its beheading. Note the theme of perilous beauty. Medea's transformation to Medusa has been interpreted in many ways but it appears that a woman in control of her sexuality was perceived as a great threat to ancient cultures.

get close enough to decapitate her. He then uses her head as a weapon before gifting it to Athena who places it on the mighty Aegis shield. Medusa is a complex analogy that can be viewed through multiple lenses. Some see her as the embodiment of female rage and power, some suggest it is the power of female sexuality. An important observation to make is her severed head being used to benefit the hero. This is a theme constantly used, once the monster or challenge is overcome, its strengths can be used for benefit. Should the monster be representative of some psychological challenge, we see confronting and overcoming it leads to its control which wholly benefits the individual. Should we put this into the theory of a strong female sexuality, one could assume that if the woman confronts and controls it, then she can wield it to great personal benefit - whether that be for good or evil is up to the individual.

Scylla & Cherybus

Scylla and Cherybus are two monster mounted only an arrows shot apart on separate rocks of a narrow sea pass. Ships passing through the pass would have to make a choice, avoiding Scylla brought them to close to Cherybus and vice versa forcing an ultimatum between two evils. The lesson here is that in life there usually is no right choice, no easy way out, either way, there is going to be a challenge and that challenge is best met head-on.

Hydra

The Lernaean Hydra is a multi-headed serpentine water monster with poisonous breath and blood. In its mythology, it is reputed for regrowing multiple heads for each one cut off. It is featured as one of the ten labors of Hercules, who overcomes it with the help of Iolaus. Together they kill the creature by cauterizing each neck as they cut off the heads until the last immortal head is left which is buried under a mountain. Psychologically speaking, the hydra looks like Hercules 'shadow', the more he fights with it the stronger it grows until he finds help to reduce its strength and remove many of its heads/issues. The shadow cannot be totally remove though, it is an irremovable aspect of the hero so is buried under a mountain representing Hercules' burial of his shadow into his subconscious.

Ghosts

The belief in ghosts, spirits, and specters is as old as man. They are present in our earliest writings from Sumeria and have continued as a phenomena up until today. They are viewed both as a literal being and a metaphorical or mythical object in countless stories. All cultures have their spin on what a ghost is, but all seem to agree that is the lingering life force of the deceased present on the material plane. From the earliest days, they were seen as the escaped life force, or breath, of the deceased, explaining their whispy, ethereal appearance. Beyond being a way to explain a life after death, ghosts also serve a purpose in storytelling. They are a link to the past, a contactable being that can communicate messages or advice that would otherwise be lost to eternity. This is evident in Gilgamesh contacting Enkidu, Odysseus travels to the underworld, nineteenth-century séances and modern Ouija boards. In all cases, the living are attempting to gain information from the dead. So why is there such fear and speculated danger behind summoning the dead? Of course fear of the unknown is ever present in humans. This is why monsters are so frightening in movies until they are finally revealed in their true form. There is also the case that dead men can't, or shouldn't, talk, perhaps the information they hold is best left unsaid. This last point carries on to malevolent spirits, the ones who cause harm, if they are still beings of free choice, the fear of revenge is still ever present, even beyond the grave.

Zombies

Zombies are a relatively new phenomena first recorded in the nineteenth century proving the continued modernity of mythology. Their forms are continuously updated and changed but keep the principal parts, a zombie is a human who has been corrupted one way or another to be a mindless living corpse that feeds on human flesh. The original corruption changes from story to story, originally a phenomena from Haitian voodoo, the zombie is created through magic. Since then a multitude of methods have been born from radiation poisoning to disease. The fear of zombies is much like other mythological monsters, there is something so human in their appearance that makes the monster so identifiable with ourselves, yet the monstrous side of the psyche has taken hold driving the lower urges of the beast on. The dichotomy of something so human and so corrupted is something we can all relate to, it is something we all fear as we border on it ourselves.

Vampires

Vampires also fall under the category of the living dead though are a creature very dissimilar to zombies. They appear in many cultures with proto like vampire creatures existing even in Mesopotamia, however, vampires proper, as we know them today come from the traditions of south-east Europe, particularly with the Balkan regions. The tales typically tell of a human who suffer through demons, spirits or other vampiric bites that result in the individual being turned after death into a vampire proper. The individuals body changes internally and externally receiving heightened perceptions and a gaunt, pale appearance and above this an inextinguishable thirst for blood. This thirst for blood gives vampires a predatory archetype as their need for blood leads to hunting both animals and humans. In modern times the vampire is usually given a dominant personality, overly confident and suave further fuelling this archetype. This gives us an opening to why there is a general fear of this monster, for no one wants to be dominated or preyed upon by an individual seemingly stronger and better than us at all levels. The monster feeds on an inferiority complex inside the mind of all of us. Along with fear, there is also an attraction in many toward the vampiric life and this is also linked to the dominant characteristics and immortality of the creature. The escape or protection from death is very appealing as it gives us hope from our own eventual demise and those that fear being preyed upon due to their own weaknesses see strength in the powers of the vampire. These powers would, of course, change the individual so that they become the predator and thus the one in power.

There are countless gods, demi-gods, demons, and monsters in mythologies around the world and we have barely scraped the surface. I could not possibly write an explanation for each one as it goes beyond this work, we have however looked at a few, and this is to give you the tools to examine others through your own critical eye. Read about the creature, find its context within the story, break down its characteristics and then ask yourself, what is it that these authors are trying to convey? It is also crucial to keep in mind that we are looking at these creatures and concepts through the lens of our own culture and ideas. The stories and mythologies that tell of these things were written long ago and we can't assume to know everything they did.

Heroes & The Heroic Cycle

Heroes

Heroes are essential to mythology. They are the central person we relate to as we watch them attempt to work through the challenges of their journey. Joseph Campbell wrote a great book called The Hero of a Thousand Faces that in essence shows us that all heroes share a set of traits. They are more or less all the same and this is part of Carl Jung's idea that all humanity shares a collective unconscious. So across cultures and times, people have been creating the same heroes and this is simply because the hero is you. When you navigate these tales you become the hero in the story, and the story becomes a kind of guide that teaches you of choices and consequences, of right and wrong and whether that idea really does exist. As you take on the role of the hero, you can use mythology as a kind of space outside of reality to experiment and observe outcomes of different actions, it becomes a safe place to learn without the danger of repercussions.

What Drives The Man

What drives a hero to do the things they do? Well, the ancient worldview was that after death, all people went to the underworld, a lifeless place of no glory or joy. So to win immortality, one must secure great fame in the life they had. The only way for you to live forever was to be remembered by those of the generations that follow. In the Babylonian Epic of Gilgamesh, our hero makes the realization that his name would only be remembered by the deeds he does right now, in this lifetime. This leads to the idea that we should live boldly, making a name for ourselves and forgetting about tomorrow. But Homer questions this in the Odyssey where Achilles talks to Odysseus in the underworld (line 486),

'Nay, seek not to speak soothingly to me of death, glorious Odysseus. I should choose, so I might live on earth, to serve as the hireling of another, of some portionless man whose livelihood was but small, rather than to be lord over all the dead that have perished."

Achilles is essentially saying that if he could live again he'd much prefer to be an insignificant peasant and live to old age than be the hero he is that lived fast and died young and is remembered for all eternity.

So we see a prime motivator for the hero is immortality that can be won in life, but even this is questioned, and as we shall see is not always the case either. Heroes might take their quests against their will, it might be forced upon them by fate. It might be forced upon them by necessity and survival, or for love, vengeance, hope, or good. The motivations and reasons for heroic action is not set in stone because the underlying lessons of each story are intrinsically different. It is useful to look at why the hero is set on their path and then observe what challenges are met and how they are overcome, very soon a pattern will be seen and an underlying story is revealed beneath the one that runs on the surface.

Gods & Heroes - A Recipe For Disaster

In classical mythology, heroes hold a kind of halfway station between the mortal realm and that of the divine, giving them a somewhat 'demigod' status, even though their explicit divinity may not exist. In many cases they are literally half god – half man, for example, Heracles is the son of Zeus and the human Alcmene, Theseus claims heritage from Poseidon, even modern stories continue the claim, Luke Skywalker is the son of the god-like Vader. This claim to divinity gains a hero the chance to work with the gods, especially with those deities that work as guides or helpers, just look at Athene hiding within Mentor in the Odyssey, or Hera assisting Jason and his Argonauts. The gods take an active role in manipulating the human world, and they do it through these heroes. However, gods are not always helpful, indeed it is often the case that mixing with the gods is a recipe for disaster. As the gods are imperfect beings, their jealousies and anger is often the bane of heroes and people trying to live. It is often seen that the worship of gods is not out of respect or love but out of fear for what an angry god could do.

Beside this, what are we seeing when powerful gods assist humans? We have to look at what the god is representing, and then we can understand what power or phenomena the hero is calling upon, or what is helping him on its own behalf. For example, a call to Hermes might well be interpreted as the Hero needing assistance in bridging the divine and mortal realms, or he needs help to dive into his own psyche for understanding. When Athena offers a helping hand or advice we might equally assume the hero is being guided by the benefits of civilization. Is she giving him modern weapons to have the edge over his opponents, or perhaps she is devising plans to outwit his competition. Both these gifts are merely the product of a working civilization to which Athena is a patron. Equally, it can be interpreted the opposite for when the hero is being hindered by a deity. Apollo lashes out at the Greeks in the Iliad and it is because of their desecration to his shrine. Being the god of truth and justice, the Greeks are paying for their wrongs toward those powers.

Heroes do not usually live in harmony with society, there is always something about them that is unsettling, that does not let them live like the others of their community. Heracles was troubled from birth and continuously trialed by Hera, Theseus was forever yearning for the opportunity to prove himself, Skywalker was restless and unsatisfied with his menial existence. In all cases, the hero is itching to leave in one way or another because they know they are being constrained by their everyday life.

Lost In The Journey

Though they struggle through their challenges during their journeys they are far more at home and even feel a certain sense of belonging in their adventure. As we discussed earlier, the journey changes will change the hero, fighting monsters drives the man further from the civilized life they hope to return to. So the longer they are journeying, the further away they are led from a life of normality.

The great tragedy of the heroic return is paralleled with modern soldiers. The phenomena of shell shock and post-traumatic stress disorder is well known and sees these people unable to return to daily life as they might have been able to before the incident. There is the hard fact, that when you fight a monster, you take on the characteristics of that beast yourself. These modern-day heroes may have done great deeds and gone through huge journeys, but in fighting the tyrannies of the world, they have still seen death, destruction, atrocities of all sorts, dealt it out, and taken it in. And what we see as a result are men and women who cannot seem to fit back into the lives they once lived. The hard fact is the heroic journey changes people, sometimes for the better, sometimes for the worse.

You Are The Hero

But why is it that we relate to the hero of the story? It is because they portray human behaviors that we see in ourselves, their interactions with the surrounding world, their handling of their inner urges and psyche – all of this is relevant to the trials we go through every day. Mythology is a virtual playground where we can tell stories or live a fantasy and see how different aspects will relate to each other. It is a tool for learning how to live life, and in this tool the hero is us.

The Heroic Cycle

Associated with his work on the monomyth, Joseph Campbell wrote about a phenomena associated with mythic heroes called the heroic cycle. In essence, it is a

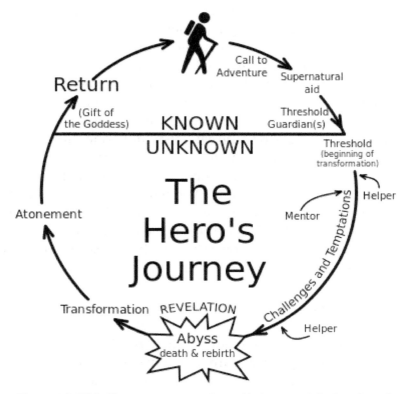

Figure 26: This diagram portrays the cyclic nature of the heroic cycle through Christopher Vogler's explanation of it.

circular diagram that maps out the path of the hero as he traverses through his journey. The map can be used to correlate the literal path of the hero and the episodes associated with him during the myth, but also show the evolution of the hero's psyche. The Campbell's heroic cycle is discussed in chapter 2, so instead, we will look at the same cycle but through the works of Christopher Vogler's The Writers Journey (2007) who divided the cycle into twelve parts as explained below.

Stage I: Departure

1. *THE ORDINARY WORLD.*

The tale begins by introducing the audience to the hero. We are shown his normal world, where he comes from, who his family is, and what culture he belongs to. He lives a regular life that the audience can relate to, however, there is an uneasiness that surrounds him as his life is stressed by forces outside of his knowledge or control pull him in various directions. The hero begins with a limited awareness to the problem which is bearing down on him.

Myths present this stage at the start of their telling to give a contrast between the ordinary and mythic worlds. It is our introduction to Bilbo Baggins and his Hobbiton home in The Hobbit, Theseus living with his mother before he journeys to Athens or Luke Skywalker trapped on his farm as an adolescent in Star Wars.

2. *THE CALL TO ADVENTURE.*

The normality of the hero's life is shaken to the core by external pressures or internal struggles. He must face the problem and in doing so recognizes that there is, in fact, a problem present. Through this recognition, the hero begins to increase his awareness of the need for change.

The call to adventure is the spark that sets the journey in motion, whether it be Bilbo's conversation with Gandalf or Luke Skywalker viewing the hologram of Princess Leia, it is the moment that gives the hero an awareness of the need for action.

3. *REFUSAL OF THE CALL.*

The hero is not yet heroic and may fear the call for adventure. His fears may be brief, he may overcome them himself or alternatively be assisted in beginning the journey by others. In any case, what is apparent is the fact that the hero is filled with fear and resists the need for change, hoping that there might still be hope in the life he has lived so far.

The refusal does not always occur and if it does it may only be momentarily. In the Hobbit, it is Bilbo's inability to sign the contract, though he overcomes this through his inner strength. For Luke Skywalker, it is when he refuses Obi-Wan and returns home instead, in this case, Luke's hand is forced as there is no home to return to.

4. MEETING WITH THE MENTOR.

The inexperienced hero meets with someone who has seen the world and knows the path. The person, friend or stranger, offer advice, equipment, or training so that the hero may find confidence to continue. This stage defines the psyche of the hero as a point of overcoming fear, but it is arrived at with the assistance of others and not through the hero's own self-confidence.

Meeting with the mentor may occur earlier or later, but it is the moment where the hero is given a helping hand. Gandalf acts as Bilbo's mentor, and Obi-Wan is Luke's. In Star Wars this stage is defined by Obi-Wan giving Luke his father's lightsaber, a magical tool that will help him.

5. CROSSING THE THRESHOLD.

Taking the help of the mentor, the hero commits to the journey and enters a new world with unfamiliar rules and values. Here we see the hero pass from the ordinary into the mythic, willingly submitting himself to change.

For Bilbo, this is setting off into the wild with his dwarven company. He leaves his home behind and has to learn to cope on the road. Theseus crosses the threshold when he begins his journey to Athens.

Stage II: Initiation

6.   *TESTS, ALLIES AND ENEMIES.*

The hero is challenged and through these tests learns to discern between friend and foe. Finding faithful allies he can continue his journey through the mythic world with the help of friends. Here the hero learns to experiment, observing dynamics that do and do not work and becoming wiser to the ways of the world.

Finding faithful friends is an integral step for the hero's development, Luke Skywalker sets a solid alliance with Han Solo in the Cantina, and Bilbo meets his allies in his home and makes his friends on the road.

7.   *THE INNERMOST CAVE*

This stage is often marked in mythology by the "chthonic" event, the episode or confrontation that occurs deep underground or even in the underworld. Bilbo faces it in the Mines of Moria, Luke Skywalker in the depths of the Death Star, in the trash-masher. Theseus undergoes this in the labyrinth itself.

8.   *THE ORDEAL.*

This is the central point of the tale and shows the hero confronting his shadow. He reaches the lowest point of the innermost cave and faces the monster where he will either be destroyed or reign triumphant. This is likened to facing death or his greatest fear, and through overcoming this death can be reborn anew. The minotaur await Theseus in the labyrinth, and for Bilbo, it is the monstrous Gollum.

9. THE REWARD.

Having defeated death, the hero is awarded a prize, this prize may be represented by physical treasure but is, in fact, the newfound knowledge acquired. Though there is great success, there is also the fear of losing this prize. The hero relinquished his old ways and life and accepts the consequences of his new self. Mythology typifies this moment with the hero settling the conflict with the shadow, for Star Wars this is Luke coming to terms with his father being Darth Vader. Bilbo is rewarded with his magic ring, and Theseus attains the knowledge of what it is to be a man and to be alive.

Stage III: Return

10. THE ROAD BACK.

The hero cannot stay in the mythic world and must return home to complete the adventure lest it be in vain. He must bring the treasure back to his society so that all can reap the reward of his labor. However, the road back is fraught with dangers and a sense of urgency may be produced by the hero being chased or hunted. This new challenge makes the hero reface the acceptance of his new life and forces a rededication to his cause. This is evident with Luke Skywalker's hasty escape from the Death Star, and Theseus' return to Athens from Crete.

11. THE RESURRECTION.

This is the height of the tales climatic telling, the hero is ruthlessly tested one last time and must face off with the final threshold guardian. Facing death and overcoming it once more leads to a moment of ecstatic realization and the conflicting polarities within the hero at the beginning are now equalized.

12.   RETURN WITH THE ELIXIR.

The hero returns home with the prize he has one which has the power to transform the ordinary world of his society for the better. From here he may choose to live in normality or continue his adventures. Having completed his journey, the hero emerges in a state of mastery over his life and has resolved the problems that plagued him in the beginning.

Heroes From Mythology

Theseus

Theseus was the rightful son of Aegeas, King of Athens, and an insignificant woman in a far off town. Growing up in the town, Theseus soon finds he outgrows his surroundings and needs to leave. He passes his father's first test to retrieve his sandals and sword beneath a boulder and takes the dangerous land route to Athens where he is challenged by an assortment of monsters which he dispatches in various ways eluding to different aspects of the mental challenges we all overcome. He seeks out Aegeas to discover who he is in the world, and in doing so is tempted into further quests to prove himself. Through these quests, he finds heartache in losing lovers and his father through his own faults where it becomes obvious that the choices we make have heavy responsibilities. Theseus does find great success, he inherits the Athenian throne and is loved by the people, furthering the prosperity of the city and continuing his quests to benefit the world. He seems to find himself in the heroic role which also causes him to be unable to rejoin society, even as a king. This eventually leads to the people questioning him as a leader, he falls from popularity which leads to his death. The heroic quest brought Theseus fame but lost him what it is to be alive.

Orpheus

Orpheus' quest is one framed in tragedy. His prime motivation is to recover his love Eurydice from the underworld due to her untimely and sudden death. He is the famous minstrel, his ability with music challenging even Apollo's, so sweet are his songs that they can charm nature, animals, man, and gods bending them to his will. The insinuation of skill with music is that one would understand emotion better than others and it is in Orpheus' inability to come to terms with loss that makes his myth tragically comic. It is Orpheus' lack of emotional control, trust, and understanding of fate that sees his ultimate failure.

Heracles

Heracles, or Hercules, as the Romans knew him, was perhaps the greatest of the Greek heroes. His mythology centers around twelve labors he had to complete to be redeemed for his horrific murder of his family. He is often seen as a brutish man full of strength and animalistic urges, highly violent and full of rage, an insatiable sexual urge and a lust for drink and action. We will spare details of Heracles for now as we will study him in detail in the chapter nine.

Bilbo Baggins

Bilbo Baggins is the protagonist of J.R.R. Tolkien's mythical novel The Hobbit. His journey follows the heroic cycle quite cleanly. He is introduced in his ordinary world where the audience is shown his regular life. He is visited by the wizard, Gandalf, who acting as a herald, mentor, and wise old man announces the journey to Bilbo. Bilbo nearly refuses the call, but on his own accord joins the journey. Crossing the threshold into the mythic realm, Bilbo learns who his true allies are and is faced by his first threshold guardian, the trolls. Overcoming them using his wit and the help of his friends he is awarded treasure in the form of a magical sword. He undergoes further challenges through Gollum in the Mines of Moria, the spiders and elves in Mirkwood, the problems in Dale, and through the dragon Smaug. He shows an emotional development from one who is fearful and timid to one who is in fact quite brave, displaying the highest bravery not in facing enemies but standing up to his friend Thorin Oakenshield. By the end of the tale, Bilbo returns to his home, however, we see that reinserting himself into his original society is impossible and he always years to reenter the mythic journey.

Luke Skywalker

Skywalker works perfectly for a modern day hero living in mythology. Portrayed as the leading protagonist in the Star Wars movies, he begins his journey in a humble setting as the adoptive son of his uncle. He is not happy here, he is restrained to menial tasks and has a great longing to explore the world. Later we find he is the son of a Jedi, an order of men with god-like abilities, and a queen giving him the same prestige of ancient half god-heroes. Skywalker's journey is one to save the world while underneath he is truly trying to find himself. Like all other great mythologies, he is guided by mysterious elders, helped by friends and challenged by monsters and 'gods'. What we see in his story is the journey of self-awakening that is common in all people. He is pushed to his limits and in doing so learns just what he is capable of. By journeying through existence more or less alone he is also forced to find where his place is in the world is and finds satisfaction in it, a lesson he would not have achieved by staying at home.

To discuss individual heroes is important as they are the key movers in their own mythological stories. But for their characteristics to make sense, the story as a whole must be studied and this is an endeavor that takes much time and space. It is true that each hero is different, in the virtual world of mythology these differences are important as they present new ways at looking at or tackling similar situations. Where Heracles might use brute strength to overcome a challenge, that same challenge might be tackled through wit by someone else with an entirely different outcome. And that is what is important in mythology as a whole, to observe alternative answers to the same problem to find the outcome you are looking for.

Mythic Places & Times

A Dream-Like State

The stories of mythology exist in a kind of dream-like state. The events are told as having taken place in this world, yet it is not this world. In Homer's epics, the Achaean's fought at Troy which has a defined place on earth, having been rediscovered in Turkey, yet Odysseus also travels to the underworld, which is not part of our reality. In the same way, many mythologies take place in a historical time, the Trojan War believed to having occurred in the Mycenaean period of Greek history, around 1600 - 1450 B.C. Yet the myths exist outside of time as we know it and continue to occur over and over.

Mythology is not fixed, some stories may be based on factual events, but the stories themselves are born in a different realm. This is the realm of Jung's collective unconscious but it can take many names, the archetypal world, the unconscious mind, or even the imagination. But do not discard mythology just because it cannot be placed definitively within history. These worlds are set aside from the material one we inhabit on purpose and are just as important and just as profane as what we see in front of us. This may seem somewhat confusing, so let's take a deeper look.

Geography Of The Ancient World

For convenience of writing, we are going to specifically look at what the ancient Greeks considered to be their world. This is because we are predominantly looking at western mythology which was dominated by Greek culture. That said, the broader meanings, thoughts, and philosophies of what is going to be said was the general belief of all peoples though they put themselves as the central figures.

The Greek world was divided into threes. The reality we inhabit, or the universe, had three parts, the heavens above, earth in the middle, and the underworld below. Each part of this universe was intrinsically connected and inhabited by the divine and mortals alike. It is fair to say that for the greater part of mythology and believe the

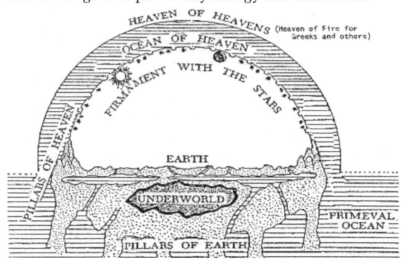

Figure 27: Taken as a cross section, the universe can be seen as such. Creation has taken place is a chasm created by the gods. This chasm is an opening in the primordial ocean that was the origins of everything.

inhabitants of each realm was divided as such - the gods lived in heaven but could and often did transcend into the other realms. Mortals were stuck to living on the earth, and the dead inhabited the underworld.

Heaven

Heaven is an ambiguous term when discussing ancient Greek mythology. A better definition would be Mount Olympus which had a fixed location in Thessaly, northern Greece. It was the center of the world and the gods inhabited glorious palaces atop its summit. Mortals were barred from entering, except on rare occasions, and this was indeed a place for the divine. In this way, it is not right to call it a 'heaven' in the sense that we would know it today. There was no reward for mortals after death if they had lived a good life for all souls would end up in the same place.

Mount Olympus was the home of the gods, but there was still the sky above and the celestial bodies which the Greeks took particular note of. Though not the habitation of the gods, this region is still important and should be considered part of heaven. The Greeks believed that the planets and heavenly bodies were emanations from the divine world, a way in which the gods could contact the mortal world and pass on messages of good tidings, warning, or wrath. In this way, we see the process of celestial divination taking place in an attempt to read the signs from the deities.

Earth

Earth is the middle ground, it is the world we know, the place humanity resides on during life where all events of importance take place. The Greeks mapped the world in a rudimentary way, dividing the land into three. Each third was a continent of its own, Europe in the north, Africa in the south, and Asia to the east. Greece itself was the midway point of each of these land masses, and Mount Olympus was the very center of the universe. This idea of a religious point being the center of all creation lived on for quite a long time with both Rome and Jerusalem vying for the position in the Christian era. This can be seen in Dante's Divine Comedy.

The Greek mind populated the earth with many fanciful creations. Elementals in the form of dryads and other semi-divine beings ran freely in the wild, governing their small area of expertise. Locations of merit were noted and surrounded with mythic meaning. For example, the Oracle at Delphi is situated in the place Apollo defeated Typhon (interestingly, some mythologies place the Oracle at Delphi in the center of the universe.) They said that the rotting carcass of Typhon gave off gasses which provided the power of Oracle.

Everywhere one looked a duality was born. Ocean and land, urban and wild, civilized and barbarous. All of this needed explaining and it seemed that the very land in which humanity lived was in simultaneous existence with the mythic world.

The Greek mind found many polarities within the world they lived. They divided the Greek-speaking cultures from foreign peoples, calling them Barbarians for they likened their speech to "bar...bar...bar...". they also differentiated between places of civilization such as cities and towns against the wilds of the world where man had no dominion. In this, we see many luminal themes in mythology where characters from the wild interact with those of civilizations. An outstanding example of this is the interactions between centaurs and people. The centaurs being half-beast, half-man are themselves a luminal creature as they stand in a halfway point between the civilized and uncivilized. Historically it is theorized that centaurs may have been a product of the early Greek encounters with the peoples of the steppe, most probably the Scythian culture. To urban Greeks, these people would have indeed seemed as if they straddled two worlds, they lived in tribes, yet were part of the wild. This same influence may be the origin of the Amazonians of mythology, where women were held with high regard and were an integral part of warrior culture. In these examples, we see the Greek mind trying to rationalize the world around them, creating categories to make sense of the world.

Figure 28: One of the earliest cartographers to divide the earth like this was Anaximander (610 - 546 B.C.). The world is divided into three major land masses with Greece in the center.

Underworld

The underworld is a place much more familiar to modern audiences. To the Greeks, it shared the same name as its divine ruler, Hades, and was typified as a hellish place where its darkness is the counter to Mount Olympus' light. All souls are bound for Hades regardless of the actions taken in life. The soul of the deceased leaves the body with much of the form of its prior self except that it is now a 'shade'. The soul is transported to the underworld and encounters five significant rivers.

Oceanus is the first, it is the 'world river' that encircles earth, and in some mythologies marks the barrier between the realm of the living and the realm of the dead. The next is the river Styx, known as the river of hatred, it encircles the underworld seven time and the soul needs the help of the boatman Charon to cross. The boatman continues his ferry across the river Acheron which is defined as pain. Lethe is the river of forgetfulness, Cocytus is that of wailing, and finally, the river Phlegethon is that of fire and leads to the deepest pits of Hades, that of Tartarus.

Charon does not, however, transport all souls across the river. Those souls whose bodies are unburied may not cross, and only those who pay the ferryman his penny will continue their journey. Once on the other side, the soul is met at the gates by the three-headed dog Cerberus who persistently guards the place of the dead. Passing through the gate, the soul can now confront the Judges of the Underworld who will decide the final destination for the deceased. Either the Fields of Asphodel, Elysium, or the Fields of Punishment.

The soul is judged to reside in one of these three destinations based on the life they had led. The Fields of Asphodel were for regular folk, those who had not committed overly heinous sins, nor performed any great deeds of note. Elysium was the home for souls who had distinguished themselves. This place was generally populated by great heroes and demi-gods who spent the rest of eternity at ease with no need for labor. It was ward for a regular mortal to gain admission, though it was possible such as in the case of Socrates who distinguished himself through philosophy. Finally, there is the Fields of Punishment, home to those who had purposefully made havoc through the world and had committed crimes against the gods themselves. Hades would define the punishment for each individual, usually in a sick mimic of the mortals acts on earth.

The last location in Hades is Tartarus. The darkest, deepest pit in all creation. It lay so far underground that the darkness itself was oppressed. This was the home of the Titans which Zeus had cast out of Olympus. Here Kronos is king and it is a place seldom seen by any other than those damned to inhabit it.

Chthonic Realms

As we are discussing the underworld, it is a good point to discuss the reoccurring theme of a 'chthonic' stage of mythological stories. The word 'chthonic' derives from the Greek term khthonios which means 'in, under, or below the earth'. It is not hard to imagine then that a chthonic realm in mythology is one that occurs underground, or to be more precise, an adventure into the underworld. However a chthonic event is not limited to only the underworld but could take place anywhere that has an underworldish nature, for example, in the Biblical Book of Jonah, Jonah's adventure inside the whale can be viewed as a chthonic stage of his journey.

As the heroic cycle deals with a process of evolution, we see the chthonic event in alignment with 'The Innermost Cave'. It is the place the hero descends into and confronts the main antagonist. Psychologically speaking this is the conscious mind descending into the abyss which is the personal or collective unconscious. By delving deep within, the mind can view its innermost fears as its 'shadow' or alternative personality. The mind can confront the shadow and either be consumed by it or overcome it and once this is done the hero will ascend from the chthonic realm victorious.

There are symbolic parallels between the chthonic realm and the woman's womb. Aside from the rudimentary visual similarities, there is also the figurative rebirth which the hero endures. Once the shadow has been overcome the hero will gain a kind of enlightenment and be forever changed. When he reemerges from the chthonic realm, he is a new man and has thus been reborn into the world. To discuss Jonah once more, we see this is what happens to him, where he originally fled from God's command, he was transformed in the belly of the whale (his chthonic realm) and when he reemerged he had the strength to go to Nineveh to complete his task.

Chthonic events are very common in mythology and can be seen in Homer's Odyssey, Virgil' Aeneid, The Homeric Hymn To Demeter, and even modern mythologies like del Toro's Pan's Labyrinth or Lucas' Star Wars. The chthonic event is terrifying, everything associated with the process of change is horrific, but it is through these darkest moments that the hero can gain the brightest light and reemerge a far better person.

Jonah & The Whale

From the Biblical Book of Jonah.

*****

There once lived a man in the land of Israel who was called Jonah. One day God came to Jonah and told him that he was to go to the city of Ninevah and tell the people there about him. But Jonah feared what he was ordered to do. The people who lived in Ninevah were dangerous, they were fearless warriors who had killed everyone who got in their way.

As Jonah traveled his heart became filled with fear, he doubted himself and above all was terrified of being killed himself. In his fear, Jonah fled from his orders and boarded a ship heading to the city of Tarshish instead. The sailors carried him safely across the Mediterranean but it was not long before the water began to turn. Dark clouds came from overhead and the waves grew like mountains. The little boat was thrown about like a leaf in a winter storm and Jonah began to howl that this was the work of the Lord against his unfaithful servant. The sailors in their panic took Jonah by the arms and hurled him into the sea, and as they did this the winds calmed and the sea became still.

Yet Jonah floated away into the vast depths of the waters. Alone and terrified Jonah cried again, but before he could truly know fear a great whale leaped from the sea and swallowed him whole. Deep in the bowels of the beast, Jonah was safe but again full of uncertainty. He prayed and begged for the strength to endure and God delivered him.

The whale spat Jonah out and again he was on the shores of Israel.

With his faith restored, Jonah traveled to Ninevah and did what was asked from him. He told the people there about his God and the people gave up their ways to worship him as Jonah did.

***

Mythic Time & The Eternal Return

We have brought up the idea that mythology exists outside the bounds of time as we perceive it. This is a complex notion but can be explained like this. Humans perceive time as linear, we define a beginning, a middle, and an end to events and this helps us sort out and categorize our daily lives and history. However, it is not the only way to perceive time and it may not even be the correct way to understand it. Time can also be viewed non-linearly, it can be seen as cyclical. This is not a new notion and may be humanities original way of defining time. For example, in ancient Egypt, the years began anew at zero for the beginning of each Pharaoh's reign. The death of the old brought about the birth of the new and the cycle repeated itself.

The scholar Mircea Eliade made huge leaps in understanding what this mythic time is. He did so by realizing that for ancient man there were two worlds, the divine and the profane (or mundane / our physical world). Following Plato's ideas on Forms and Jung's theories of archetypes and the collective unconscious, Eliade explained that true existence was that of the divine world and that the profane was only an imitation of the divine. So we see that there is a divine space and a profane space, but also that there is a divine time and a profane time. Now, because our profane world is in imitation of the divine, it made sense to ancient people that the telling of myth and the enacting of ritual was a way to draw power from the divine as it mimicked that world in a more pure way than that of everyday life.

To use a modern example, a church is a divine space built within a profane city. By entering the church, the person is essentially entering a representation of the divine world. When the priest begins the sermon, that space enters the divine time. By hearing the words of the gospels, the audience travels to a mythic time while they sit in a divine space. This works through archetypes. The church, the gospels, and the time all merge to mimic and portray the archetypal patterns that only exist in the divine realm.

In this, we see that the telling of mythology, the practice of rituals, and the rites of religion all bridge a gap between the divine and profane world. They bring universal archetypes into the sphere of everyday life. This is how time can be viewed as non-linear, Eliade said that,

In imitating the exemplary acts of a god or of a mythic hero, or simply by recounting their adventures, the man of an archaic society detaches himself from profane time and magically re-enters the Great Time, the sacred time.
- Mircea Eliade, Myths, dreams, and mysteries (1967, Pg. 23)

In this, mythology and religion act as a kind of vehicle that take the individual back to the divine time. By transcending linear time like this we see how the mythic world is always alive and can be revisited again and again, and by revisiting this divine space, the existence of the individual is given reason and value.

People have always held this cyclic value of time, especially when considering their mythologies and beliefs. The people of Mesopotamia would reenact the events of the Enuma Elish mythology every new year, the Australian Aboriginals would annually repaint their rock paintings, and Christians celebrate Christmas and retell the stories of the Nativity each December. By celebrating these yearly events, time in a sense only exists in a closed circle. The new year is often symbolic for the birth of creation, so every year we return to this date and the world is recreated. The repeating of the stories keeps them alive, it allows us to escape from the mundane, linearly-timed world so that we can reenter that mythic time and experience the divine for ourselves.

As a side note, it is also interesting to consider that for many cultures, the celebration of mythic time was a way in prolonging the life of the profane earth. In these societies, the link between the divine and mundane is overstated, the belief that the mundane world cannot exist without the divine led to the belief that ritual and myth had to be repeated to add strength to the divine world, keeping the profane from disappearing. In this way, the 'new-year' was quite literal as they performed the rites to keep everything in existence for another yearly period.

A Herculean Task

A Herculean Task

This account of the life and labors of Heracles is given to us from the Greek mythographer Apollodorus. Writing somewhere in the first or second century A.D. he is sometimes given the prenomen title *Pseudo*-Apollodorus to differentiate him from the earlier philosopher of the same name. Our Apollodorus, that of the second century, recorded a great number of classical Greek mythologies in a chronological telling of events called the *Bibliotheca*. He makes an account of creation through the earlier writings of Hesiod before discussing the gods and the deeds of various lineages and heroes. His section devoted to Heracles (*Hercules* in Latin) is quite lengthy and simple enough to read through. It is a systematic telling of events, not divulging into depth with details and never asking the hows or whys. However, the account is easy to read and allows us an opportunity to put everything we have learned so far into dissecting an entire tale.

The Birth Of Heracles

Before Amphitryon reached Thebes, Zeus came during the night and made the one night as long as three. He made himself look like Amphitryon, slept with Alcmene, and told her what had happened with the Teleboans. When

Amphitryon arrived and saw that his wife did not welcome him home, he asked the reason. After she said that he had arrived the night before and slept with her, he learned from Teiresias of the encounter she had had with Zeus. Alcmene bore two sons, Heracles, the older by a day, to Zeus, and Iphicles to Amphitryon. When Heracles was eight months old, Hera sent two enormous serpents into his bed because she wanted to destroy the infant. Alcmene called to Amphitryon for help, but Heracles stood up, throttled them, one in each hand, and killed them. Pherecydes says that Amphitryon, wishing to know which of the boys was his son, put the serpents into the bed. When Iphicles fled and Heracles confronted them, Amphitryon knew that Iphicles was his.

The mythic cycle of Heracles opens expectedly with information of his parentage and details of the world in which he is born into.

Heracles can make claim to a divine lineage as his father is Zeus, yet is brought up by the mortal Amphitryon who himself is a great general of Thebes. The opening passage relies on the assumed knowledge of the reader to know that Amphitryon was away with the Theban army who were fighting the Teleboans. During his absence, Zeus came to his wife Alcmene and impregnated her with Heracles. This sequence of events is told in detail in Plautus' comedy *Amphitruo* for those who are interested.

What we have seen so far is that Heracles is born from Zeus and the mortal Alcmene, he is a Theban, and he has a wholly mortal twin brother named Iphicles.

Heracles' Youth

Heracles was taught to drive chariots by Amphitryon, to wrestle by Autolycos, to shoot a bow by Eurytos, to fight in armor by Castor, and to play the lyre by Linos, who was Orpheus' brother. After Linos had come to Thebes and become a Theban, he was slain by Heracles, who hit him with his lyre (Heracles killed him in a fit of rage because Linos had struck him). When some men prosecuted him for murder, he read out a law of Rhadamanthys that said that any man who defends himself against an instigator of unjust violence is innocent. In this way, he was acquitted. Afraid that Heracles would do something like that again, Amphitryon sent him out to tend his herd of cattle. Growing up there, Heracles surpassed everyone in size and strength. It was obvious from his appearance that he was Zeus' son, for his body was four cubits tall, and a fiery radiance shone from his eyes. He also did not miss when he shot a bow or threw a javelin. When he was eighteen years old and out with the herd, he killed the Cithaironian lion, which used to rush from Mount Cithairon and ravage the cattle of Amphitryon, as well as those of Thespios.

Thespios was king of Thespiai, and when Heracles wanted to kill the lion, he went to this man. Thespios entertained him as a guest for fifty days and had one of his daughters (he had fifty of them by Megamede daughter of Arneos) sleep with him every night before Heracles went out to hunt, for he was eager for all of them to have children with Heracles. Though Heracles thought that he was always sleeping with the same one, he slept with all of them. After overpowering the lion, he wore its skin and used its gaping jaws as a helmet.

When he was returning from the hunt, he ran into some heralds sent by Erginos to collect the tribute from the Thebans. The Thebans paid tribute to Erginos for the following reason: One of Menoiceus' charioteers, named Perieres, hit Clymenos, kin of the Minyans, with a stone and wounded him in the precinct of Poseidon in Onchestos. When Clymenos was brought to Orchomenos, he was barely alive. As he was dying, he directed his son Erginos to avenge his death. Erginos marched against Thebes, and after inflicting many casualties, he made an oath-bound treaty that the Thebans would send him a hundred cows of tribute every year for twenty years. As the heralds were going to Thebes to get this tribute, Heracles met up with them and mutilated them. He cut off their ears, noses, and hands, tied them around their necks, and told them to take that back to Erginos and the Minyans as tribute. Enraged by this, Erginos marched against Thebes.

After Heracles got armor and weapons from Athena and became the commander, he killed Erginos, routed the Minyans, and forced them to pay double the tribute to the Thebans. It happened that Amphitryon died fighting bravely in the battle. Heracles received from Creon his oldest daughter Megara as a prize for bravery. He had three sons with her, Therimachos, Creontiades, and Deicoon. Creon gave his youngest daughter to Iphicles, who had already had a son, Iolaos, with Automedousa daughter of Alcathos. After the death of Amphitryon, Rhadamanthys, the son of Zeus, married Alcmene and, exiled from his county, settled in Ocaleai in Boiotia.

Heracles had already been taught archery by Eurytos. Now he got a sword from Hermes, a bow from Apollo, a golden breastplate from Hephaistos, and a robe from Athena; he cut his own club at Nemea.

After his battle against the Minyans, it happened that Heracles was driven mad because of the jealousy of Hera. He threw his own children by Megara into a fire, along with two of Iphicles' sons. For this, he condemned himself to exile. He was purified by Thespios and going to Delphi, he asked the god where he should settle. The Pythia then for the first time called him by the name Heracles; up until then, he had been called Alceides. She told him to settle in Tiryns and serve Eurystheus for twelve years. She also told him to accomplish ten labors imposed upon him and said that when the labors were finished, he would become immortal.

This passage depicts the years of Heracles youth and sets up the motive for the rest of Heracles adventures and begins to foreshadow the themes that define the hero. To begin with we see the young man being trained in the arts of war by other heroic figures of renown. Heracles first act of impulse is displayed when he murders Linos, to which he defends was in line with the law showing the audience that he is also quite smart and cunning. So from the beginning, Heracles is displaying conflicting characteristics that will later define him. These conflictions cause the people around Heracles to fear him which is why we see him as a young man ushered away to be a cowherd.

The act of sleeping with all of Thespios' daughters is sometimes referred to as Heracles "thirteenth labor" and is an important addition to the mythic cycle as we reaffirm Heracles weakness in his base urges. He struggles to control his appetite for sex and violence, and though in this case it is condoned, it will not always be and this will lead to difficulties. In another sense, we see Heracles unwittingly being taken advantage of by Thespios as the hero has no idea that he is sleeping with all the man's daughters in the hope that he will impregnate them all. Though there seems to be no repercussions in this episode, it foreshadows what is to come.

Heracles' goal to obtain the Cithaironian Lion is important. It is his first real achievement as a hero. You will remember from our discussion on archetypes and the tarot cards that the eighth card, "strength", held the image of a lion, to which I explained as,

The Strength card symbolizes the man's acknowledgment of the beast within. Taking time to meditate and focus his energies internally, he finds that he still cannot control life and that it will guide his emotions. In the quiet, he finds his inner beast, acknowledges its existence, and finds strength in it. However, he still must develop, as merely acknowledging the beast means that the strength is still not sourced from himself.

This applies to Heracles in full. For him, this inner beast is his Cithaironian Lion and represents the passions that give him strength, yet he has no power over. They drive his actions and in a way protect him, which is why we see him wear the skin as an armor. We will see through the rest of this story though that the lion's skin cannot protect the hero from himself, nor can it negate the monstrous deeds he performs and so he must still develop.

Figure 29: This Tarot card (c. 1465, Ferrara, Italy) is entitled Forteza which today is translated as Strength, but better suits the meaning Fortitude. This is fitting when considering Heracles as his true strength isn't in his physical body, but within his mind shown by his will to continue even when defeat is imminent. Heracles was no doubt an influence in the design of this card's artwork as we see the central figure wearing the skin of a lion and wielding a club.

The last episode depicted that with the Oracle needs a little bit of fleshing out to truly understand. Hera's hatred toward Heracles was present before his birth and was a product of her jealousy toward the disloyalty of her husband Zeus. Her first act of vengeance took place at the time of Heracles birth where Hera had made Zeus promise that the next male born of Perseus' line would one day be high-king of Mycenae. Zeus agreed, believing this destiny would be for Heracles, but Hera was cunning and in one set of mythic cycles we see that she binds up the birthing canal of Alcmene so as to prolong her pregnancy. This was done so that Eurystheus could be born first and take the throne in place of Heracles. This may seem like a minor detail, but the importance lies in the theme of the Olympian gods cleansing the earth of the old order and replacing it with the new. They sought a hero to do their bidding on earth, and it now appeared that Eurystheus would be the one. This is a theme of husband versus wife, or male against female, as these deities backed different men. It also creates a foundation for the rest of Hera's attacks on Heracles, as we will see that it was Hera who told the oracle to send Heracles to Eurystheus who gives Heracles his labors, and it is Hera who is behind most of the hardships which Heracles encounters.

Labor I: The Nemean Lion

After Heracles heard this, he went to Tiryns and did Eurystheus' bidding. First, he commanded him to bring back the skin of the Nemean Lion. This animal, Typhon's offspring, was invulnerable. When he was going after the lion, he came to Cleonai and was put up as a guest by Molorchos, a poor man. When Molorchos wanted to sacrifice a victim, Heracles told him to hold off for thirty days; if he returned from his hunt safe and sound, he told Molorchos to make a sacrifice for a god to Zeus Soter {"Saviour"}; if he died, he told Molorchos to make a sacrifice to himself fit for a hero. When he got to Nemea and tracked down the lion, he first shot it with his bow. When he found that it was invulnerable, he brandished his club and pursued it. When it fled into a cave with two entrances, Heracles blocked up one entrance and went after the beast through the other. Getting it in a headlock, he held on, squeezing until he choked it. He put it across his shoulders and brought it back to Cleonai. He found Molorchos on the last of the thirty days about to offer the victim to Heracles in the belief that he was dead. Instead, Heracles sacrificed it to Zeus Soter and then took the lion to Mycenae. Terrified by Heracles' demonstration of manly

The episode with the Nemean lion is a chthonic event, occurring underground, so we would be safe to interpret this as a journey into the heroes unconscious. There is a resounding parallel between this and the Cithaironian Lion, and in some mythic cycles, Heracles actually wears the Nemean Lion's fur as armor. With this we can say that Heracles is again meeting the unconscious source of his power and confronting the base urges that control him.

Our hero displays intelligence in trapping the lion first showing the audience that he is not simply a strong man, but one

Figure 30: Hercules and the Hydra, Antonio del Pollaiolo, circa 1475.

242

that can use his mind too. His failure to slay the beast outright using strength teaches the audience that sheer brawn alone is not enough to overcome your adversaries, but the power of the mind must be applied.

Heracles use of the bow first is also important. As with Apollo and Artemis, the bow can be seen as an instrument of distance, keeping yourself away from your quarry. In this way, one could interpret a kind of emotional distance being kept during the early stage of the episode. This of course failed and it is because the Nemean Lion is an aspect of Heracles psyche to which he must literally wrestle with to overcome, showing the audience that the unconscious mind is a personal sphere that cannot be dealt with from afar.

The success of a man who can take control of his unconscious mind is shown to us by the fear it causes for Eurystheus who now keeps Heracles away from himself. It shows the strength that is gained through such an adventure, that though gained internally, shows externally once attained.

This mythic episode is also a ritualistic explanation for why the people at Cleonai sacrifice a lion each year, and why they have such a strong worship and devotion to Heracles.

Labor II: The Lernaian Hydra

The second labor Eurystheus commanded Heracles to perform was to kill the Lernaian Hydra, which had been raised in the swamp of Lerna and was making forays onto the plain and wreaking havoc on both the livestock and the land. The Hydra had an enormous body with nine heads, eight of them mortal, and the one in the middle immortal.

Heracles mounted a chariot driven by Iolaos and traveled to Lerna. He brought his horses to a halt and found the Hydra on a hilt by the Springs of Amymone, where she had her lair. He shot flaming arrows at her and forced her to come out. As she did so, he seized her and put her in a hold, but she wrapped herself around one of his legs and held on tight. Heracles got nowhere by smashing her heads with his club, for when one was smashed, two heads grew back. An enormous crab came to assist the Hydra and pinched Heracles' foot. Because of this, after he killed the crab, he called for Iolaos to help. Iolaus set fire to a portion of the nearby forest and with the burning pieces of wood, he scorched the stumps of the heads, preventing them from coming back. Having overcome the regenerating heads in this way, Heracles then cut off the immortal one, buried it, and placed a heavy rock over it by the road that leads through Lerna to Elaious. As for the Hydra's body, he ripped it open and dipped his arrows in her bile. Eurystheus told Heracles that he should not have to count this labor as one of the ten, for Heracles had not overcome the Hydra by himself, but with the help of Iolaos.

There is some background behind Lerna that should be of interest to anyone who wants to grasp Heracles second labor in full. Firstly, Lerna is a district in Greece, near the Isthmus, which is characterized by its sacred springs and swamps that were mythically gifted to the land from Poseidon. The area was incredibly sacred for a vast period of time with modern archaeology dating its inhabitation to well before the Mycenaean Period. Geographically, Lerna sits in the vicinity of Eleusis, and Demeter was ritually connected with the Lernaean Mysteries. The natural springs, lakes, caves, and mythology all led to Lerna being seen as a gateway to the underworld - which brings us to the Hydra.

The Hydra is linked to Lerna through age, the monster is incredibly old like Lerna itself and in this way is seen as a remnant of the pre-Olympian chaotic age which is further explained as it is an offspring of the monstrous titans Typhon and Echidna. The Hydra is a chthonic creature, it is associated with the underworld, and therefore symbolic of Heracles subconscious. What we might infer from the details so far is that Heracles is confronting an aspect of his subconscious which is very old, it is a remnant of old thinking, perhaps his old ways, and must be destroyed or overcome to allow for a new way of thinking. In fact, this is essentially what the labors of Heracles are doing, by ridding the earth of evil monsters and creating a better world in his mythic cycle, the audience learns the virtues of shredding away the negative attributes of the mind to create a new state of being.

Now, this Hydra did not only exist in the myth of Heracles. It was universally agreed that the Alcyonian Lake in Lerna was an entrance to the underworld and that it was guarded by the Hydra. For two quick examples of interest, Emperor Nero felt it important in the first century A.D. to investigate the matter for himself, rowing his boat to the center of the lake he had his men throw weighted ropes overboard until they hit the bottom. However, they never did reach the lake floor and after a time the exercise seemed to confirm that the lake was bottomless. In his work *Isis & Osiris*, Plutarch wrote of the lake, saying that any who swam across it was sucked down by the Hydra, whom he called the "Keeper of the Gate". This, of course, being the gate of the underworld.

Our interpretation of the Hydra can continue now where we can suggest that the Hydra is symbolic for the aspect of the mind that stops one from entering the sub and unconscious. If we recall back to our discussion on Carl Jung, we might say that the Hydra is the ego.

The Hydra does not necessarily have to be the ego, it is not a perfect fit, and we could easily create a rational argument to say that the Hydra is the archetypal shadow of the hero as well. However, what we are going to see now is that the ego is actually a composition of the self and the shadow and this is why Jung says that to obtain enlightenment one must assimilate the shadow so that the individual can exist with both light and dark aspects in balance.

However, we digress, the Hydra can be said to be the shadow or the ugly side of the ego which the individual does not accept as themselves and tries so hard to suppress. This fits with the myth as we see Heracles attempting to cut the heads from the Hydra with the result being that multiple heads regrow from each severed neck. In a symbolic way, we are seeing the result of one who tries to destroy the shadow instead of assimilating it. Each head of the Hydra can be likened to an "ugly" aspect of the ego which Heracles does not accept in himself. He cuts off the neck, trying to destroy these "ugly" aspects but finds that new forms of the shadow emerge instead. From a psychological standpoint, you cannot destroy the shadow, you cannot remove the negative. Instead, the individual has to accept these features of the psyche and bring them under his own control. This is how we see Heracles defeat the Hydra. Unable to overcome the monster alone, he calls for help, and knowing the beast can never truly be destroyed (symbolized by its one immortal head), he instead buries it under a mountain representing the heroes subconscious.

Heracles does not bury the head just anywhere but places it along the Sacred Way, a road that ran from Athens, through Lerna, and to Eleusis. There may be significance between this and the Eleusinian Mysteries as if the mythographer is telling his audience that everybody must face the Hydra on their journey to enlightenment.

Finally, we see that Heracles may use the success of the labor to his benefit. He dips his arrows into the Hydra's blood creating the most potent of poisoned tips. This is synonymous with him wearing the lion skin as armor. Essentially, once the challenge has been overcome, the hero becomes better for it, psychologically this works as the mind becomes stronger and full of understanding. First, he won the lion skin which protects him, then he won the arrows which he can use for offense.

Labor III: The Cerynitian Deer

The third labor Eurystheus commanded Heracles to perform was to bring the Cerynitian Deer alive to Mycenae. This deer was in Oinoe. It had golden horns and was sacred to Artemis. Because of this Heracles did not want to kill or wound it, so he pursued it for an entire year. When the beast was wearied by the chase, it fled to a mountain known as Artemisios and then to the Ladon River. When it was about to cross this river, Heracles shot the deer with his bow and captured it. Putting it on his shoulders, he hurried through Arcadia. But Artemis, with Apollo, met up with him and was ready to take the deer away. She reproached him because he was killing her sacred animal, but he made the excuse that he was being forced to do it and said that the guilty party

Heracles third labor looks at his challenges in a new light. Though we are working through Apollodorus' version of the tale, I am referring to a broader telling which you can access by looking into the works of other classical authors. After Heracles had overcome the Nemean Lion and Lernaean Hydra, it was clear that physical conflict was going to be relatively easy for him to gain victory

It is at this point in the mythic cycle that we see Hera and Eurystheus come together to scheme a new plan that that could put a stop to Heracles. They decided they must attempt a new approach where the hero is not allowed to harm the creature he pursues. They then chose a creature with astonishing speed, reputed to be able to outrun an arrow in flight. But on top of all this, the Cerynitian Deer was sacred to Artemis and in this way, Hera and Eurystheus secretly hoped to incite the goddess' anger against the hero.

Heracles completes the labor using a new set of characteristics that have not really come to the foreground yet. Firstly, we see patience in his determination, spending an entire year on the chase. We see intelligence being employed when sheer strength cannot be. This is related to waiting until the deer has been slowed down in the river and thus can no longer be faster than an arrow in flight. Then we are shown Heracles piety, and how he approached the goddess with honesty rather than deceit.

An interpretation of the meaning behind the Cerynitian Deer can become quite complex. It has been stated that the deer, a doe, may have been influenced by reindeer - as the females of that species bear horns, whereas deer in Greece do not. This also links to Heracles tracking it through Hyperborea which is a northern land. This could be the source of the mythic animal but does not help us progress in understanding the meaning behind it. Rather, we should look at what the deer is symbolizing.

In spirituality, enlightenment can be likened to deification, a process which Heracles labors are forcing him to undergo. A perfect being holds in equal proportions all aspects of the psyche including both masculine and feminine qualities. The Cerynitian Deer may be representing this, as the doe is feminine but bears horns like its male counterparts. These horns are further emphasized by being golden and therefore pure. This could be further implied by Heracles being confronted by both Artemis and Apollo. Twin gods that display the male-female dichotomy in balance.

This episode then could be seen as Heracles pursuing the deer to awaken his feminine aspect as it is essential in his progress toward becoming a god.

In other accounts of the myth, Heracles promises Artemis to return her deer safely. He takes the doe to Mycenae and demands that Eurystheus come and take the deer from him himself. As Eurystheus approaches, Heracles puts the deer down in front of him and it springs away. Eurystheus is outraged and Heracles laughs saying, "You have to be quick." This is a minor detail, and quite humorous, but it is essentially saying that everyone who is on the path to deification must catch their own Cerynitian Deer and that it cannot be achieved until the individual is at a stage of progression where they are ready to do so.

Labor IV: The Erymanthian Boar

The fourth labor Eurystheus commanded Heracles to perform was to bring the Erymanthian Boar alive. This beast was causing destruction in Psophis by making attacks from a mountain they call Erymanthos. Traveling through Pholoe, Heracles stayed as a guest with the Centaur Pholos, the son of Seilenos and an ash-tree Nymph. This Centaur offered Heracles meat that was roasted, but he himself ate his raw. When Heracles asked for wine, Pholos said that he was afraid to open the Centaurs' communal storage jar. Heracles told him not to worry and opened the jar. Not much later the Centaurs scented the odor and came armed with rocks and fir trees to Pholos' cave. Heracles repelled Anchios and Agrios, the first to grow bold enough to enter, by hitting them with burning firewood, and he shot the rest with his bow, pursuing them all the way to Malea. From there they fled to the home of Cheiron, who had settled at Malea after being driven from Mount Pelion by the Lapiths. Heracles shot an arrow from his bow at the Centaurs, who had surrounded Cheiron. The arrow went through Elatos' arm and lodged in Cheiron's knee. Distressed by this, Heracles ran, pulled out the arrow, and applied a drug that Cheiron gave him. Cheiron, with his wound unable to be cured, left to return to his cave. He wanted to die there but was unable to do so because he was immortal. Prometheus offered himself to Zeus to become immortal in Cheiron's place, and that is how Cheiron died. The rest of the Centaurs fled, each to a different place: some came to Mount Malea; Eurytion went to Pholoe; and Nessos went to the river Euenos. Poseidon took in the rest at Eleusis and concealed them within a mountain. As for Pholos, he pulled an arrow out of a corpse and marveled that such a small thing could kill such a large

foes. The arrow slipped out of his hand and fell on his foot,
killing him instantly. When Heracles returned to Pholoe and
saw that Pholos was dead, he buried him and went to hunt
the boar. He chased it from a thicket by shouting, and when
it tired out, he forced it into deep snow, lassoed it, and
brought it to Mycenae.

We see now for the first time Centaurs in mythology. You
will note some of the characteristics we have already
discussed, that they are civilized to a point but still have
quirks of the wild displayed in their eating of raw meat
and their use of primitive weapons such as stones and
sticks. This is displaying the luminal characteristics of the
Centaurs and shows the encroaching dangers that exist on
the borders of the wild and civilized worlds.

There is also a commentary on the effects of alcohol
here and how it can lead to damaging outcomes. This is
shown through the Centaurs inability to restrain
themselves from the drink and their violent obsession in
gaining it for themselves. Of course, this occurs through
Heracles own ignorance which in itself shows the reader
that pride begets the fall. It is clear that should Heracles
have listened to Phobos and not opened the wine, then this
tragedy would not have occurred in the first place.

The episode where Pholos admires the devastating
effect of Heracles arrows is a commentary on the brutality
of warfare. But as the arrows are dipped in the blood of the
Hydra, it is also suggesting the Centaur's amazement at the
effects of Heracles transformation so far, and how so much
strength is gained through overcoming hardships and
successfully learning the lessons they bring.

This episode with the Centaurs foreshadows the
meaning of the Erymanthian Boar. The boar is symbolic

of over-indulgence, of earthly desires and addiction. This is synonymous in our society when you refer to someone as a gluttonous pig. This aspect of the psyche must be tempered, controlled, and removed for someone looking to achieve spiritual enlightenment.

Heracles drives the boar into the deep snow, symbolic of 'cooling down' these passions, and then captures and ties it up so that it cannot continue to devastate the landscape - symbolic for the destruction of the mental faculties resulted from unrestrained desire. Heracles uses a mix of force and intelligence in navigating the labor suggesting that such a task of self-control necessitates both active and passive action from the individual. He then offers is up to Eurystheus who is horrified that such an accomplishment could be possible.

Labor V: The Cattle of Augeias

The fifth labor Eurystheus commanded Heracles to perform was to clear out the dung of the Cattle of Augeias in only a single day. Augeias was the king of Elis. According to some, he was the son of Helios, according to others, of Poseidon, and according to still others, of Phorbas. He had many herds of cattle. Heracles came to him and, without revealing Eurystheus' command, told him he would clear out the dung in a single day if Augeias would give him one-tenth of the cattle. Augeias promised he would, but did not believe it was possible. Heracles called upon Augeias' son Phyleus to act as witness. Then he made a hole in the foundation of the stable and diverted the rivers Alpheios and Peneios, which flowed near one another, and caused them to flow in after he made an outlet through another opening. When Augeias learned that this had been accomplished at Eurystheus' command, he

would not render payment and went as far as to deny ever
having promised to do so in the first place, saying that he
was ready to be brought to trial over the issue. When the
judges had taken their seats, Phlyeus was called by Heracles
as a witness against his father and said that he had agreed to
make a payment. Augeias, enraged, ordered both Phyleus
and Heracles to depart from Elis before the vote was cast. So
Phyleus went to Doulichion and settled there, and Heracles
came to Olenos to the house of Dexamenos to help, he killed
Eurytion when he came for his bride. Eurystheus did not
count the labor among the ten either, because he said that it
was done for payment.

The clearing out the dung of the Cattle of Augeias is a
metaphor for cleansing the mind of falsehood.

Imagine the literal task Heracles must perform. He
comes to the stables and sees row after row of cattle in
their stalls all eating fodder and defecating where they
stand. With only a shovel in his hand, he could clean the
barn one load at a time, but he would find that the waste is
regenerated quicker than he removes it. This, of course,
renders the task as impossible to complete.

The dung itself is representative of the lies that
surround our life, these could be the lies told by others,
but more importantly, it is the lies we tell ourselves. If we
tried to rationalize or argue each lie in turn, then this
would be like using the shovel, more would generate as
each is faced in an endless cycle. Our pre-enlightened
mind is like the cattle stalls and so must be cleaned, but
this must be done in a unified push, like the flooding rivers
that washes away all the waste at once.

The Labor teaches that the dirtiest work can be performed
without losing face and in a dignified manner and that to

the spiritual man no activity is degrading. Considered in its
analogical implications the Labor shows that the Holy Ghost
alone is able to effect a cleaning up of Ahankaric dirt within
the soul. No amount of "psychological shuffling" (which is
only "spadework") can bring the same result.
- Dr. G.H. Mees, The Revelation in the Wilderness

What we are essentially seeing is that all the falsehood and all of the lies we believe must be swept away in one action of spiritual truth. This is given further meaning in Heracles order to clean the stables in one day - for to spend any longer would drag the task out and cause it to be impossible.

The two rivers used by Heracles, the Alpheios and Peneios, are named after two sons of Oceanos. They can be seen as symbolically representing involution and evolution when they combine we see the mind moving inward and changing. This is essential for the internal purification of the mind.

Lastly, this labor was not accepted by Eurytheus because Heracles asked payment for the service. This is an important point because it tells us that spiritual development is not one that should involve incentives from the mundane world. Heracles has overlooked the rich rewards that are paid from the work itself.

Labor VI: The Stymphalian Birds

The sixth labor Eurystheus commanded Heracles to perform
was to chase away the Symphalian Birds. There was the city
of Stymphalos in Arcadia in a marsh called the Stymphalian
Marsh, which was covered in thick woods. Countless birds
took refuge in it out of fear of being eaten by the Wolves.
When Heracles was at a loss how to drive the birds from the

woods, Athena got bronze castanets from Hephaistos and gave them to him. By rattling these on a mountain situated near the marsh, he startled the birds. They could not stand the racket and took to wing in fright. In this way, Heracles shot them.

To interpret this short episode we must look at the key details and how they interact with each other. Unfortunately for us, Apollodorus has neglected to give his readers a background in what they Stymphalian Birds are. In brief, they are violent man-eating birds, made of bronze, sacred to the god of war, Ares, and are laying waste to the land around them.

In this labor, we see the classic contrast between Athena and Ares. Athena represents the 'civilized' approach to warfare, that where rationality and a cool head are employed, and Ares represents the bloody mayhem of battle.

Because Athena is helping Heracles, we might conclude that in this instance, she is trying to reinstate a civilized manner to a particle of warfare that has spiraled out of control. The Stymphalian Birds could represent soldiers who are out of control and thus sacred to Ares. Heracles becomes a vehicle for the attributes of Athena to try and pacify or rectify the problem.

He calls out the wrongdoers using the brass clappers and they flee for fear of being prosecuted by the civilized law. Heracles manages to shoot some as they fly away, but, in the end, the task is ineffective because many escape back to the sacred island of Ares. This could easily be a commentary on the problems of a militaristic state showing the audience the ease in which a force can fall out of control and of how it is impossible to kill such an organization once it has been birthed.

   The true victory for Heracles is in having gained the inner strength to call out against injustice and this is what the author is conveying to the audience in an attempt to keep a harmonious civilization - the way in which Athena intended it. However, The Symphalian Birds do not only represent external injustice but can equally symbolize the power for wrongdoing inside each of us. It is easy for an individual to become part of the raging mob - or flock - and it is only through developing our inner strength that we can break away from this. Heracles' arrows can be seen as outward expressions of intellect used to strike down our own unjust thoughts and are essential to employ for his own spiritual and mental development.

Labor VII: The Cretan Bull

The seventh labor Eurystheus commanded Heracles to perform was to bring the Cretan Bull. Acusilaus says that this was the bull that carried Europa across the sea for Zeus, but some say that it was the one sent forth from the sea by Poseidon when Minos said that he would sacrifice to Poseidon whatever appeared from the sea. But they say that when he caught sight of the beauty of the bull, he sent it off to his herds and sacrificed another to Poseidon and that the god, angered by this, made the bull go wild. Heracles went to Crete after this bull, and when he asked for help capturing it, Minos told him to take it himself if he could subdue it. He captured it, carried it back, and showed it to Eurystheus. Afterward, he let it go free, and it wandered to Sparta and all of Arcadia, and, crossing the Isthmos, it came to Marathon in Attica, where it plagued the locals.

This labor is essentially showing Heracles righting the wrongs of others and to truly disseminate the myth, we have to look at where it started which was with the wrongs of King Minos.

Now the story of King Minos can fit into the mythic cycle of Theseus as it set up his conflict with the Minotaur, or it can stand as its own mythic cycle. To paraphrase the events very quickly, King Minos

Figure 31: Heracles forces the Cretan Bull into submission. Engraving by Bernard Picart, 1731.

wanted to offer a sacrifice to Zeus, so he prayed to Poseidon to give him a sacred bull. Poseidon granted the prayer and sent King Minos a beautiful bull from the sea. Minos loved the beauty of this bull so much that he did not want to sacrifice it. He replaced this bull with an ordinary one from his own flock believing that no one would notice. Having cheated the gods we go on to see the disastrous effects of his decision. Some of the consequences included the birth of the Minotaur and the bull creating havoc throughout his land.

The underlying question here would be, what is sacrifice? Can you just offer anything up to the gods and it be okay? Obviously not, in this story, we see that the gods instantly recognize the difference between a mundane and a divine sacrifice. If we ignore the outer layer of the myth, we can see that a sacrifice is not that of sacrificing an animal to appease a deity but is something freely chosen to display the inner strengths of the individual. It is the surrendering or giving up of something precious or loved. In this way, sacrifice takes bravery, fortitude, and stamina - all heroic traits.

In this myth, Minos has promised to sacrifice something precious to himself, the sacred bull. But he lacks the fortitude to do so. However, he has already promised he would and now that he has gone back on his promise, the thing that was most precious to him has now become his greatest problem.

Psychologically this would imply the dangers of obsession. Unable to part with the bull, it has now become a liability to the king where it was once a joy. This is a pretty straightforward commentary. The myth is also suggesting to the reader that promises of sacrifice should be thought out, think about your promises before you make them. What are you as an individual able to give up? It would have been far better for Minos to have promised something simpler like sacrificing a normal bull and seen it through rather than swearing to sacrifice something he couldn't and have the guilt of failure eat him up.

The consequences of guilt are the meaning behind the sacred bull devastating the landscape. The landscape is symbolic for Minos' mind, before his failure, it was green pastures and beautiful. After his failure to commit to a promise it is ravaged by his guilt.

So Minos' mythic cycle is teaching the audience the truth behind sacrifice, that it is indeed the surrendering of something precious to the individual, and anything less than this is merely an imitation of a much purer act. That sacrifice is hard and that it takes a strong character to be able to fulfill. The story is showing us that promises should be thought out and only made with the intention of actually being fulfilled. And we, of course, see the consequences of failure. But how does this fit in as a labor of Heracles?

Heracles goes to Crete to capture the bull, he does so, takes it back Eurystheus and then releases it into the wild. He does not covet the sacred bull and does not have any wish to keep it. Instead, Heracles does what he has promised to do and then releases the bull which can be seen as a sacrifice in its purest form as he freely gives it up. Heracles completes the task that Minos could not do and we see the hero the better for it as he advances further along his path toward godhood.

Labor VIII: The Mares of Diomedes

The eighth labor Eurystheus commanded Heracles to perform was to bring the Mares of Diomedes the Thracian to Mycenae. Diomedes was the son of Ares and Cyrene. He was king of the Bistones, a very warlike Thracian tribe, and owned man-eating mares. So Heracles sailed with his willing followers, overpowered the men in charge of the mares' mangers, and drove them to the sea. When the Bistones came out under arms to rescue them, Heracles handed the mares over to Abderos to guard. Abderos, a son of Hermes, was a Locrian from Opous and Heracles' boyfriend. The mares dragged him to death. Heracles fought the Bistones, and by killing Diomedes he forced the rest to flee. He founded a city, Abdera by the tomb of the slain Abderos, and then took the mares and gave them to Eurystheus.

Eurystheus released them, and they went to the mountain called Olympos, where they were destroyed by the beasts.

To look into the meaning of this episode we are going to have to pick apart the meanings of the mares as well as that of Dimoedes. To begin, we have to look into what horses represent to humanity in general. It is commonplace to attribute strength, power, and wild freedom to them. Diomedes has these horses under his command, so we can infer that he exhibits the same traits or at least uses them as a vehicle. Diomedes himself is described as the son of Ares - the god of war, and also the king of the very warlike Thracians. There is no doubt then that he is a violent, militaristic man who is obsessed with power.

As we have seen from the Creten Bull, an obsession with anything is dangerous to the individual - but an obsession with violence and power is deadly to everyone. This is obvious through the description of the mares as *man-eating* and leaves the audience with the impression that Diomedes bears the archetype of the power-mad monarch who has no concern for the welfare of his people.

The actions of Heracles in this labor truly reveal him as being the son of Zeus. One of Zeus' most important attributes is justice, and Heracles now becomes the vehicle through which justice is distributed. In one broad sense, we are seeing a righteous Zeus (justice) confronting an obsessive Ares (warfare). The result being that Diomedes is fed to his own horses and is symbolically destroyed by his own greed for power and strength. Having consumed their owner, the horses are then set free and naturally destroyed themselves showing us that without someone to drive them, these obsessions have no power on their own.

The episode with Abderos is most likely a later addition to the story as it appears to act as an explanation for the city of Abdera. This kind of addition is commonplace in mythology, especially with Heracles for the individual cities and towns strived to become part of his mythology in a way to advance their reputation in the Greek world.

Labor IX: The War-Belt of Hippolyte

The ninth labor Eurystheus commanded Heracles to perform was to bring the war-belt of Hippolyte. She was the queen of the Amazons, who used to dwell near the river Thermodon, a tribe great in war. For they cultivated a manly spirit; whenever they had sex and gave birth, they raised the female children. They would constrict their right breasts so that these would not interfere with throwing a javelin but allowed their left breasts to grow so that they could breastfeed. Hippolyte had Ares' war-belt, a symbol of her preeminence over all the Amazons. Heracles was sent to get this belt because Admete, Eurystheus' daughter wanted to have it. Assembling some willing allies, he sailed with one ship and landed on the island of Paros, where the sons of Minos dwelled, Eurymedon, Chryses, Nephalion, and Philolaos. It happened that those on the ship disembarked, and two of them were killed by the sons of Minos. Angry over their deaths, Heracles killed the sons of Minos on the spot, blockaded the rest of the population and besieged them until they sent ambassadors and appealed to him to take whichever two men he wanted in place of those who were killed.

So he ended the siege and took with him Alcaios and Sthenelos, the sons of Androgeos son of Minos. He came to Lycos son of Dascylos in Mysia and was his guest. When

Lycos and the king of the Bebryces fought, Heracles aided
Lycos and killed many Bebryces, including their king
Mygdon, a brother of Amycos. He took away a large portion
of the Bebryces' territory and gave it to Lycos, who called the
whole territory Heracleia.

Heracles sailed to the harbor in Themiscyra, and Hippolyte
came to him. After she asked why he had come and promised
to give him the war-belt, Hera made herself look like one of
the Amazons and went among the populace saying that the
strangers who had come were abducting the queen. Under
arms, they rode down on to the ship. When Heracles saw that
they were armed, he thought that this was the result of some
treachery. He killed Hippolyte and took the war-belt, and
then he fought the rest, sailed away, and landed at Troy.

It happened at that time that the city was in difficulties
because of the wrath of Apollo and Poseidon. For Apollo and
Poseidon, desiring to test the insolence of Laomedon, made
themselves look like mortals and promised to build walls
around Pergamon for a fee. But after they built the walls,
Laomedon would not pay them. For this reason, Apollo sent
a plague and Poseidon sent a sea monster that was carried
up on shore by a tidal wave and made off with the people in
the plain. The oracles said that there would be an end to the
misfortunes if Laomedon set out his daughter Hesione as
food for the sea monster, so he set her out and fastened her to
the cliffs near the sea. When Heracles saw that she had been
set out, he promised to save her if he would get from
Laomedon the mares that Zeus had given as compensation
for the kidnapping of Ganymedes. After Laomedon said that
he would give them, Heracles killed the sea monster and
saved Hesione. But Laomedon refused to pay up, so Heracles
set sail threatening that he would make war against Troy.

*He landed at Ainos, where he was the guest of Poltys. On the
Ainian shore, when he was about to sail off, he shot and
killed Sarpedon, Poseidon's son, and Poltys' brother, because
he was insolent. Coming to Thasos and conquering the
Thracians who lived there, he gave the island to the sons of
Androgeos to live in. He set out from Thasos to Torone, and
after being challenged to wrestle by Polygonos and
Telegonos, sons of Proteus son of Poseidon, he killed them in
the course of the match. He brought the war-belt to Mycenae
and gave it to Eurystheus.*

This labor pits the forces of love and honesty against hate
and lies. Coming to the land of the warlike Amazons,
Heracles knows that he would never be able to win a fight
against them with the numbers he has on his side. So
instead, he tries a new tactic which is telling of his internal
evolution so far. He speaks with the queen, Hippolyte, with
honesty and tells her why he has come. She appreciates his
truth and freely gives up her war-belt to him. So the
audience instantly see's the power that passive truth has
overactive lies, and how love can easily outdo violence as
the quest is completed without bloodshed.

However, this point needs to be established, so the
alternative must also be displayed. We see that Hera
spreads rumor through the Amazons which they easily
believe because they are so plausible. This is a
commentary on political deceit and the problems of a
'mob rules' mindset that often besets a society.

Now we come to the spiritual pinnacle of this tale which
is that of the war-belt. This can be seen as the
psychological shield each person holds to protect them self
from the judgment of society. It could be seen as an
outward projection of ego that allows an individual to cope

and defend itself from judgment. This construct of the mind is absolutely necessary for the development of a person, but at a certain stage of life, it must be removed to allow for spiritual progression. What we are seeing then is Heracles acting as a catalyst, or as a spiritual teacher to Hippolyte who is at the stage of letting her defenses down so she can progress. This is the deeper meaning of why Heracles acts with love instead of force. The tragedy, of course, comes when Hippolyte is killed by the mob which only happens after she lets her defenses down, another kind of commentary on the ego shielding against society.

Heracles then takes the belt and returns to Eurystheus who give it to his daughter. A girl in youth who is need of this kind of mental protection. The question may arise of why one would want to remove their defenses, especially considering the fate of Hippolyte. This could best be described through the likeness of a castle. By hiding inside its stone walls, the individual is indeed protected from the outside world, but the walls also act as a prison in which the person is trapped within. The castle should be seen as a tool for progression instead of a lifestyle choice. By developing strength within the walls, one can then leave its safety to experience the world around them.

Aside from the psychological importance of this story, there are some other facets we should look into. There is a beautiful description of the Amazons and their mythic culture which is probably a commentary on some of the tribes in eastern Europe and Turkey encountered by the ancient Greeks. Their society is maternal, centered on the feminine aspect, but in a surprising turn of events, they take on masculinity through deforming their own bodies. We are given a practical explanation of why the right breast is removed, but it could also be seen as a way that these warrior women could take on the dual roles of a nurturing mother and as a super masculine fighter.

We are also given some aetiological explanations for place names such as Heracleia, and a ritualistic story of human sacrifice at Troy. This latter explanation was probably a later addition to explain the outrageous custom or rumor of human sacrifice.

Labor X: The Cattle of Geryones

The tenth labor Eurystheus commanded Heracles to perform was to bring back the Cattle of Geryones from Erytheia. Erytheia (now called Gadeira) was an island lying near Oceanos. Geryones, the son of Chrysaor and Callirrhoe daughter of Oceonos, lived here. He had a body that was three men grown together, joined into one at the belly but separated into three from the waist down. He had red cattle, which were herded by Eurytion and guarded by Orthos, the two-headed dog that was the offspring of Echidna and Typhon. So traveling across Europe in quest of the cattle of Geryones, he killed many wild beasts before arriving in Libya. Going to Tartessos, he set up as tokens of his journey two facing pillars at, the limits of Europe and Libya. When he was made hot by Helios during his journey, he pulled his bow back and took aim at the god. Helios marveled at his courage and gave him a golden cup in which he traveled across Oceanos. Arriving in Erytheia, he camped on Mount Abas. The dog sensed his presence and charged him, but Heracles hit it with his club and killed the cowherd Eurytion when he tried to help the dog. Menoites, who was there pasturing Hades' cattle, reported what had happened to Geryones, who caught up as he was driving the cattle along the Anthernous River. He joined battle with Heracles, was

shot by an arrow, and died. Heracles put the cattle into the
cup and sailed over to Tartessos, where he gave the cup back
to Helios.
He went through Abderia and arrived at Ligystine, where
Ialebion and Dercynos, the sons of Poseidon, stole the cows.
But Heracles killed them and went through Tyrrhenia. One
of the bulls broke loose at Rhegion, swiftly plunged into the
sea and swam to Sicily. Traveling through the nearby
territory, the bull came to the plain of Eryx, who was king of
the Elymoi. Eryx, the son of Poseidon, incorporated the bull
into his own herds. So Heracles handed the cattle over to
Hephaistos and hurried off in search of the bull. He
discovered it among the herds of Eryx who said that he
would not give it back unless Heracles wrestled and beat
him. Heracles beat him three times and killed him during the
match. He took the bull and drove it along with the others to
the Ionian Sea. When he reached the top of the Adriatic Sea,
Hera sent a gadfly against the cattle, and they were scattered
throughout the foothills of Thrace. Heracles chased after
them; he captured some and took them to the Hellespont, but
others were left behind and afterward, were wild. Because he
had such a hard time collecting the cows, he blamed the
Strymon River and, whereas in the old days its streams used
to be navigable, he filled it with rocks and rendered it
unnavigable. He brought the cows and gave them to
Eurystheus, who sacrificed them to Hera.

Heracles labor in obtaining the cattle was relatively easy, it was the journey to them and the journey home which was troublesome. If we look at this mythic task as if it were any normal, mundane project of some length then we can view the story as saying it is always the unexpected events which will draw out and complicate things. Like a long road trip, it is the unexpected breakdowns, booked out motels, or gas stations just out of reach that leads to the complications of the journey. Yet Heracles pushes on through all the hold ups and overcomes each issue as it comes, the trip takes longer than expected but through enduring persistence, he completes what he set out to do.

Figure 32: The monstrous Geryones whom Heracles dispatched is found in Dante's inferno where he is described as the monster of fraud. Here the monster is depicted in Gustave Dore's famous wood engravings showing us the widespread popularity for classical myth and the way in which it influenced writers through history.

This is an outer layer interpretation of the myth and to delve deeper into it is to dive into the world of the occult and ancient mysteries. Three is a sacred number, it represents completeness, perhaps a symbioses of mind-body-spirit all working in harmony. We actually see this number come up a lot in mythology, the earth is divided into three continents (Europe-Asia-Africa), the universe into three spheres (heaven-earth-hades) and the mind into three partitions (rational-emotional-animal). When the three are balanced then spiritual enlightenment is near, and this is why we see the number become prevalent in the last three labors of Heracles. We see the three-headed giant Geryon (labor ten), next is the three Hesperides (labor eleven), and lastly, the three-headed dog Cerberus (labor twelve).

The interpretation that Heracles is now reaching the final stages of obtaining godhood and enlightenment is strengthened by the geographical location of each of these last tasks. Eurystheus is now literally sending him to the ends of the earth, and more importantly, he is sending Heracles to the west - the place of death where the sun sets each day. If we look at a map of how the ancient Greeks saw their world, the heroes descent into the underworld in the final labor is like crossing the veil and finally obtaining that spiritual completion. These last labors have been journeying to the ends of the earth, where his ego slowly dies until he can slip through to the underworld and truly achieve completion. However, we are not there yet. Let's look at the Cattle of Geryones closer before we go on.

We see on his journey to the cattle, that Heracles is barred by the two-headed dog Orthos. In mythology, this dog is actually the brother to the three-headed Cerberus which we will encounter later. Now the two heads of this dog are symbolic of duality, and specifically the duality within the mind. What we are observing in Heracles mythic cycle is the distillation of the mind until it reaches enlightenment, and at this advanced stage, Heracles must now face the negative attributes of duality. This duality presents itself in contradictions of thought which gives birth to self-doubt. Heracles very quickly and swiftly deals the death blow to Orthos and literally crushes that doubt. And this is how it is to be dealt with, and we see that it has to be destroyed outright because it allows Heracles to move forward and the doubt does not return to disturb him. So the author is telling his audience that when you are on the journey, destroy any inclinations of doubt outright lest it holds you up and plagues you.

The issue with duality continues though as Heracles encounters the triple-headed giant Geryones. Heracles shoots the giant in the stomach, the place where all three aspects of the monster join into one. Symbolically this represents reducing plurality back to unity, which is the goal of the spiritual path in all occult systems. To remove the idea that you are one of many and to replace it with the understanding that all are one is the crowning achievement of enlightenment.

It may be worth mentioning now that the two pillars of Heracles at the ends of the earth may be symbolic of unifying this duality. Perhaps by sailing between them, one can be seen as finding the middle path between polar opposites. This aspect of the story may have been taken as literal later on and the Rock of Gibraltar given as the locale in an attempt for aetiological reasoning.

Now, on his return home, we see Heracles being plagues by Hera once again. She sends down a gadfly to disperse his cattle which takes him a great amount of time and effort to recover. This episode works in a similar fashion as that of *The Tower* card in the tarot. The great tower Heracles has built up to this point, symbolized by the herd of cattle (where each is representative of a different aspect of his hard earned beliefs), is destroyed and scattered by Hera. This destruction is devastating, but it allows Heracles to build a new dynamic belief system so he can freshly incorporate the knowledge of unity.

The episode with Eryx may be a ritual explanation which Frazer would describe as a *year-king,* similar to what we see in the Theseus mythic cycle when he wrestles Cercyon and has most likely been added to explain the customs of that land. Heracles anger at the Strymon River is an aetiological addition to explain why the rivers waters are poor for boats to navigate.

Labor XI: The Apples of the Hesperides

Although the labors were finished in eight years and one month, Eurystheus, who would not count the Cattle of Augeias or the Hydra, ordered Heracles as an eleventh labor to bring back the Golden Apples from the Hesperides. These apples were not in Libya, as some have said, but on Mount Atlas in the land of the Hyperboreans. Ge had given them as a gift to Zeus when he married Hera. They were guarded by an immortal serpent, the offspring of Typhon and Echidna, which had a hundred heads and used to talk with all sorts of various voices. Alongside the serpent, the Hesperides named Aigle, Erytheia Hesperia, and Arethousa stood guard. So Heracles traveled to the Echedoros River. Cycnos, the son of Ares and Pyrene, challenged him to single combat. When Ares tried to avenge Cycnos and met Heracles in a duel, a thunderbolt was thrown in between the two and broke up the fight. Traveling through Illyria and hurrying to the Eridanos River, Heracles came to some Nymphs, daughter of Zeus and Themis. These Nymphs pointed out Nereus to him. Taking hold of him as he slept, Heracles tied Nereus up though he turned into all sorts of shapes. He did not release him until he learned where the apples and the Hesperides were. After he got this information, he passed through Libya. Poseidon's son Antaios, who used to kill strangers by forcing them to wrestle, was king of this land. When Heracles was forced to wrestle with him, he lifted him off the ground in a bear hug, broke his back, and killed him. He did this because it happened that Antaios grew stronger when he touched the earth. This is why some said that he was the son of Ge.

He passed through Egypt after Libya. Bousiris, the son of Poseidon and Lysianassa daughter of Epaphos, was king there. He had to sacrifice foreigners on an altar of Zeus in accordance with a prophecy. For nine years barrenness befell Egypt when Phraisios, a seer by profession, arrived from Cyprus and said that the barrenness would end if a foreigner were sacrificed every year to Zeus. Bousiris sacrificed the seer first and then went on to sacrifice those foreigners who landed on his shores. Heracles too was seized and brought to the altars. He broke the chains and killed both Bousiris and his son, Amphidamas.

Passing through Asia, he came to Thermydrai, the harbor of the Lindians. He loosed one of the bulls from a cart-driver's wagon, sacrificed it, and feasted. The driver was unable to protect himself, so he stood on a certain mountain and called down curses. For this reason, even today when they sacrifice to Heracles, they do so with curses.

Skirting Arabia, he killed Tithonos' son Emathion, and, traveling across Libya to the outer sea, he received the cup from Helios. Crossing over to the continent on the other side, on Mount Caucasus he shot down the eagle that ate Prometheus' liver and that was the offspring of Echidna and Typhon. He freed Prometheus after taking the bond of the olive for himself, and to Zeus, he offered up Cheiron, who was willing to die in Prometheus' place despite being immortal.

Prometheus told Heracles not to go after the apples himself, but to take over holding up the sky from Atlas and send him instead. So when he came to Atlas in the land of the Hyperboreans Heracles followed this advice and took over holding up the sky. After getting three apples from the

Hesperides, Atlas came back to Heracles. Atlas, not wanting to hold the sky said that he would himself carry the apples to Eurystheus and bade Heracles hold up the sky in his stead. Heracles promised to do so but succeeded by craft in putting it on Atlas instead. For at the advice of Prometheus he begged Atlas to hold up the sky because he wanted to put a pad on his head. When he heard this, Atlas put the apples down on the ground and took over holding up the sky, so Heracles picked them up and left. But some say that he did not get them from Atlas, but that he himself picked the apples after killing the guardian serpent. He brought the apples and gave them to Eurystheus. After he got them, he gave them to Heracles as a gift. Athena received them from him and took them back, for it was not holy for them to be put just anywhere.

The reader should not overlook that the details from the events in the Garden of Eden in the Biblical *Genesis* are uncannily similar to those in this story. We have sacred apples guarded by a serpent that are linked to the first primordial man and woman - Zeus and Hera. It should be of interest to us than of what these apples represent as they are the focal point of the episode. In his work *On Heracles*, Herodorus writes about these apples and their relation to Heracles,

These are the apples the myth says he took away after killing the serpent with his club, that is to say, after overcoming the worthless and difficult argument inspired by his keen desire, using the club of philosophy while wearing noble purpose wrapped around him like a lion's skin. Thus he took possession of the three apples, i.e., three virtues: to not grow angry, to not love money, and to not love pleasure.
- Herodorus, On Heracles

So we see an ancient interpretation is in line with our idea that Heracles is journeying toward enlightenment.

There are three events in this episode that can be interpreted through Frazer's ideas of ritualistic interpretation. They are; wrestling with Antaios, the sacrifices of Bousiris, and cursing Heracles during sacrifice. Each of these appears to describe, and thus explain, the certain customs of certain people. I believe this is the case for the third event, but the first two I believe are linked with Heracles journey to enlightenment.

The giant Antaios is a son of the earth goddess Ge and grew stronger when he touched the ground. This could be symbolic of materialism, where Antaios represents the aspect of the psyche that desires for material wealth which grows stronger when it is surrounded by such. Heracles overcomes Antaios by lifting him into the air, for the soul this is removing itself from the material world and placing itself in the realm of the spirit - the air. So Heracles is raising his perception of the world from the mundane to the spiritual.

Now Heracles did not know where to find these apples, so he sought out Nereus who could answer his question. He wrestled Nereus as the sea god changed into every different shape and substance imaginable but held on until he received his answer. This appears to be a commentary on the ego and the way in which it behaves when it fears the inevitable 'ego-death' which occurs during enlightenment. Heracles holds onto Nereus and does not let the shape-shifters illusions distract him from his goal. He gains the knowledge of the location of the apples, in the land of the Hyperboreans - or paradise, which is symbolic of gaining insight into attaining his godhood.

Heracles in his travels toward the land of the Hyperboreans comes across Prometheus and frees him from his daily torture. This is important, we have talked about Prometheus before but now we will pull the threads of his meaning out a bit more. Prometheus' name means *forethought* and is telling of the aspect of the mind which is always thinking, always curious, looking for answers and ways to progress. However, he is chained to a rock and has his liver eaten every day by an eagle. This is telling us that his goals will never be fulfilled, he will never know everything. Yet the liver regenerates and the next day is eaten again. This side of the psyche will never rest of its own accord. It will never stop, yet it will never succeed. So Heracles frees it and in doing so releases himself from the need to know everything, it is the psychological acceptance that humanity and the individual will not find all the answers to life and that this is okay.

Heracles' last encounter is that with Atlas. It is at this time that Heracles must take on the role of the Titan and hold up the sky himself for a while. This may be symbolic of Heracles obtaining a direct link to the divine and for a period sharing in the knowledge of the gods. This kind of interpretation can be met as the sky is symbolic of the heavens. This task is not easy, nor is it enjoyable, being described as taking the weight of the world as we see often in portrayals of Atlas. However, it does allow Heracles to secure the apples, and these he can take away with him.

Labor XII: Cerberos

The bringing back of Cerberos from the house of Hades was ordered as a twelfth labor. Cerberos had three dog heads, the tail of a serpent, and along his back, the heads of all sorts of snakes. When Heracles was about to go off to get him, he went to Eumolpos in Eleusis because he wanted to be initiated into the mysteries. Since he was unable to see the mysteries because he had not been purified of the killing of the Centaurs, Eumolpos purified him and then initiated him. He came to Tainaron in Laconia Where the cave that leads to the house of Hades is located. He made his descent through it. When the souls saw him, they all fled except for Meleagros and Medousa the Gorgon. He drew his sword against the Gorgon in the belief that she was still alive, but he learned from Hermes that she was just an empty phantom. When he went near the gates of Hades' realm, he found Theseus together with Peinthous, the man who tried to win Persephone's hand in marriage and for that reason was in bonds. When they caught sight of Heracles, they stretched forth their arms so that they could rise up by means of Heracles' might. He did take hold of Theseus by the hand and lift him up, but when he wanted to raise up Peirithous, the earth shook and he let go. He also rolled Ascalaphos' rock off. He wanted to provide some blood for the souls, so he slaughtered one of the cows of Hades. Their herder, Menoites son of Ceuthonymos, challenged Heracles to wrestle. Heracles grabbed him around the middle and broke his ribs. Menoites was saved when Persephone begged for mercy for him. When Heracles asked Plouton for Cerberos, Plouton told him to take him if he could defeat him without any of the weapons he carried. Heracles found Cerberos by the gates of Acheron, and, encased by his breastplate and covered entirely by the lion's skin, he threw his arms around Cerberos' head and did not stop holding on and choking the beast until he prevailed, even though he was being bitten by the serpent that served as his tail. So he took Cerberos and returned, making his ascent through Troizen. Demeter turned Ascalaphos into an owl;

Heracles showed Cerberos to Eurystheus and then brought him back to the house of Hades.

All of Heracles labors so far have led him to this final task. Each challenge has refined his character and soul to a point where he can finally undergo his chthonic adventure and journey into the underworld. As discussed earlier, the underworld is a symbolic feature of mythology to denote the individual journeying past the conscious mind and into their sub- and unconscious where they will face their shadow.

However, an individual cannot simply waltz into the underworld on their own accord, it is a dangerous land where the hero has just as much chance of perishing as they do of succeeding. Despite all his refinement, Heracles

Figure 33: Hercules leads Cerberos out of the underworld by a chain in an etching by Nicolo Van Aelst, 1608.

still needs to prepare himself for the journey ahead and this is why he goes to Eleusis.

Eleusis is home to the Mysteries of Demeter, and it is here that he is purified of all his blood guilt to date and is indoctrinated into the Eleusinian Mysteries. This prepares him for 'death' with the divine knowledge that all people are immortal and that the 'death' Heracles will endure when he ventures into the underworld is only the destruction of his own materialistic ego.

The underworld, or subconscious mind, is usually off limits to the living which is why it is guarded by the monstrous Cerberos. In modern psychology, we perceive the world around us through the eyes of our ego, but this is only a minute part of the much larger psyche. The greater body of the mind includes the subconscious and unconscious mind which is only unlocked through dreams. However, humanity has known the power of psychotropic drugs for unknown millennia and these allow the waking mind access to these deeper depths of the psyche. During the rites at Eleusis, the psychedelic drink, *kykeon*, was consumed by initiates allowing them an experience with the divine. As Heracles underwent these initiations in preparation for his journey, we can conclude that he had gained the key to his own underworld or subconscious.

This is why he enters the underworld unchallenged, Cerberos does not block his entrance as it would have for any other living mortal.

When he enters the underworld, all the spirits flee from Heracles and this is because of the refinement of his soul from the previous labors. These spirits might represent all the fears and weaknesses of Heracles unconscious mind but he has overcome them. When Meleagros and Medousa confront him, Heracles feels fear but has the bravery to attack them with his sword instead of fleeing. They only have the power to defeat him through fear, much as our own negative thoughts can only affect us if we allow them too. This is why Hermes reveals the true nature of the spirits. Hermes here is acting a *'psychopomp'*, or an intermediary between worlds, or an intermediary between the conscious and unconscious mind. So in a way, Hermes rationalized what these phantoms truly are so Heracles knows not to fear them.

Heracles then came to Theseus and Peirithous who were trapped by Hades within the underworld. It is worth mentioning now the beautiful intricacies of Greek mythology and the way in which separate mythic cycles become intertwined within each other creating a living and breathing world. It is important to understand this separate myth, so I will quickly paraphrase.

Theseus and Peirithous agreed to marry the daughters of Zeus. Theseus chose Helen of Troy and kidnapped her, Peirithous chose Persephone, the wife of Hades. So the two heroes went to the underworld to kidnap her but Hades knew of their intentions. He had the pair sit at his feast table but fooled them, having them seated in the chairs of *forgetfulness* from which they could not get back out. This is where Heracles finds them.

Heracles manages to free Theseus, but Peirithous is forced by Hades to remain. This episode is symbolic in portraying the role of intent and spiritual evolution. Because Peirithous came to the underworld with ignoble intentions he is trapped there forever, giving the audience insight into the consequences of failing within their own subconscious. Theseus was there to help his friend, he also failed in the underworld but retained his purity and so could be freed. This is a commentary on the various perspectives of intention and purity and how they play out during the journey for spiritual enlightenment.

Next comes Heracles encounter with Plouton (Hades himself), where we see a peculiar episode take place. Heracles asks permission to take Cerberos. This is important because it shows our hero paying respect to the powers of the underworld, or to interpret this, he is respecting the powers of his own unconscious which is terribly important in understanding and accepting love for ones whole being. With the struggle with Cerberos to come, this can be seen as Heracles encounter with his shadow, he is accepting its existence and bringing it into himself without succumbing to it.

Heracles defeats Cerberos without any weapons and only bears his armor and the cloak of the Cithaironian Lion. This is telling us that his only defenses are those that he has won through his hardships and is symbolic of the inner strength that he has attained. It is bringing to a point that all of Heracles deeds to date have in fact led him to this moment, the final conflict. So Cerberos can be seen as Heracles shadow which he successfully defeats.

Cerberos is taken to Eurystheus before being returned to guard the gates of the underworld so that future individuals who attempt the same journey have the opportunity to face their own shadow.

Eurystheus freed Heracles from performing any future labors under his command. Heracles had paid his penance and had transformed his self from a mortal living in ignorance to a hero full of divine knowledge. This is why he was granted deification by Zeus after his death.

After The Labors

The mythology surrounding Heracles continues after the twelfth labor, but I have omitted them from our analysis on purpose. It is my own belief that the mythic cycle of Heracles involving his labors is in itself a complete unit having a beginning, middle, and end, and did not need the additional stories that were added. It appears that with the increasing popularity of Heracles, more stories were added to credit certain towns, places, and people with having been associated with him. There is no doubt that these later stories are also important and hold many mythic truths that are quite valuable, but you will find that the character of Heracles reverts back to its origin displaying no spiritual advancement that he worked so hard to obtain through his twelve labors. It is because of this that I have left them out of our study so that we can focus on his spiritual journey.

Over-Arching Interpretations

Throughout the telling, we broke down individual aspects of Heracles' twelve labors but that did not give us the opportunity to look at the message as a whole or to observe overarching themes.

It should be clear to us now that the twelve labors are steps that Heracles is taking that will eventually lead him to a kind of spiritual awakening or enlightenment. This is the same enlightenment sought after by religious ascetics, occult practitioners, spiritualists, and philosophers. The journey is archetypal through the theories of Carl Jung, the stencil is more or less the same for all people and a set of experiences during the journey are experienced by everyone who pursue it. These twelve labors are mapping out these experiences as we slowly watch the evolution of Heracles' character.

Each of the labors encountered is an aspect of Heracles psyche, they display a negative trait in which he must use the positive to overcome. In doing so, he manages to accept the negative poles of his inner being and negate them by finding the strength to display the positive instead. In this way be bridges the opposing poles of his psyche to find enlightenment through the middle path. This may be the hidden meaning behind the Pillars of Heracles. If you imagine each pillar as a polar opposite of an emotion or character trait (i.e. love and hate) then the waters between them are the middle ground or balance. By sailing between the emotional extremities, one can safely navigate these hazardous water and reach paradise, the land of the Hyperboreans.

That is what this mythic cycle is telling. Yet there are other aspects interwoven that are of interest to us. It was mentioned earlier, but we will now elaborate, that there is an odd theme involved of woman versus man or femininity against masculinity. This is portrayed as Hera's hatred toward Heracles which is truly a vengeance against his father, Zeus. Each of the monsters Heracles fought was created in the pre-Olympian, primordial age. These are seen as belonging to the Earth-Goddess, and hence they are earthly representations of Hera's wrath. Heracles is the son of Zeus, so in a similar fashion, he is seen as the earthly representation of the Sky-God. He slowly works his way through the land and destroys or banishes each representation of the Earth-Goddess and installs in their place the rulership of the masculine Sky-God. This is an artistic way to explain the subjugation for maternal societies and their replacement for a masculine dominated world view which is what we see in classical Greece.

Following the same dialogue, these events also show the world going from a place of chaos to one of civilized order. This is reminiscent of the Titanomachy in Hesiod's *Theogony* and may be simply another way of explaining the same fundamental message. Heracles is destroying the chaotic monsters of the land to create order which is patronized by the Olympian gods under the leadership of the masculine Zeus.

Figure 34: Heracles is flanked by the goddesses Vice and Virtue in Annibale Carracci's the Choice of Heracles (c. 1596).

The Pursuit Of Virtue

We are introduced to Heracles as a the archetype of a Greek warrior. He is the strongest man on earth and seems to know no fear. He excels in learning the arts of war and does not flee from battle. All this is shown to us and he might well be admired for his youthful greatness, however, he has a darker side. He is impatient, he killed his teacher Linos. He has a weakness for women and drink. And most frightening of all, he was cruel in his dealing with the Minyans and horrific in his madness that resulted in the death of his family. It was this final point that Heracles came to a crossroads in his life and was forced to choose which way he wanted to lead his life. Either through lustful vice or through the pursuit of virtue. It is this moment that the Greek scholars called the *Choice of Heracles*.

Heracles chose to pursue virtue, and in the Greek world, this was called *pathos*, the virtuous struggle against trials that would lead to the immortality of the soul. For those interested, this episode is written beautifully by Xenophon, a student of Socrates, in his work *Memorabilia*.

The Heroic Cycle Of Heracles

The mythic cycle of Heracles can be seen in a micro or macrocosmic way. The microcosmic would have us interpret the mini mythic cycles for each of his twelve labors. This can be done as each is a small myth in its own way, however, we are going to look at the larger picture and explain the entire myth in the terms of Joseph Campbell's monomyth.

The Ordinary World
Prior to the beginning of his labors, we are introduced to Heracles and his life from infancy. This sets us up for his 'ordinary world' - or at least the world that he is used to. We see him grow up in Thebes and learn the ways of a

Greek warrior and even take part in some fights with the Minyans. He is married and fits well into his society.

Call To Adventure

Despite the relative normality of Heracles' life, not all is well, and this is shown to the audience through the fits of rage that regularly plague him. One such episode really brings this to the forefront and that is the killing of his family. The guilt he receives from this is the catalyst that leads to his adventures.

Refusal Of The Call

The version of Heracles' myth given to us by Apollodorus does not give us a refusal of the call. However, in other recitations of the story, Heracles breaks down after murdering his family and wishes to kill himself. This in its own right is a refusal to take proper action. It is only through the advice of Theseus does Heracles find the strength to seek atonement.

Meeting With The Mentor

He travels to Delphi to speak with the Oracle and is told to go to Eurystheus and complete ten labors which will absolve him from the guilt of his murders. This is the advice given to him which can be seen as a meeting with the mentor but also sits with the call to adventure.

Crossing The Threshold

Once Heracles has agreed to perform the tasks for Eurystheus, he crosses the threshold properly and enters the realm of mythology as he undergoes his first labor.

Tests, Allies, Enemies

This stage of the heroic cycle makes up the bulk of the stories associated with Heracles. It is all ten of the labors he undergoes until he must travel to the land of the Hyperboreans. Heracles is tested through the labors, meets the few friends that help him on his journey, and discovers the enemies who will try and stop him.

Approach To The Innermost Cave

The innermost cave is Heracles descent into the underworld, and it can be argued that all his labors constitute the approach to this final episode. However, it is better to say that this stage is defined by Heracles travels to the land of the Hyperboreans as this is a geographic journey literally to the ends of the world before the Ocean-River gives in to the boundaries of Hades. However, I believe the approach is better defined as the preparations seen in the twelfth labor before venturing to the underworld. I think Heracles' approach to the innermost cave is his time spent at Eleusis as this was a period where he learned the final mysteries of life that would truly prepare him for what follows.

Ordeal

The climatic ordeal for Heracles is undoubtedly his confrontation of the hell-hound Cerberos. As Jung explains the final ordeal as the encounter with one's own shadow, this can be the interpretation we use for this episode. It is his last task before he may re-emerge from the underworld.

Reward

The reward that Heracles wins is not anything physical. The myth portrays a plethora of items that he 'wins' along the way like his lion coat and poisoned arrows, however, these are symbolic for the evolution of his mental faculties. Heracles true reward for his adventures is enlightenment, and this is what he brings back from the underworld.

The Road Back

The road back does exist for Heracles though I have omitted it from our study. It involves a number of extra myths, adventures, and events that take place after Heracles completed his twelve labors and shows the audience the problems with a hero returning to normal life, which for Heracles is impossible.

Resurrection

Heracles is literally resurrected in his mythology. Upon his mortal death, the gods deem that he has lived a life worthy of deification and take him up into Mount Olympus, granting him immortality.

Return With The Elixir

Finally, the return with the elixir can best be interpreted as the positive impact each of Heracles' deeds has done for society. As we discussed, he removed the old chaotic ways of the world, represented through each monster, and replaced them with the order granted by the sky god, Zeus.

The Roman Hercules & Beyond

The Romans loved Heracles, his name is found in the Latin as *Hercules* which was given to them through the Etruscans (where he is called *Hercle, Heracle,* and, *Herceler*) who themselves indoctrinated the myths from the Greeks. In this way we see the way in which cultures mix and mingle, the Greek colonies and traders in Italy would have been in direct contact with the Etruscans and through them, the mythology of Hercules spread and remained on the peninsula.

Figure 35: Here we see a posthumous bust (191 A.D.) of the Roman emperor Commodus. He has likened himself to Hercules as can be seen from the lion's skin, club, and apple of the Hesperides.

Because of the wide popularity of Heracles, everybody wanted to be associated with him in one way or another. Cities would compete for his birthplace, others would claim the hero passed through during his adventures. The world became alive with monuments and markers of the achievements of the hero and many individuals tried to draw a direct hereditary link to him, proclaiming that they were descended through one of Heracles many love affairs.

Rome was not innocent from this kind of *Hercules-mania* and we see many later Herculean myths directly associated with Rome and Latin culture. One of these is Hercules defeat of Cacus, who was rampaging across the Roman countryside. Hercules was also linked with Rome itself, the Aventine Hill being named after the hero's son, *Aventinus*. His story with Cacus not only relates Heracles with the city of Rome but is also used as a ritual and aetiological explanation for the location of the *Ara Maxima*, which was later the cattle market for Rome called the *Forum Boarium* which still holds ruins of temples to *Hercules Victor*.

Hercules held many stations in the general Roman belief system with shrines to him being found from Hispania through Gaul. He was held as a local deity, often called upon by expecting mothers due to the hero's victory over the hardships of his infancy. His prowess in combat was appreciated by the people, Mark Antony held him as his personal patron god and the Emperors Commodus and Maximian modeled themselves after the hero showing us his widespread appreciation in Latin culture.

The myth of Hercules spread throughout the ancient world and archaeological digs have found a number of club pendants, called *Donars Clubs*, that come from Germany dating to the second and third century A.D. Tacitus write about the love of Hercules from the Germanic Tribes, likening him to the proto-Thor god *Þunraz*. It has been postulated that these amulets later developed into the hammer of Thor found later in the Viking period.

The myths of Hercules lost their relevance in society until the resurrection of the love of classical culture during the Renaissance. During this time the mythic cycle of Hercules had a resurgence and scholars found many points to raise in the pursuit of virtue.

However, over time, the understanding of the myths true meaning was forgotten and people could only interpret Hercules as literal and saw him as slow, stupid, and acting as a buffoon. Episodes of complex symbolism, such as Hercules shooting an arrow at the sun, Helios, was interpreted as an inflated ego and a childish tantrum leaving society to believe the labors were merely a set of enjoyable stories to read.

This is where society stands now and many still do not realize the sacred importance of Hercules' mythic cycle. However, through the skills we have learned, we can read into the true depths of the story and see how it is a kind of ancient 'road-map' into achieving enlightenment. And beyond that, we can enjoy the intricate meanings behind the many philosophical thoughts woven throughout the story.

Hercules was the greatest hero of classical Greece and it was not because he was an idiot. It was due to his pursuit of virtue and his victory over incredible odds. He was the greatest hero because he raised himself from the life of an ignorant mortal to the enlightenment of godhood.

Modern Mythology

Adult Lives

For most of us it is hard to fathom why mythology could be important in our modern and adult lives. We no longer live in the archaic world of our far-off ancestors. In fact, in our modern world, we have become as powerful as the gods of ancient cultures. We can travel at unprecedented speeds, across the land, into the heavens, and deep into the oceans. Like Zeus' thunderbolt, we can destroy cities in seconds. Our technological advances allow us to manipulate the very essence of life, creating our own living monsters. So how could we, having achieved so much, need the mythic tales of our ancient ancestors? It seems that for all our achievements, we have delved deeper and deeper into the folly of shortsightedness. We have overloaded ourselves with information which is so readily available to us every day that we have become monstrous consumers, only valuing things with a monetary value. We have forgotten how to live and this is where mythology can save humanity.

One facet of society that has always existed is the human will and desire to tell stories. These stories unite us and make us human. They define our consciousness and make us self-aware, distilling the essence of what it is to be human. We have talked about the great men who have studied mythology, and all agree that the mythic patterns and archetypes shape how we as humans define and interact with the world around us. These stories put humanity into a retrospect with the rest of existence. They show us how to live.

For you see, even with our world rapidly advancing, human nature has not changed. We might see ourselves very differently to our ancient counterparts, but people have always and will always experience love and hate, fear and courage, hope and despair, and the rest of our wide scope of emotions. You can read the ancient stories and still feel the power of their universal truths and they might even remind you of what it is to be alive.

These mythologies of a lost time still apply to us today. We see the heartbreaking heroic return in the issues associated with repatriated soldier. Their struggles with post-traumatic stress disorder and the inability to return to the life they left behind is recorded nearly verbatim in the classical stories. The monstrous creatures are revealed in our darkest fears, the myths teach us how to deal with them while we turn our heads and try to blur the lines and fight our fear of aging, loss, and heartache. Then we can look at specifics, observe Dionysus and his attitude to drink and drugs. His followers revel in inebriation and we see the productive attributes of blurring social boundaries and the destructive side of problematic drunkenness. In Hesiod's Theogony, Zeus tells us that fire will be "a great plague to you and all of mankind," and here we are still trying to figure out how we can balance our dependence on combustion energy with its potential for catastrophic disaster.

Though you may not know myth, myth knows you and this is starkly obvious in the society we live. Companies use the archetypal images to speak to your subconscious.

Wear Pandora jewelry and be an all-gifted woman, consume Minotaur or Red Bull energy drinks to regain your strength, beware of Trojan Horse viruses that may come to you unexpectedly. Mythology is alive in our modern world. But it is not just in consumerism, we live in an age of great connectivity and we are lucky that our arts are still flourishing. The aspects of mythology have been passed down and are alive and well in the books we read, the music we listen to, the games we play, the art we admire, and the movies we watch. Mythology is not set, it is not stagnant, and it never has been. The stories are continually updated and evolve to meet the needs of new audiences. The concepts are reinvented and continue to inspire us. Mythology is still with us and its study is vitally important as it is integral to our self-definition, giving value to our lives. And so, I think it is important for us to explore this modern mythology, to see how close they come to those of the ancient world, and to see if we can apply some of the lessons we have viewed so far in these new works.

J.R.R Tolkien's The Lord Of The Rings

The Lord Of The Rings is a work of literature penned by J.R.R. Tolkien in the early 20th century. It exists in its own mythic world, constructed out of a "mythic-soup" of inspiration that the author was inspired by through his study of classical cultures. Tolkien stressed that his story was not allegorical and did not portray the political actions of his time. Despite this, many scholars have linked the tale to the events of his time, namely the build-up and execution of World War II. As he lived and wrote through this time, it is not hard to imagine that Tolkien would have been influenced by the current affairs of his era and that this influence would have found its way into his writing. With this in mind, a euhemeristic study of the Lord of the Rings may be well founded. But I do not believe that the true importance of the story lays here, perhaps an influence, but no more. Instead, I think that Tolkien used his literature to portray teachings that can only be found through the use of internal theories, namely through the psychoanalysis of characters and the decipherment of the vast ocean of symbolism that he created.

What Is The Ring?

The One Ring is the central point of focus in Tolkien's tale, yet its meaning is shrouded in mystery and is only alluded to in passing quotes. However, what it represents is of the utmost importance in understanding what it is that the story as a whole is trying to teach us. There is so much emphasis placed on the control and destruction of the Ring that it would seem a folly to overlook what it is actually representing.

To begin our deciphering of the symbolism, it may prove useful to look at the authors words directly, in a letter he sent in 1958, Tolkien writes about the One Ring.

"I should say that it was a mythical way of representing the truth that potency (or perhaps potentiality) if it is to be exercised, and produce results, has to be externalized and so as it were passes, to a greater or lesser degree, out of one's direct control."
- J.R.R. Tolkien, Letter #211, 1958

Through his words, we can see the long-standing tradition of representing metaphysical, abstract ideas through the use of physical objects in a mythological setting to show how they might play out in various situations. In Tolkien's case, he is using the ring to represent an odd phenomena - that all people have the potential to exercise action and this action will produce results. But for the results to be produced, the action must take place. However, at the moment that the action is externalized, the individual loses control of whatever reactions may take place afterward.

For example, a game of football is taking place, one of the players has the ball, he has the potential to shoot for the winning goal. He does so and scores, winning the match. He had the power to score that last point, but no longer has any power for the events that follow. For in scoring the final goal he may cause riots in the stands, people may be crushed and killed. Alternatively, there might a gratuitous roar as the audience breaks into celebration. The player held the original decision, the potential power, but through exercising it, lost direct control of the actions that followed. This is in effect what the One Ring represents. However, it is clear through the omniscient fear toward the Ring that it must represent more than this and that Tolkien has only told us half of the true meaning.

When keeping in mind that the ring is symbolizing potential power, one can begin to analyze the above. When you hold the potential for action, you gain strength as the exercising of that action is in your own hands. As you invest your time and energy into securing a successful outcome for the potential action, your (potential) power grows. However, should your plans be ruined before they are exercised, then you have not only lost the original power, but also that of the time and energy you spent building it up.

Gandalf explains to Frodo that the Ring has a will of its own, tying in with Tolkien's expression of a loss of control on exercised action. Gandalf also says that the Ring wants to be found, and this could be taken to mean that the potential for action wishes to be exercised, and that the individual in control of that potentiality has to take care of when, or if, it is put into action. Perhaps this is why we only see Frodo only use the ring in times of carelessness or necessity. He is aware that it needs to be controlled, and only under those dire circumstances does his mind, weakened through fear or carelessness, actually use the power he holds.

Slowly we start to see what Tolkien is trying to teach through his mythic symbolism. The ring literally represent the power that is held by all people. That power can be used for good, but its resulting effects are out of the hands of the individual and so can lead to good or evil reactions. The episodes entailing the One Ring are essentially showing the control, restraint, and forethought needed when contemplating the exercising of this power. In other words, our actions will bear consequences that are out of our control, so we need to be wise in the decisions we make.

The second half of the interpretation of the ring, which Tolkien did not express was in the nature of it being evil. The dark lord Sauron created the ring in darkness, in the dread realm of Mordor, by an evil lord, and for wicked intentions. The Ring is in essence evil, and through our interpretation so far, can now be seen as the potential to do evil actions.

Now, because the One Ring represents this abstract idea of an individual's potential to do evil, we see that different character react in drastically different ways to the effect of its power. This experimenting of varying scenarios is classic in mythology and allows us to observe how different character will act to the same stimulus. Sauron intends to use the power for selfish and evil deeds, bent on becoming overlord of the world. Isildur and the other men of Gondor want to use the ring to extend their power and defend their land. Lady Galadriel would use it to make herself a queen of the world, full of power and loved, yet feared by all people. Gandalf expresses that he would try to use the power for good, but through him, it would wreak havoc. But what is interestingly observed through Tolkien's narrative, is that no matter who bears the ring, it will always inevitably turn the wearer to evil and corruption. It is plain to see that evil actions, even if intended for good, will only lead to evil consequences. This could be a commentary on the corruptive nature of power as a whole. As Abraham Lincoln put it,

"Nearly all men can stand adversity, but if you want to test a man's character, give him power."

   This could not be truer when interpreting the interaction of the Ring with the characters in The Lord of the Rings. For example, we see Boromir struggle with the temptation of gaining power to the point that it destroyed him. Sauron is forever working to regain the power he lost and chases his goal regardless of the price. Galadriel is tempted but resists her inner urges. Gandalf fears what may become should he hold such power. Aragorn has no interest in the glory of bearing the ring of power. And most interestingly of all, though corrupted beyond repair by it, the only character to give the power of the ring away as a free choice was Bilbo, Frodo, and Sam. This interaction with the ring goes a long way in representing the corruptive aspects of power and how different personalities succumb, struggle, or overcome the evils of power.

Through this one object, the ring, Tolkien shows his audience through mythic symbolism how our choices have consequences, and how power can corrupt an individual.

Fellowship of the Archetypes

Frodo

Despite the continual oppression from external danger, Frodo's path is one of internal struggle. He is the ring bearer which is clearly a task that only he was strong enough to endure. This is seen by the reactions of everyone else on merely looking at the ring, let alone possessing it. Frodo sets out on his journey with a warm heart and full of optimism and it is these qualities that he must hold if his task is to be successful. Time and time again, Frodo is trialed by the ever presence of danger from both good and evil beings which are bent on taking away his possession. But it is the corruptive power of the ring which dictates Frodo's evolution in the story as we see his pure heart battle with the yearning temptation to wield the power of the ring. In the end, the ring is destroyed, but Frodo failed in its undoing, refusing to release it into the chasm of Mount Doom. But Frodo carried it all that way without fault, and his final failure may be because this was an impossible task for anyone. Its final destruction may even elude to the ever-present power of higher beings or divine providence. Frodo's return to the Shire and everyday life is a classic representation of the returned hero and we see that he simply cannot cope nor reintegrate into the life he was knew and loved. He has endured too much and been corrupted to heavily by his task and that is why we see him leave with the elves. And so we see Tolkien depicting the self-sacrifice of individuals all around us, who with open hearts do amazing feats in the name of good and yet are punished by a tormented mind forever after.

Sam

Sam acts as the ultimate protector of Frodo, though he lacks fighting prowess, he is instead rich in loyalty and love for Frodo. Sam's path is one of faith and reliability, he promises to never leave Frodo's side and never does. His challenge is to have the continence to always keep going, and this is trialed many times yet he never falters. His loyalty to Frodo was so much that when he believed his friend was dead, Sam picked up the ring to continue the mission. And when he found Frodo alive, Sam did not hesitate to return the ring to its rightful bearer. It is because we see Sam's choices to continually take the moral high ground that he returns to the Shire in a better state than he had left it. His heroic return is the opposite of Frodo, using the successes of the journey to improve his life, having the confidence to pursue the woman he loved and to build a life of happiness.

Aragorn

Aragorn's path is one of evolution. Born as the heir to the throne of Gondor, he cowers away from the position and we meet him as the anonymous ranger from the north, Strider. He has chosen to live as the shadowy ranger because it gives him the opportunity to stay away from his true role in the world. He hides from it because he fears the responsibilities of his destiny. However, as the story of The Lord of the Rings unfolds, we see the development of Aragorn from the forgotten Strider to the loved King of Men. Yet his transformation does not occur overnight but through enduring long lasting hardship. None of the challenges he faces are in vain and each supplies a lesson through experience which brings Aragorn closer to his ultimate state.

There are four stages to Aragorn's development, the first is his declaration at Elrond's council that he is the heir to Isildur, effectively accepting his identity. He conquers his inner urges to take the Ring from Frodo, showing to himself and the rest of the world that he has a good heart and iron will. He proves his valor and determination when he fought with the men of Rohan, showing the kingdom of men that he has the quality of a leader. Aragorn then accepts the gift of Isildur's reforged sword from Elrond, accepting his heritage and willingness to ascend to his seat of power. And finally, he shows compete acceptance of his new station as king by ordering the Men of the Mountain to fight with him knowing full well that they will only fight with the true king of Gondor.

His later coronation is only a visual ritual, for the internal transformation was already complete. Through Aragorn, we see that you cannot irk away from your destiny, but must accept and face it. Through self-control, hardship can be overcome and turned to the strength needed to rise to your proper station in life.

Gollum/Sméagol

Gollum serves as the trickster character in Tolkien's works, he is both humorous and helpful yet dangerous and deceitful. This duality is a clear portrayal of the parliament of the mind, and we often see Gollum fighting with himself internally on which actions to take. He is struggling with the evil urge to take the ring and the goodwill to help his master, Frodo. For much of the narrative, Gollum is able to overcome his dark nature showing an incredible strength of the mind through denying the darker urges that constantly nag him.

To quickly gloss over the other characters does not do them justice, but must be done in order to save time and space. Gandalf represents the Wise Old Man and a Mentor to the fellowship, often giving advice and wisdom in place of action knowing that the heroic journey of his friends would be stunted by his interference. Gimli and Legolas are helpers of the hero, yet can also represent industrialism and nature respectively. In the beginning, they are distrustful of each other yet find a common respect and love by the end allowing for a symbiotic nature. Merry and Pippin are both helpers of the hero and trickster-like characters adding a light-hearted aspect to the adventures. Elrond acts as a herald, announcing the journey for the heroes, and in places as a Mentor, shedding light and information where it is needed. Saruman can be seen as a Threshold Guardian to the fellowship, Gandalf's shadow, and in stark comparison to the Gimli-Legolas relationship, as a representation of industry exploiting nature resulting in its own demise. Lady Galadriel is a Mentor but also allows for a meeting with the goddess. Arwen acts as Aragorn's Anima, she is the feminine side of the hero which he must accept as part of himself. From early on in the tale we see that she bears the qualities that Aragorn strives for, in fact, she is so accepting of her role in society that she can freely give it away, not out of fear, but through love.

Themes Of Mythic Interest

Tolkien's work through The Lord Of The Rings is that of a genius, he layers the eternal truths of human nature with fanciful stories full of ethical experimentation. He undoubtedly makes commentary on the state of the world of his own time, but seamlessly integrates the state in which the world has always been. There are a plethora of lessons, commentaries, truths, and questions throughout his stories, and we will focus on some of the episodes and imagery which correlates with mythology proper.

To begin, we should take note of the evil fortifications which Sauron has built and inhabited, namely that of Dol Guldur, The Black Gate, and his primary residence, Barad-Dur, in Mordor. What is interesting to note is that Sauron's towers collapse as the ring is destroyed. We can see a direct link in imagery to the tarot card, The Tower. Following the cards interpretation, these dark fortifications of Sauron represent his belief system and the belief of all people in Middle Earth that they are wrestling constantly with a dark power. However, when the ring is destroyed, so too is Sauron's power, and as his belief in himself collapses, so to do the towers that he has built up. The fortifications are destroyed through a catastrophic event and the people are free of them. Through their destruction, the people of Middle Earth can rebuild a new future with purer foundations.

Tolkien also wrestles with a long-standing question of what the consequences of immortality are. For living forever must lead to surviving the death of everything and everyone who is mortal. The challenge put forth by the author is this, how is an immortal being affected by their love for a mortal. How do they deal with the inevitable loss of their love? This question is raised through the relationship of Aragorn and Arwen with a continuous commentary from Elrond. Arwen's belief being that death cannot be feared until you have gained something in life, and of course, this is added to by the fact that a life is not worth living unless you have gained something to lose. It is the two sides of the coin and they cannot be balanced. Arwen knows that if she does not love Aragorn then there is no point in living, yet the cost of that love will be great through its loss. Though put in an immortal/mortal perspective, the question is perfectly valid in the real world, for death will take us all. To love will inevitably lead to loss, but this is part of the human experience.

The possibilities and questions of an extended life are expanded further through the unnaturally long life of Bilbo and Sméagol, which was granted through their possession of the Ring. Here we see the negative attributes of a faux immortality. For these characters, the extended lifespan is a curse resulting in wasted years and decrepit health. Tolkien must have been influenced from the Greek myths of the Sybil, or perhaps Tithonus. In these tales we see mortals granted a wish from the Gods, they asked for immortality but forgot to ask for everlasting youth. The result, of course, being a life that lasted forever with the body slowly withering away to a husk with no hope for the release through death. To bring the position of Arwen forward again, we see that this is her fate but in her mental faculties. After the death of Aragorn, she will surely be faced with an endless life of grief and sadness. So we are being shown that death should not, in fact, be feared, it is a release from this world, a gift given to us for the alternative is an unimaginably horrid torture. This torture of an endless life is depicted through the Ringwraiths, they were once men who sought immortality through the power of magical rings, the reward for their desire being an existence of neither life nor death, but rather an empty enslavement to mere existence itself.

The links Tolkien makes to classical mythology are extensive but not altogether obvious. Looking at particular characters, you will find similarities with familiar heroes and gods, but this is not the author copying or attempting to cheat archetypes. For an example, the character Aragorn has an uncanny resemblance to Virgil's Aeneas. Both are born of noble blood, both endure a fall and are forced to wander the wilderness where they find their true selves, both are tempted by women (Eowyn and Dido), both are tasked to restore or build great cities (Minis Tirith and Rome), and both are married to women associated with these cities (Arwen and Lavinia). Gandalf has parallels with both the Greek Hermes and the Norse Odin. Through both, we see him as a link between the mortal and divine worlds. He acts as a helping guide for his charges. He travels at great speed, yet is usually on foot. And like the wandering Odin, Gandalf is depicted as an old man, yet is as strong and as nimble as a youth, wears a dark cloak, and is aided by his staff. Lady Galadriel is often likened to the Greek goddess Athena or Circe. She is feared by outsiders who do not know her and even shares similar titles, "Witch of the Golden Wood". Many feel threatened by her presence yet she is, in fact, a patroness of heroes, much like Athena.

Tolkien links courage and its various forms throughout his work. It is a misconception that the courageous know no fear for if there is no fear to overcome than courage cannot exist. In this, Tolkien places his characters in situations of absolute fear to see how they will react to the situation. Sam and Frodo must face a journey where the odds in their favor may as well not exist. Yet they show courage in their unrelenting pursuit to do good. The experimentation here is to see what drives the heroes, for Sam, it is undoubtedly due to his loyalty and love for Frodo, from which he would lay down his life to protect. For Frodo, he is driven by his desire to do good and overcome evil. These acts of bravery are contrasted by those of other characters. Take for example Boromir, he shows outstanding bravery, but for him, it is about his personal glory and even to his dying breath he only wishes to be thought of by others as brave. For him, courage comes through a desire for reputation, it does not come from goodness and so we see that he is willing to use others to secure his reward. It is in stark contrast to the courageous purity displayed by the other members of the tale. This theme of selfless courage in the face of impending doom must have been taken from the heroic narratives of the Norse. In their tales of the apocalyptic Ragnarok, we see a similar theme where the gods and their allies, knowing they are destined to lose, still go to the fight in defense of the world. It is a lesson of righteousness fueling courageous acts in the hope to bring goodness into existence. It is the selfless desire for pure good.

Finally, before we look at other modern mythology, I believe it is important to look at some uncanny similarities between Christianity and The Lord Of The Rings. The final scene of the destruction of the ring should not escape your critique as the last moments of Jesus Christ's life. Frodo is essentially bearing the evils of the world through the Ring, just as Jesus carried our sins. Like in the Biblical description, Frodo collapses on his march up Mount Doom and is carried by Sam the rest of the way acting like Simon of Cyrene for Jesus. To bring this parallel to a close, both Frodo and Jesus say "It is done," at the moment of destruction. Gandalf too is likened to Christ in his selfless acts in the Mines of Moria. Here he sacrifices his plans, his hopes, and his life to help the Fellowship further their journey to defeat evil. He faces off the demonic Balrog and falls. But like Christ, is resurrected in an immortal, pure form. Lastly, we must look at the fate of Boromir as it holds the teaching of redemption. Here we see a man who has failed through sin, betraying his friends through the folly of his own desire. Yet he redeems himself in his last moments, selflessly sacrificing himself for his friends in an act of goodwill. He defends Merry and Pippin in vain, but purity of his act saves his soul and he can die knowing his last acts were out of goodness. To finalize this thought, the words of Gandalf add weight to the interpretation, "But he [Boromir] escaped in the end... It was not in vain that the young hobbits came with us, if only for Boromir's sake."

The Tale Of Tithonus

There was once a Trojan king named Laomedon. His wife was the water nymph Strymo and by her, king Laomedon had two sons, Tithonus and Ganymede. The brothers grew up as princes and one day the Titan, Eos, goddess of the dawn, swooped down to earth and kidnapped the pair. She was inflamed with desire and yearned to have the brothers as her lovers. Eos loved Tithonus so much that she begged

Zeus to gift him immortality. The chief of the gods grumbled and asked if this is really what Eos wanted. She begged him again and again until he gave in and granted her hearts wish. Zeus gave Tithonus immortality so that he would live forever. But as the days turned into months, the months into years, and the years into decades, Tithonius began to grow old. His skin loosened and his hair grayed, his eyes dulled and the youth Eos had loved was fading into an old man. She could not fathom what was wrong. Time continued to flow and Tithonius youth and vigor became a distant memory. His strength withered away until he could no longer bear to lift his arms or raise his head yet he would not pass from this life. Eos was heartbroken, she took her lover and hid him away in a golden room. Tithonius babbled in his madness and wished for death, yet it never came. His body shriveled and dried up, it became the prison of his mind. No release came for Tithonius for he had been granted immortality, but his lover had forgotten to ask for everlasting youth.

Some say Zeus pitied Tithonus and transformed the husky remains of his body into a cicada, forever living but singing for deaths embrace.

***

Jim Henson's Labyrinth

Directed by Jim Henson and produced by George Lucas, Labyrinth was a movie released in 1986. It has all the hallmarks of a great Hollywood film but is layered with mythological themes which both Henson and Lucas had been experimenting with in their earlier films (The Dark Crystal and Star Wars respectively). The film follows the mythic journey of the teenager Sarah as she makes her way to recover her lost brother from Jareth's (David Bowie) labyrinth empire, however, in the end, she finds a lot more in that maze then she could ever have imagined.

Sarah's Heroic Cycle

Labyrinth is interesting in that it portrays the mythic cycle through the eyes of the feminine, casting the central protagonist as a teenage girl on the precipice of puberty. As the viewpoint of the journey is through the feminine perspective, we see a flip too many of the images we are used to, however, in the long run, the message and journey is the same. Using the heroic cycle talked about in chapter 11, we can begin to analyze Sarah's story.

Stage I: Departure

1. THE ORDINARY WORLD.

We meet Sarah in the beginning of the movie as a girl who is completely engrossed in her own fairy tale. She is pretending to be the princess of her make-believe fantasies and the symbolism is evident by the excess of stuffed toys, posters, and fairy tale books that she surrounds herself in. However, this is a false world that she has constructed in an attempt to escape from the regular life she leads which is filled with the internal conflict of her mind. She sees her stepmother as a "wicked witch" and is wrestling with her place in the new family dynamics, the false fantasy she has constructed is an attempt to run from confronting the things that she fears.

2. THE CALL TO ADVENTURE.

The call to adventure comes to Sarah when she curses her baby brother, calling on the Goblin King to come and take him away. To her surprise, the wish comes true and the adventure is announced by Jareth who challenges her to resolve the issue she has created. This is a mirror to her own juvenile psyche. Unable to find her place in the family, she lashes out at those that have disturbed her order (her step-mother and baby brother). In her own mind, she had already pushed them away and it is this confliction within her mind which her journeys through the labyrinth are dealing with.

3. REFUSAL OF THE CALL.

It is important to note that Sarah does not outright refuse the call to action. The heroic cycle is a rough guide that myths usually do not completely fit. Stages may be presented in different orders, repeated, or nonexistent altogether. It is this variation which makes all myths the same in nature but different in character, it is why Campbell called his great work The Hero With A Thousand Faces - it is the same hero, but with different presentations.

4. MEETING WITH THE MENTOR.

Hoggle meets Sarah as she is transported to Jareth's world and acts as a kind of mentor by offering Sarah advice on how to navigate the maze. It is through his advice that we see Sarah gain the confidence to begin, but her immaturity shows as she does not heed all of Hoggle's advice.

5. CROSSING THE THRESHOLD.

The threshold is crossed in the moment that Sarah arrives in the realm of the Goblin King. This is symbolized when the fairy, whom she thinks is sweet, bites her on the nose and shatters her illusion that all is well. Jareth has given her 13 hours to complete the maze and save her brother initializing the quest for Sarah. At this point the concept of mythic time should be obvious as the 13 hours given is purposefully ambiguous and we see on her return that in the real world hardly any time had passed at all.

Stage II: Initiation

6. TESTS, ALLIES AND ENEMIES.

Sarah meets many characters along the way but must choose wisely on who to trust. Some of the characters include a re-meet with Hoggle, the beast Ludo, Sir Didymus and Ambrosius. Each of these characters test her in one way or another, whether it be Sarah's quick judgment of Ludo or her over trusting of Hoggle. In any case, these friends help her in her journey and teach her lessons that will later transition her into an understanding of what it is to be an adult. This stage is defined by the many riddles and obstacles that Sarah must overcome, each leading her closer to Jareth's castle and her baby brother.

7. THE INNERMOST CAVE.

The innermost cave is the "Escher-esque" stage of the palace, it is the innermost part of the labyrinth itself and Sarah must enter it alone. The confusing chamber is symbolic for the chaotic state of Sarah's mind. It is now that she must pull all the threads of what she has learned together to make sense of her journey and be successful.

8. THE ORDEAL.

Sarah confronts Jareth and he does all in his power to confuse and allure her to his control. However, in a moment of clarity, Sarah remembers what it is she has to do. She recites the line of the play she had forgotten earlier and states to Jareth, "you have no power over me!" This line has several levels, firstly it shows that Sarah had the power within her all the time. She had only forgotten the line from the beginning but the knowledge had followed her the whole way through. Secondly, it shows that the heroes shadow does not have power of the hero unless it is allowed. It is the dark side of the psyche and Sarah knows that in the end, it is her that has the power and not him.

9. THE REWARD.

Sarah is rewarded with her baby brother's safety, but also a new appreciation for life now that she has confidence in her own abilities. She has gained confidence, learned responsibility, and acquired a level of self-respect which allows her to transition into adulthood.

Stage III: Return
10. THE ROAD BACK.

The road back for Sarah is simple, for as she breaks the spell of Jareth, she is instantly transported home.

11. THE RESURRECTION.

Because the road back is simplified, the resurrection does not really occur.

12. RETURN WITH THE ELIXIR.

Sarah's return home shows her act with a renewed appreciation and understanding for her world. She has successfully bridged the gap between her conflicting views. This is evident with her care and love for her baby brother, shown by tucking him into bed and has gained a new respect for her step-mother. Sarah has successfully transitioned into her new stage of life and we know this as she symbolically packs away all the toys and images of her childhood.

Themes & Symbols

Labyrinth is packed with symbolism and long-standing themes from classical mythology. The movie plays with archetypes and through all of this shows the audience some of the mythical truths that are abound in every good tale.

To begin, the fact that Sarah is cast as a pubescent girl is no accident. The story itself is a kind of "coming of age" tale, where an immature Sarah must evolve her psyche to live in an adult world full of responsibility. This time of transition is mystical period, the world within the Labyrinth is neither day nor night adding emphasis on this symbolism. The journey is magical, it is luminal, it is a period of transition both physically from girl to womanhood and mentally from immaturity to responsibility. This is taken straight out of classical mythology and is part of Jung's collective unconscious.

Greek culture played out the same theme through the initiation rites of Artemis where a girl would undergo numerous trials to pass into womanhood.

The labyrinth itself is a chthonic realm, a kind of womb from which Sarah must pass through to be reborn. However, this rebirth is that of the mind and because of this it is an ever-changing place where things are not what they seem. The paths twist and turn and she must solve riddles and outwit monsters to further her progress. The imagery of the maze constantly changes and this is a parallel for the changing understanding within Sarah's mind. The music for Labyrinth was composed by David Bowie, and the lyrics are very specific to the metaphors for transition. Below is a segment of the song Underground which is worth considering as it depicts loss as a sacrifice for acquiring physical and mental treasures.

Underground - David Bowie (1986)

Down in the underground
You'll find someone true
A land serene
A crystal moon

It's only forever
Not long at all
Lost and lonely
That's underground

The lyrics are purposefully ambiguous to add to the mythic feel of the events occurring. But deciphering them is relatively straightforward, deep in the underground (the psyche), you can find a land serene (peace of mind). However, lost and lonely one can lose their way in the underground and never gain that serenity. It is a warning that Jung also emphasizes when one confronts the shadow. To go deep into your subconscious can be a terrifyingly dangerous adventure, the rewards are richer than can be imagined but there is also no promise of success or return. After all, there is just as much chance of being consumed by the shadow as there is of overcoming it.

It should come to no surprise to us that Sarah's shadow is Jareth. However, it does come as an often overlooked fact though that 99% of the characters in Labyrinth are male. This is quite purposeful and meaningful as it shows us that Sarah is struggling to come to terms with life in a male-dominated world. Jareth is both the shadow and animus to Sarah, and by her working with the male characters during the journey she slowly comes to term with how to assimilate her animus into herself and understand the masculine mind. This is how she learns that Jareth is part of her and therefore does not actually have power without her, making Sarah stronger than him.

As she deals with these males she learns to follow her intuition, making decisions on who to trust and who not to. These in themselves offer her a great many teachings including the nature of trust, betrayal, and redemption. This lesson comes to her through the actions of Hoggle. A little creature who at first is genuinely friendly and helpful to her but later betrays her trust and offers her to Jareth. It may be interesting to note the episode where Hoggle offers Sarah a peach that bewitches her to a new fantasy land. This is a parallel to the ancient Greek tale of Demeter, where Hades fools Persephone with a pomegranate seed which traps her in the underworld. Hoggle, full of remorse, redeems himself and Sarah learns two great lessons, the first being the virtues of forgiveness, the second that in the end, she can only ever rely on herself and her own resources.

With this idea of Sarah only being able to rely on herself, we see an interesting theme which has begun to present itself. Sarah no longer obeys the authority of others, she disobeys and challenges Jareth, defying his threats and urges on toward his castle. This is symbolic for Sarah beginning to think for herself rather than letting those of "higher-authority" do the thinking for her. Of course, now that she starts to think for herself, she has taken the first steps toward attaining adulthood and independence.

At the beginning of the film we saw that Sarah surrounded herself with fairy tales and a careful look at these images shows us that they are in fact all the characters within the labyrinth. This beckons the question of whether the labyrinth is real or another one of Sarah's fantasy constructs. The answer is both and this will be elaborated on soon. First, let's look at what Jareth is. Jareth is Sarah's minotaur, he is the Goblin King but also the only male adult in this world. He is the monster Sarah must face and acts as the villain, but she is also alluded to his seductiveness. He is wise in the knowledge he imparts to her, yet wicked in his dealings, and these polarized qualities show us how Sarah is stuck in the process of transitioning in her understanding of the world. In the end, Jareth is still just another construction of Sarah's fantasy world, and this is evident in his words to her,

"I have done everything you wanted."
"I am exhausted living up to your expectations."

Jareth is a construct of Sarah's mind, created by her to understand that not everything in life is easy and that you must take the good with the bad.

So, the Labyrinth is another one of Sarah's fantasy constructs, though this one is very different to her playing as a princess at the start of the movie. The variation is in that at the beginning, Sarah used her fantasies as an escape, but in the Labyrinth, the fantasy is used to understand life. In this way, it is clear that the mythological world can be either destructive or productive based on whether you are looking for an escape from life or for knowledge on how to live in it.

Led Zeppelin's Stairway To Heaven

For our last subject on modern mythology, I wanted to look at the world of music. It seems fitting to end this work in the place that it begun, for our earliest tales were undoubtedly told through song and verse. So as we come full circle, it should also be apparent that mythology exists in many forms, some less expected than others.

The decision to use Led Zeppelin's Stairway To Heaven (1971) was not an easy choice to make. There is a surplus of modern songs that deal with mythic themes and are symbolic, however, popular modern music does not follow all the rules which we have discussed so far and so necessitate a deeper study into the meanings of the lyrics. The poetry of Robert Plant seemed a perfect point to display this due to his widespread popularity, but also because he appears to be very knowledgeable in the secrets of symbolism and mythic truths.

The social historian Erik Davis gives us insight into the importance of Stairway To Heaven (Barker, David, 33 1/3

Greatest Hits, Volume 1. Pg. 201), describing it as resonating to the listener in a primordial way. This is true, the song sings to archetypal features that are true to all people and we are going to discover why.

Interpreting Stairway To Heaven - Led Zeppelin (1971)

There's a lady who's sure all that glitters is gold
And she's buying a stairway to heaven
When she gets there she knows, if the stores are all closed
With a word, she can get what she came for
Ooh, ooh, and she's buying a stairway to heaven

This first verse sets the listener up in the same way that first stage of the mythic cycle does (The ordinary World) where we are shown a glimpse of the hero in daily life. Here we have a lady who is cynical and shows her immaturity through a reliance on wealth. She believes that she is above others and can even buy her way into heaven (a realm of the spirit) with the materials she has accumulated.

There's a sign on the wall but she wants to be sure
'Cause you know sometimes words have two meanings
In a tree by the brook, there's a songbird who sings
Sometimes all of our thoughts are misgiven
Ooh, it makes me wonder
Ooh, it makes me wonder

The wondering talked about here is the beginnings of questioning this material world. The woman who is so sure of her accumulated material wealth is wondering what it really is worth, she is starting to question her reality. In terms of the mythic cycle, this is the hero discovering or coming to terms with the fact that not all in their world is right. The woman has been fooled by the world to think that the mundane is all there is to existence, but nature is suggesting that her thoughts might be misgiven.

There's a feeling I get when I look to the west
And my spirit is crying for leaving
In my thoughts, I have seen rings of smoke through the trees
And the voices of those who stand looking
Ooh, it makes me wonder
Ooh, it really makes me wonder

The thoughts of the second verse are extended here, the realization that the mundane world is false is growing and now the character is not only questioning reality but yearning for change. Nature is not alone now, and we see members of humanity living in harmony, the smoke offering further messages that there is a world beyond what is in front of us.

And it's whispered that soon if we all call the tune
Then the piper will lead us to reason
And a new day will dawn for those who stand long
And the forests will echo with laughter

A new world exists, but it is still distant. The new dawn of understanding will come but only for those that are true to the spiritual path. Those that have attained the knowledge can show the way to those that have not, and through this unity, humanity can be led into a new way of thinking and reason. Understanding of true reality for the totality of mankind, of course, will be a joyous time.

If there's a bustle in your hedgerow, don't be alarmed now
It's just a spring clean for the May queen
Yes, there are two paths you can go by, but in the long run
There's still time to change the road you're on
And it makes me wonder

There are of course many paths that can be taken in life, but many are false and do not take the traveler to the destination of enlightenment. Plant is telling us that the point of change will be disruptive to our lives, we will fear the unknown as it "bustles our hedgerow" and we may even refuse the call. However, while we are alive, there is always time to change our path of ignorance and join those who are traveling the truer way.

Your head is humming and it won't go, in case you don't
know
The piper's calling you to join him
Dear lady, can you hear the wind blow and did you know
Your stairway lies on the whispering wind?

This verse is a throwback to the stage of the heroic cycle defined by the refusal of the call. The hero knows not all is right but is too afraid to do anything about it. The verse speaks to this as the persistent voice inside one's head, the humming, that won't go until action is taken. Again we are reminded that the stairway to heaven cannot be bought as eluded to in the beginning, but in fact exists in the spiritual realm, elusively living on the ever-changing "whispering wind."

And as we wind on down the road
Our shadows taller than our soul
There walks a lady we all know
Who shines white light and wants to show
How everything still turns to gold

As the sun sets lower into the horizon it casts a long shadow and so we see the journey coming toward an end. The woman from the start appears again but in a new form, she has completed her metamorphosis and this could also supply us with a meeting with the goddess. She now reveals that indeed all things do turn to gold, but the gold is symbolic of the wealth of wisdom and understanding, not materiality.

And if you listen very hard
The tune will come to you at last
When all are one and one is all, yeah
To be a rock and not to roll
And she's buying a stairway to heaven

Hard work, persistence and patience are the keys for successfully navigating the spiritual path. To keep your senses open and aware, the "tune" of realization will inevitably come. And when that realization is made, plurality and individuality dissolve and an understanding of one's true place in the universe is found. From this epiphany, the soul no longer "rolls" around the world looking for answers but is firm and eternal like a rock.

Symbols, Rituals, And Rock N Roll

The lyrics of Stairway To Heaven is a kind of spiritual quest, it is sympathetic to the mythic world and takes the listener back to a time of paganism. The lyrical symbolism is quite explicit on this manner, conjuring images of "May Queens", "Pipers", and "Rings of smoke through the trees." It seems to take our imagination back to a time where materiality did not reign supreme but the spiritual and mythical had at least an equal footing on humanities view of the world. In this way, Plant's lyrics take the listener away from the mundane world and allows a journey into the mythic time talked about by Eliade (chapter 12).

The musical composition of the song itself is symbolic in the overarching message that is being portrayed. There is the journey that takes place and this is heard by the dawdling beginnings that slowly yet consistently build in tempo until there is a climactic crescendo. This Journey is that of the lonely individual, who slowly comes to realize that they are part of a community. What seemed like a duality between one and many is bridged together so the differentiation no longer exists. The climax fades out and we hear the resonating voice of Plant as he finalizes the song a capella. This finishes the piece where we left off, with the individual, but now the individual is not lonely for he knows he is one part of a whole.

As the music for the song drives us through the journey, we can say that the songs reacts to the individual in the same way that ritual does. It takes the listener through an experience that teaches a rawer, more primordial understanding of the message. This experience is of course reinforced by the lyrics which give definition to the foundation of meaning.

Plant's poetry is a stroke of genius in that it crystallizes the definitive meaning of all mythologies and presents it to a modern audience. He modernizes the paths of the Tarot, the heroic cycle of Campbell, and the archetypes of Jung. Plant uses the symbols of his own culture but still grafts these truths into a classic rock song, creating a platform that delivered a universal teaching to countless people across numerous generations.

The message he delivered lays within the lyrics them self. He is saying to the listener that when one is inexperienced and immature, the only thing that seems to matter in life is the material world. This world will try and fool you, it will try and keep you in a life of ignorance - but there is hope. If you can see through the lies and trickery and keep your mind open to the experience of life, you will accumulate wisdom, the true gold of this world. This knowledge will build and you will learn that you are not alone in this world and will find love for your fellow human beings. Love and wisdom will take you on the true path to salvation and grant you your freedom from the prison of false material wealth.

Mythology Lives On

We have studied many examples of mythology, both young and old, in our journey and it should be clear now that mythology does not only exist in the world of our distant ancestors but surrounds our lives today. The stories and songs of old tell truths of human nature and the world around us that are still of the utmost importance today.

Mythology still lives and breathes, it has evolved and changed, yet the message stays the same. To know the message and to understand the symbols will bring you closer to enlightenment and adds depth and meaning to your life.

The deciphering of mythology is a titanic subject, it is as deep as it is broad. With countless cultures to explore and an infinite amount of interpretations to consider, the task may seem endless. But the journey is far from fruitless, as you learn more and more about the tales you will see deeper into the reality that we live and a new understanding of the world will begin to emerge.

Start slowly and you will be rewarded. Throughout this work, I have included numerous mythologies and made reference to a number of stories both ancient and modern. In many cases, these were only made in passing in an attempt to pique your interest with hopes that you will seek them out in their original forms and read them for yourself. We live in a time where the wealth of humanities literature is at our fingertips and I urge you to take advantage of this blessing. Go and explore the great writings and decipher their inner meanings, knowledge is power and these works can be used as a mirror to see into your own life, to give it meaning, and to give your life a newfound quality.

The complexity of mythology should now be acknowledge and I have to admit that many aspects of mythological interpretation have been mentioned in this book prior to their fuller explanation. For example, I mentioned the non-linear aspect of time in the Wheel of Fortune Tarot card (Chapter 9) but only discussed this phenomena in depth in Chapter 12. This, unfortunately, could not be avoided and occurs in many places. My advice for those that wish a fuller appreciation of mythology is once this book has been read through, turn back to page one and begin again. What you will find is that terms that did not wholly make sense in the first read will now be clear, and through this, a greater understanding can be comprehended.

If this has been your first dive into the depths of mythology then I welcome you to the journey.

About Robert D. Jones

Robert Jones has been studying classics his whole life. His passion is in ancient cultures and languages, and the study of mythology has been integral in his own life's development. This is his first published full length work where he endeavored to share the importance of mythology with the world in a way that it can be applicable to the readers own life. Robert has since written several Epic Fantasy novels which you can find with his other work on his website.

ROBERTJONESAUTHOR.COM